THE FENNEL FAMILY PAPERS

THE
Fennel
Family
Papers

A NOVEL BY

William Baldwin

Algonquin Books
of Chapel Hill

1996

Published by
ALGONQUIN BOOKS OF CHAPEL HILL
Post Office Box 2225
Chapel Hill, North Carolina 27515-2225

a division of
WORKMAN PUBLISHING
708 Broadway
New York, New York 10003

This is a work of fiction. All names, characters, places, and incidents are either products of the author's imagination or are used fictitiously. No reference to any real person is intended or should be inferred.

Library of Congress Cataloging-in-Publication Data

Baldwin, William, 1944–
    The Fennel family papers : a novel / by William Baldwin.
      p.   cm.
    ISBN 1–56512–069–8
    I. Title.
    PS3552.A4518F46   1996
    813'.54—dc20   95–32556
                                                                          CIP

10   9   8   7   6   5   4   3   2

ACKNOWLEDGMENTS

Thanks to all my Algonquin pals—especially Shannon Ravenel, Katharine Walton, Tammi Brooks, Robert Rubin, and Ina Stern. And thanks to copyeditor Bettye Dew for referring to my punctuation as "light, quite open." For kindnesses past and present I'd like to thank my friends—especially Randy and Claudia McClure, Richard Reeves, Stephanie Waldron, Liz Dawson, David Blair, Patty and Jim Fulcher, Billy Dinwiddie, Bernadette Humphrey, Snowdie and Edmund Kirby-Smith, Dan and Erica Lesesne, Tom and Gail Fleming, and L. R. Cannon. And finally, for assistance in unlocking life's mysteries, a special thanks to our local librarian Pat Gross and the staffs of the Charleston Library Society and the National Archives.

To A and Malc

What does it mean then, what can it all mean? Lily Briscoe asked herself, wondering whether, since she had been left alone, it behoved her to go to the kitchen to fetch another cup of coffee or wait here. What does it mean?

—VIRGINIA WOOLF, *To the Lighthouse*

CONTENTS

THE FENNEL FAMILY PAPERS

BOOK ONE

The Fennel Papers—

Port Ulacca, South Carolina, 1963

IN THE BEGINNING

If the Fennel family had not invented fire, they had at least delivered it to America. Yes, and the responsibility for this Promethean legend had been passed down to that high priestess of the flame, Miss Camilla Fennel.

"A private lighthouse," the old woman expounded. "A private light."

Professor Paul Danvers nodded politely and adjusted the knot of his tie. He did not feel well. It was hot for May, unseasonably so, but he'd worn the tweed jacket anyway. Paul wasn't easygoing with people, but he would compensate with the clothes and good posture. The young man had planned for this meeting, planned well, or thought he had. If he wanted the family to entrust him with their place in history he could not afford to have his credentials questioned, either as a scholar or as Ginny's suitor.

"It was not a lighthouse then." Camilla spoke from the head of the table. "It was just a large bonfire, but the Fennels tended it from the very beginning. It was the only private light operating

in the New World. The Fennels were granted a charter, a charter from the king. A patent. It was called a patent." She brought
chalk-stick fingers to the broad lace collar of her lavender dress.

"Ah," Paul ventured and lowered his gaze. The aged linen
cloth glowed with a soft yellow incandescence. Each piece of the
mismatched tableware caught some portion of the light and held
it. He sipped his water. Outside, wisteria whispered and tapped
at the window screens. The sickly sweet smell of its flowers cut
through the strong grease odor of supper. Okra, tomatoes,
chicken, potatoes—except for the rice everything on the table
was fried and none of it had agreed with him. Paul felt the nausea rising in his throat. Then, sweet salvation, a cool breeze billowed the muslin curtains.

He closed his eyes and drew a deep breath. When they
opened, the ship's lantern that hung above the dining room table
was gently rocking. The dim pool of light it cast shifted to and
fro, curiously distorting the family members seated below. Light
to dark. Dark to light. Though immobile, their faces seemed to
be expressing a wide range of emotions. From sad to happy, the
lantern swung, and back again from elation to despair.

Having excused herself from the table, Ginny's mother gave
Paul a tiny wave and slipped from the room. He nodded at the
retreating figure, took another sip of water, and glanced across
at Ginny and at her invalid father. The girl alone seemed
immune to the magic of the lantern. Her face, with its perfect
symmetrical features, remained a perfect oval mask of inscrutability. Paul could not guess what she was thinking or whether
she was even thinking at all. Only now was he beginning to realize how little she had told him about her family and this house
with its strange servant. Though he'd known her for an entire
semester and had spent the previous Saturday night with her at
the Armada Inn, Paul was taken by surprise. He had, of course,

read Ginny's essay mentioning her parents, Adam and Azalea, and the Fennel lighthouse and her grandfather, Captain Jack Fennel. And at their first interview she had spoken of Great-Aunt Camilla and the family papers. But he could remember nothing else.

Ginny dabbed her father's lips with a napkin, then brought a spoon of mashed potatoes to his mouth.

"The only private lighthouse operating in the New World," Camilla said. "A charter from the king, Dr. Danvers. Are you listening, Dr. Danvers?" Paul nodded quickly, though in fact his mind had wandered. "The patents were only granted to persons of substance and education," the old woman continued. "This speaks well of my family, especially when one remembers their patent was the only one of its kind granted. They were of necessity exceptional men, men of constant habit and good order—temperate, moral, conscientious, and above all watch-ful—and this same laudable conduct was, of course, required of their families."

"A patent from the king," Paul repeated. "That is remarkable." The nausea had passed and he managed a smile.

"Of England," Azalea said, returning from her trip to the powder room. Stepping just inside the circle of lamplight, she presented herself for inspection—neat, plump and shiny—and all but Paul ignored her. Carefully she smoothed the folds of her double-knit suit and began to pull on a pair of white gloves.

"What are you talking about, Azalea?" the old woman snapped.

"The king of England. That's who granted the charter."

Camilla dismissed Ginny's mother with an imperial wave and went on. "The family's contribution to this country's wealth and commerce did not go unnoticed by the founders of our repub-lic, Dr. Danvers, for immediately following the Revolution this patent, in a slightly altered form, was renewed. Not that they

could have done otherwise, considering the Fennel contribution to the war effort and their steadfast devotion to the cause
of freedom."

"We still have the charter," Azalea said. "It's in the family
papers, isn't it? There's so much in those boxes I can't remember what's been preserved."

At last. Collaborating proof that Paul was not on a fool's
errand. Yes. Yes, indeed. What graduate student had not heard
of the Fennel family papers? They were legendary, an almost
mythical body of primary sources on which a career could be
built. Many careers, perhaps, for there were trunks filled with
papers—even rooms, whole houses. The collection reached far
back into history. Some said the Norman Conquest.

"Woman," Camilla hissed.

"I just thought he might like to know which king," Azalea
said. She continued to worry the last glove onto each finger of
her hand and cast sideways glances at Paul. Her hair was dyed
bronze, and in preparation for going out she'd sprayed it into a
frozen bronzelike wave. Her face too had taken on a metallic
glaze. Eye shadow and liner gave her an expression of wonderment, and she'd lipsticked onto her mouth a slightly crooked but
prominent smile.

"I was not aware that you shared in the ownership of the
papers," Camilla said.

"I meant to say your papers." Azalea averted her eyes to the
worrisome glove.

"You seem to forget you are only a Fennel by marriage."

Yes, Paul thought, and thank God for small favors.

Miss Camilla was the real thing, all right, for she had the
beaklike nose and sunken eyes that Paul recognized from the
portrait in the parlor. They were also the features of Adam Fennel whom his daughter was attending with such devotion. And

thank God for grand favors, Ginny resembled neither side of the family.

Paul watched as Adam made his feeble chewing motion. The man was paralyzed. Neither arms nor legs could move and he had to be tended like a baby—well tended, it seemed. His dark hair was cut short and he was clean-shaven and freshened with talcum powder. His clothes were spotless and pressed. Even the bib was unsoiled. Was this for Paul's benefit? No. Ginny was too practiced at what she was doing, and what she was doing made Paul uncomfortable. The spoon came down and the man's throat constricted as he swallowed. The neck seemed impossibly long. It stretched up and out, straining away from the ruined body. The tiny bloodshot eyes blinked continually, and though Ginny's father appeared to have no control over them, Paul suddenly felt he was being watched in return.

He turned to Azalea and realized for the first time that she wasn't even forty years old. Yes, it would be easy to feel sorry for her, but Paul's own position was all too precarious. It was Camilla's approval he needed in order to see the papers. The papers would tell what had happened at the lighthouse over a century before—explain the events that had changed the course of history. This information Professor Danvers could convert into an article, and this article would gain him tenure, and then he could consider his future with Ginny Fennel. And then and only then could he afford to feel sorry for Ginny's mother. In the meantime he would smile and nod at everyone.

"Well, I'm off to play bridge," Azalea said. The glove was finally in place. "How do I look?" The question was directed at Paul, but once more Camilla responded.

"I guess we know what kind of bridge that is." The old woman gave a murmur of disgust.

Paul was baffled. He smiled at Camilla, nodded, and then

smiled at Azalea. "I don't know much about card games," he said. This was true. Card games had been played in the dorm, but he hadn't joined in. In fact, he'd never owned a pack of cards, and when his mother was alive, he'd never seen cards in their apartment.

Camilla snorted again.

"You look fine, Momma," Ginny said. It was the first unsolicited comment she'd made since the meal began.

"Thank you, Virginia."

"Yes. You do," Paul said. But that sounded insincere and adding "You really do" sounded even worse.

"I guess we know what kind of bridge that is," Camilla repeated to herself. As she lay aside her fork Paul could see the tendons rippling beneath a pale, almost transparent flesh. A half-dozen silver bracelets slid up her forearm as she patted the bun of silver hair and turned her glittering sunken eyes on Paul. Her severe lips twisted into a sneer.

"Summer people!" She spit the words out. It was an invitation for Paul to share her disapproval of anyone not by blood a Fennel.

"You'll love dessert, Paul," Azalea whispered. "You're having ambrosia."

"The Fennels are really the last of the old families still intact," Camilla continued.

With caution Paul shifted his gaze from one to the other. Not wanting to hurt Ginny's mother. Not wanting to be involved at all.

"Ambrosia is the food of the gods," Azalea added.

"Azalea! Please. Dr. Danvers is an educated man. Certainly he knows that ambrosia is the food of the gods."

Both women waited for his response. Helpless, he looked across the table—and made contact with the equally helpless

Adam Fennel. Ginny was oblivious to everything but feeding her father.

"I really don't know much about food," Paul said and smiled at each woman. This was true. If anything, he knew less about food than about card playing. In the tiny apartment he'd shared with his mother he had done most of the cooking and mostly he'd opened cans of tuna fish. For a year he'd eaten in the college cafeteria and then it was back to tuna fish in an apartment of his own. "Supper was delicious, really," he added and tapped his plate with his fork for emphasis.

"We have a cook," Camilla said.

"A very good cook," Azalea added.

Camilla raised a small dinner bell and rang it with vigor.

"Da Bena!" Azalea shouted.

"I rang."

"You know she won't answer the bell."

"I rang," Camilla repeated and turned on Paul. "Da Bena has been with the Fennels her entire life. She was my da, my nurse. She also raised Adam and Virginia, and she cooks for the family and aids Azalea in the housekeeping. Now that Ginny is away she has again taken on the care of Adam."

From the kitchen came the sound of a pot clanging and then padding footsteps. The door opened and an arm swung like a tentacle into the room.

And the room went dark. Paul grabbed at the table edge, rattling silver against china.

"A fuse," Azalea whispered.

"Azalea," Camilla hissed.

The light flickered, shone faintly, and then renewed itself brighter than ever.

"There, Paul," Azalea said. "A fuse."

But Paul's attention was to the approaching servant. Yes, he'd glimpsed her when they first arrived. Seeing her then he had refused to believe his eyes.

The ancient black woman was as tall as he—a slack six feet, but thin. Gangling. Her bulging joints were the loosest of hinges, and the skin that hugged the bones seemed a single layer of dusty parchment. A mummy. A mummy pitched from the tomb— except for the costume. The woman wore a housecoat of light blue terry cloth over a turquoise T-shirt advertising motor oil. A man's straw hat was pressed over gray-white curls and tied on with a red bandanna knotted beneath her chin. The affect was comic but hardly laughable.

Standing on one foot like a giant stork, she scratched her heel beneath a faded pink bedroom slipper, and surveyed the diners. Her small wizened face expressed nothing. Here, Paul thought, could be the source of Ginny's own emotionless veneer, but then the bulging chocolate eyes fell on him and she smiled, revealing rows of piano-key teeth. The smile was inviting, but at the same time monstrous.

LEROY

"This is Dr. Danvers," Camilla said.

"Da Bena, he was raving about your cooking," Azalea said.

"So dis the one." The mummy servant spoke with the thick accent of the coastal blacks. And this odd vestige of African speech was made even stranger by the musical lilt in her voice. "So dis the boyfriend."

"Oh, hush," Azalea half whispered. "You're going to embarrass Virginia."

"Lovin' a man ain't nothin' to be shame of."

Ginny continued to tend her father.

"Da Bena is right as always," Camilla said to Azalea.

"I didn't mean to imply that she wasn't. It's just that Paul would tell you, if he wasn't a gentleman, that a statement like that puts him in an awkward position."

"Yes. Dat so if he be a gentleman for true."

"See," Azalea said. "Da Bena agrees with me."

Camilla was about to reply when the door to the hall gave a shudder and swung open hard.

"Leroy!" Azalea cried. "We had given up on you."

There had been several mentions of a "Leroy" since their arrival, and Paul was aware of the empty place set beside him.

"Paul," Azalea continued, "this is my brother, Leroy Ramona. Leroy, this is Virginia's friend from the university, Dr. Danvers. He insists that we call him Paul, so you must also call him Paul."

Leroy grunted a welcome and stepped into the circle of lamplight. Paul nodded and in return for the nod, Leroy gave a brief smile. It was the crooked-mouth smile of his sister. A half-completed expression. He was young. In his mid-twenties— Paul's age. His hair was long. It trailed like a horse's mane down a thick neck and almost touched the broad shoulders. He was short, no taller than his sister. He stood before her now, shifting his weight from one foot to the other and cracking his knuckles. Muscles bulged beneath his clean white T-shirt and well-laundered jeans. Here was a physical threat. Not just to Paul, but to the entire world.

"Miss Camilla, I goin' serve the ambrosia now." Da Bena's half-sung words ended the silence, and Paul turned his attention from the intruder to the others. Only Azalea had so much as glanced in her brother's direction.

"Gin!"

Now Leroy's presence was harder to ignore, for as Da Bena left the room he stepped behind Ginny. Leaning over her shoulder, he kissed her roughly on the mouth. His large obscene hand lingered on her breast. Unaware of his own anger, Paul jumped from his chair, which tipped behind him with a crash. He stooped to regain it and then, embarrassed by the attention he'd drawn, murmured "Sorry." And there was nothing left to do but propose a handshake. "Pleased to meet you, Leroy," Paul said.

Azalea's brother eyed the offered hand for a suspicious moment. Then, abandoning his niece, he leaned across the table and shook.

"Ramona with an *R*," Leroy said.

Paul felt the delicate bones in his palm and fingers crumbling in the man's grip. Tears welled in his eyes. Helpless, he looked around at the other members of the Fennel household. Adam blinked in helpless staccato as Ginny went back to wiping his chin. Azalea stared in dumb admiration at her brother's broad back. That left Camilla to observe Paul's facial contortions, but instead of coming to his rescue she leaned forward and whispered something he couldn't hear.

"Excuse?" Paul whispered back as evenly as possible. His body was beginning to curl inward. His free hand clutched at the aged linen tablecloth.

"Summer people," the old woman hissed. "The Ramonas are summer people."

"Leroy! Stop that!" Azalea screamed and pounded her brother across the shoulders with tiny white-gloved fists.

Leroy grinned and gave Paul's hand one final squeeze. Something broke. Paul could feel it and even heard the snap of bone. He surrendered and fell over into the almost-emptied gravy bowl. Only then did Leroy release his hand.

"Oh, Paul! I'm so sorry. Please forgive me!" Azalea shrieked. "Leroy's just a boy. He doesn't know his own strength."

Leroy smiled.

Adam blinked.

Ginny stared at her father's plate.

"Summer people," Miss Camilla whispered for the fourth time.

Da Bena arrived from the kitchen with a clatter, balancing six bowls of ambrosia on her tentacle arm.

Paul slumped into his chair and pulled his throbbing hand into his lap. It had to be broken.

"Oh, Paul, Paul," Azalea murmured as she circled behind Camilla. "Please let me help you." Reaching his side, she swept up a napkin and began to mop the spilled gravy from the front of his shirt.

"Dem old accident have a way of happenin'," Da Bena crooned as she slipped a bowl of dessert in front of him.

"Let me see it, you poor boy," Azalea went on, and against his will she tugged his hand into view. There was nothing to see. Just a slight red puffiness, but giving a soft moan, the woman who he hoped was to be his mother-in-law brought his mangled fingers to her lips and kissed them.

"For heaven's sake, Azalea, remember where you are," Camilla shouted.

"Yeah, Azalea," Leroy added with a snicker.

Azalea dropped the hand and stepped away embarrassed. The crooked smile seemed even more pitiable and Paul knew he must somehow come to her defense.

"Paul's all right, Momma," Ginny said suddenly. "You go on and have a good time."

"Virginia . . ." her mother said. "Virginia, I'm sorry I can't spend the rest of the evening with you, but I have a bridge date."

"I bet we know what kind of bridge that is. Right, Aunt Camilla?" Leroy looked at the old woman for support but instead received a contemptuous glance.

"Go on and play that game, honna. Bena goin' be right here the whole night long."

"Thank you, Da Bena. I won't be late." Azalea placed a quick nervous kiss on the side of her husband's head, gave the white gloves a final tug, and left through the door where Leroy had entered.

"Thank God," Camilla muttered. "Perhaps now we can carry on a civilized discourse." She raised a fruit-laden spoon to her lips. Six silver bracelets slid up her wrist and halted at the lavender lace cuff.

"Amen," said Leroy, beginning to circle the table.

With Azalea gone, Paul felt truly alone and truly vulnerable. He'd dealt with bullies before, more than his share of them. As a boy he'd run—and then later, especially in the dorm, he'd just ignored them and suffered whatever abuse came his way, and plenty did. Someone was always beating on his door late at night or tossing flaming toilet paper through the transom. He had ignored them as he would like to ignore Leroy now.

But behind him he heard a creeping step. He should have let the uncle embrace his niece. Leroy's touching of the breast was no doubt an accident. Yes, Paul had overreacted. He must be careful never again to jeopardize his chance at the family's papers. He flinched and shrank into his chair. Leroy brushed by him to sit in the empty place and began to heap a plate from the remnants of dinner.

"Looks like I'm scraping the bottom of the pot here, Professor. Guess that'll teach me to show up on time." There was no malice in his voice. Not a trace. Paul meant to nod but the gesture came out as a cringing shrug.

"You should apologize," Camilla said suddenly. She had finished her ambrosia.

"Ma'am?" Leroy questioned.

"You heard me. Apologize to Dr. Danvers."

"For what?" Leroy spoke like a small child.

"You know very well for what."

Leroy laid down his fork.

"I'm sorry, Paul. Hope there are no hard feelings." Leroy's sheepish glance passed from Ginny to Camilla and then to Paul. He seemed quite sincere, genuinely contrite.

"No harm done," Paul mumbled and concentrated on his ambrosia. Surely the worst was behind him. He had met them all, paid the price, and somewhere ahead lay the fabled Fennel papers.

"Dr. Danvers," Camilla said. "After supper I would like to speak to you about some family documents. I would value your opinion, as a professional historian."

The old woman had read his mind.

A DEATH IN THE FAMILY

Could she? Could Camilla actually read his mind? Of course, the very notion brought forth the worst possible memories. "Cunt hound." The words came whispering. They demanded—crowded out all reasonable thought. Paul smiled at the old woman and declared that he would be happy to take a look at her family papers. "Cunt hound!" The inside voice came wailing now but there was no escape. All eyes were fixed on him. Even Ginny's father happened to be facing his way. Paul willed himself to think of something else but the scenes of other meals eaten in that other place spilled in.

"Cunt hound," Paul's mother said, looking up from her book. "That's all he ever was."

"Why don't you eat, Mother?" her son asked. A small portion of tuna fish casserole was on the plastic plate before her. The remaining surfaces of the tiny kitchenette were crowded with books and papers. Paul ate standing up, holding his own plate several inches below his chin.

"And why don't you close your mouth when you eat, Paulie?

You can't imagine what it sounds like. Much worse than when you breathe. Much worse."

"I'll try." Paul's reply lacked commitment.

"I can't get over how much you're beginning to look like him. Have I told you that?" His mother took off her reading glasses, wiped them on the edge of her skirt, and returned them to the reddened bridge of her nose. "Those thick lips especially. You lose thirty pounds, grow a mustache, and pick up a pipe and I'll have another cunt hound on my hands."

Paul didn't know whether he looked like his father or not. His mother had kept no photographs, but the boy had searched the college yearbooks until he found a Greek professor who shared his name. Still, he couldn't be sure. His own acne was so bad and the quality of the print so poor that a comparison was impossible. Anyway, Paul had come to doubt his mother on most things. If she said they looked alike then they probably didn't.

"Let me show you something, Paulie," she said, sliding back her chair.

"Please finish eating," Paul begged.

"No. No. Now I just want to show you something. We might forget."

"Please," Paul whispered as he trudged behind the woman.

"Here!" she exclaimed, her voice thick with theatrical menace. "This is where I found them." A small hole marred the black vinyl cover of the sofa and she stuck her finger into it. "Do you see the stain?"

"Yes, ma'am," he answered. Of course, there was no stain, and Paul was beginning to doubt there'd ever been one. But over the years his mother's repeated jabbings had poked that hole in the plastic.

"He was standing here, with his pants down around his ankles, but still wearing his coat and tie, mind you, and the girl, this student, was sprawled out here on my sofa in my living room and they'd left this most god-awful stain right here." For the ten-thousandth time the finger punctured the sofa.

"Yes, ma'am."

"Cunt hound! That's all he ever was and you're no better. Don't shake your head at me—I know what you are."

Paul prayed his mother was just going through a stage. Perhaps she had some self-healing disease of the brain and eventually she'd stop screaming that obscenity at him. He waited, but nothing changed. And he had no one to confide in and really nothing to confide other than this single obsession with the stain. Outside the apartment she managed fine. He watched in dumb amazement when she crossed the campus on the way to class. Occasionally he would even spy her on the arm of Dr. Whitman. She'd be gazing up at her escort with wide-eyed coquettish interest. Out there she was fine, but in the apartment it was always the same—until Paul's junior year when he returned one day to find her lying cold and stiff beside the sofa. Her finger hung from the hole it had opened. "Aneurysm" the report said. The doctor suspected she'd had it for years.

Paul gave up the apartment, which was reserved for faculty anyway, and moved into the dorm. It was then that he lost thirty pounds, grew a mustache, and began to smoke a pipe. He never became a cunt hound, though. Far from it. After several clumsy attempts at romance including a particularly disastrous date with a graduate student, he had settled for platonic relationships. Or, more precisely, none at all. Word went around that he was "funny." This covered a multitude of abnormalities but at least was not as damning as outright "queer."

And in this uncertain state he'd labored through the years, remaining a virgin until the time weeks before when Ginny had carried him to the Armada Inn on Atlanta's Peachtree Street and relieved him of his burden. Then she had brought him to this place.

"Dr. Danvers?"

"Augh," Paul replied.

"Sir?" Camilla stood at the head of the table. She watched him with slight shoulders drawn back. The light from the ship's lantern flickered twice but did not fail.

"Ma'am?" Paul answered.

"Would you care to come with me?"

"Yes, ma'am. Yes, ma'am. Of course." Paul rose with haste and again his chair pitched backwards. The room was empty. Even the dishes were cleared away. What had transpired while he was lost in dismal reverie? Where were the others?

"The others have gone." Again Camilla had read his mind.

ANISE, BASIL, CHERVIL,

AND THE OTHERS

I was born in the house my father built," Camilla said as she led Paul down the dark hall.

Through the crack in one door came a faint flickering blue light and the disconcerting sound of canned laughter. A television was on. Perhaps it was this that disoriented him further. Something had. On first arriving he'd experienced a slight loss of equilibrium for which he could compensate. Now, walking the short distance from the dining room he had stumbled twice and even bumped the wall.

Of course, he'd experienced a similar sensation often in the past. Since boyhood he had suffered from a paralyzing vertigo often accompanied by nausea. As a result he avoided heights— at least those where open spaces were involved. He suspected some inner-ear disturbance or even an aneurysm like the one that felled his mother. But the doctors at the infirmary could find nothing wrong. They insisted that the problem was all in his mind. He knew better but it was useless to argue.

Yes, life was a hard, hard journey but Paul had made that difficult first step. The parlor was attained. With relief he accepted the chair Camilla proffered, and when she gave permission he retrieved his pipe from the tweed coat and began to stoke it. He was careful to cross his legs and doubly careful that the crease of his forward pants leg fell in a straight line to the top of his shoe. He brushed the edges of his mustache, half fearing that during supper it had somehow been damaged or even ripped from his lip. It had not.

He struck a match, causing the dull pain in his hand to sharpen. He flinched but held tight. The flame flared above the pipe bowl. He inhaled. He exhaled. This was cultivated self-assurance that he hoped would not be lost on Miss Camilla Fennel. He glanced over the pipe stem and his two cupped hands. She was facing not him but the portrait that hung above the fireplace.

"Every post and lintel, every door and sash was gathered on the beach by my father, Captain Jack Fennel, during his more than half-century as keeper of the Fennel light." Now the old woman turned. Her own hands were clasped tightly in front—held as if an aria was to be sung. "I believe I mentioned at dinner that my family tended the light on Dog Tooth Shoal for over three centuries, and I am sure that such men as Anise, Basil, and Chervil Fennel are not strangers to a student of our state's history such as yourself."

She paused, but Paul realized too late he was meant to comment.

"The injustice of it!" she went on fiercely. "The injustice. These men—all the Fennels have led lives of heroic simplicity—the maintenance of the flame, that flame which has been the salvation of so many lives, that was the principal mission of their lives." She unlocked her fingers so that an accusing one could be pointed in Paul's direction. "Do you know the duty of the light keeper?" she demanded. Paul smiled—a forced gaiety.

Shook his head no. She clasped her hands once more. "You are to light the lamps every evening at sun-setting, and keep them constantly burning bright and clear till sun-rising." Paul sucked on the pipe, coughed, nodded. Her voice rose an octave. "Dr. Danvers, that ancient instruction could serve well as the Fennel motto. A life spent primarily in the service of humanity, in steadfast devotion to the interest of others—until, of course, these last sad years." She pointed again. This time in the direction of the television's blue flicker. "An age of darkness which has come not just here to Port Ulacca, but I fear the entire world." Her hand hovered like a small white bird, then clutched for the mantel's edge.

And Paul wanted very much to agree. He removed his pipe in order to say "Yes, that's true," but she would not give him time.

"These were men of strength and vigor," she raced on. "Men who with the help of their wives and families brought to this wilderness a measure of civilization and order that was the envy of their neighbors. Envy! Dr. Danvers, do you know what envy does to people?"

Paul shook his head yes and then no.

"It poisons them," she concluded.

Paul was no longer certain what they were discussing. He poked the pipe as if meditating on a response. For some reason his left palm had begun to hurt as well.

"Yes, ma'am," he said finally and hoped this would be taken as an agreement. The old woman was satisfied. She began again.

"Anise! Basil! Chervil! History has not treated these men well. It has cast them in a dark light and accused them of villainy. All without proof. But they have been convicted and what has been done to them cannot be undone. This is not our concern here, though, is it, Dr. Danvers?"

"No, ma'am." Paul risked a meek confidence at this point,

for he thought their concern was with Jack Fennel. He hoped that, anyway.

"Our concern here is with this man, my own dear father, Captain Jack Fennel." The clawlike hand released the mantel's edge and floated reverently upward. She faced the portrait. "See how the eyes follow you about the room?" She glanced back at Paul. She waited.

Paul rose from the chair and studied the canvas with a studied appreciation. The surface was blackened with age and the room barely lit. Still, this was the distinct Fennel face, the small eyes, the beaked nose—but as the old woman had claimed, there was evidence of a pioneer vitality. The pictured man had a hardness about his features that had eroded over the following generations.

"Yes," Paul said. "Yes, indeed."

"The eyes, Dr. Danvers," Camilla snapped.

Paul took several tottering steps and the eyes did indeed follow him. But this came as no surprise. He had passed beneath this foreboding gaze on his arrival to the house. In fact, the first words Azalea had spoken to him were "See how the eyes follow you?" Not "Hello" or even "Welcome." Just "See how the eyes follow you."

"Uncanny," Paul had remarked on that first passage. He decided to risk it again. "Uncanny," he said to Camilla now. Though it wasn't so uncanny, considering the room was no more than eight feet wide. It would have been impossible for the portrait not to command the narrow space.

"See, see. It's in the eyes," Camilla whispered as Paul returned to his chair. He recrossed his legs and once more took up his pipe. "A man of strength and vigor like all the Fennels before him," Camilla exclaimed. "He designed and built this house when he was almost sixty. He built it for Jewel, my mother, a young woman who was fated to never know more of life than this house. The same I suppose could be said for me. Though I did travel at one time, my experience has not been great."

The old woman indicated the framed photograph on the end table beside him. And juggling it and the pipe into the light, Paul made out a white-bearded gentleman seated in a broad rattan chair and beside him a girl standing stiff in a high-collared dress.

"Very distinguished," he said. She snatched it from him and perched herself on the edge of the upholstered Victorian sofa.

"There are many pictures. In addition to the papers there are many priceless photographs."

"I'd be interested—"

She cut him off. The retreat to the Victorian sofa had only been a strategic withdrawal.

"We lived here in Port Ulacca, the Captain and I, until his death, at which time I returned to the Fennel light to live with my half-brother Jack Junior and his wife Liza. He could be generous. Jack Junior still had the revenues from his patent, and he enjoyed treating his wife to certain frivolities. A gentleman, Dr. Danvers, and I don't have to add, a true Fennel. He helped to build the Panama Canal, you know?"

Paul didn't know. He'd never heard of Jack Junior.

"I will be happy to speak to you at some other time about this period in my life. But what concerns us now are the papers of my family. Most importantly, my father's papers. Virginia wrote that you wished to study them and perhaps to do an article. Is that true?"

Paul lurched forward in his chair and gripped the pipe with both good hand and bad. When he'd first met Ginny she had mentioned the papers to him, but he thought he'd successfully concealed his interest. Were his motives that transparent? Was Ginny so astute? After reading her essays for a semester he found the idea that she would write home truly bizarre. He had assumed she would always telephone.

"Yes. Yes, I would." Paul rose to his feet and, crossing to the fireplace, went through the motions of cleaning his pipe. He needed time to think.

"There is more than an article, Dr. Danvers. There is most certainly a book. At my father's death I inherited several large cartons brimming with materials, and over the years I have filled several more from various sources. Anything that was of possible interest was tucked away for one reason and one reason alone. And what was that reason, Dr. Danvers?"

Once more she pointed her bony accusing finger at him. Crossing to the fireplace had been a mistake, for he was now exposed. From up above, the eyes of the portrait burrowed into his skull. Paul nodded. Hummed. Cleared his throat. Yes, the interview had been out of his control from the beginning, and the news that Ginny had realized his ulterior motives with such ease had left him standing naked before this old woman's assaults.

"Why, Dr. Danvers? Why was this material preserved?"

Paul bowed towards her. Here was his chance.

"You wanted to help the historians."

"Help the historians!" Camilla shrieked and sprang from the sofa. "It was to protect him from those very people. Even before his death he was the victim of their lies, a victim like all the Fennels, of others' envy. The envy of smaller, lesser men, men of the shadows, not men of deeds and valor."

Men like you. That would surely have been her next phrase if Paul had not thrown himself into this final breach.

"And you wanted to be able to defend him from these libels."

"Yes," Camilla said with a sigh. "Yes. Yes. Yes. That's it exactly." She sank into the chair Paul had vacated an eternity before.

"I'd like to help. I'd like to have a look at what you have." And for the first time since he'd entered the house he spoke with sincerity. Perhaps he and Miss Camilla could help one another—a symbiotic relationship. The bee and the flower. A book for him. Justice for her. But what sort of justice? Past historians had treated the Fennels fairly. Some had been more than fair.

"Danvers?" Camilla asked suddenly.

"Yes, ma'am?"

"Was your family originally from Charleston? There were several families of Danvers living there."

"No. I don't think so." Paul had no idea where his father's family had come from. He had never heard his mother mention a family home, and he'd lacked the courage to ask.

"They were connected in some way to the Lovages of Savannah. Surely your father would have mentioned them."

"He died when I was very young." A desperate lie, but this poverty of relations shamed him. It was unfortunate to have relatives who were not mentioned in the history books. It seemed unforgivable to have none at all.

"Surely your mother knew?"

His mother had mentioned his father's name in connection with only two places, Mexico and Sweden, places which were for her the capitals of sexual license. His father had come from one and gone to the other, but he couldn't be certain which. Did it matter? Paul struck boldly.

"He was Swedish."

"Danvers?"

"He just took that name. His own was too difficult to pronounce."

"Ah. And your mother? Who was she?"

"She was a history instructor at State."

"I mean who was she?"

"Ma'am?"

"What family did she come from? What was her maiden name?"

"Vetch." At last Paul could tell the absolute truth about something. "Her first name was Rosemary. Her friends called her Rose."

He could see that Camilla's lips were handling the syllables of Rosemary Vetch with some distaste.

"I have never heard of anyone named Vetch," she said finally.

"It's an old name," Paul added with assurance. "Dr. Whitman says there was a Vetch family at Caladium as early as 1690."

"Dr. Whitman?" Camilla struggled from the chair. "The author of *Whitman's History?*" She beat the upholstery with angry fists.

True, the questions about his own family had caught him off guard. True, Dr. Whitman was a historian. But how could Paul have known not to mention the name? To mention it simply in passing? "Yes," Paul admitted. "The author of *Whitman's History.*"

The old woman stood before him stiff with rage.

"This interview is at an end, young man. In the morning I must ask you to leave this house. Were you not a guest of my grand-niece I would send you out into the night. Follow me, please."

Beneath the disapproving glare of Captain Jack's portrait, Paul was led stumbling from the room and up the stairs. The house was now dark and silent. No help for him on any side. She shushed his bumbling apologies with a finger to her lips and moments later deposited him at the door to his room. Now was worse than never but he stepped out to block her path.

"Miss Camilla, surely you aren't going to let my knowing Dr. Whitman stop this research."

"That man has done a great disservice to this family," she hissed back. "I cannot in good conscience allow an acquaintance of his access to my family papers. You must leave in the morning. I will not change my mind, and there is nothing left to discuss."

"Dr. Whitman is the head of my department, Miss Camilla. I can't not know him."

"Stand aside."

"Miss Camilla, Dr. Whitman defended the Fennels," Paul wailed at last.

"Stand aside, you villain."

Paul did and watched her disappear down the darkened hallway. Camilla Fennel was taking with her his hope for a very modest fame and fortune. He was not thinking only of himself, but of Ginny as well. Their futures were intertwined—and until this blunder the Fennel papers had been woven soundly into their mutual tapestry. Still, it could be worse. He had not claimed, as he might have, that Dr. Whitman was a close friend of his meager family. But what, after all, was so terrible about that? Compared to what others had written, Dr. Whitman had been generous—generous to a fault considering what he had recently told Paul in private.

But such reasoning brought slim consolation. How his enemies in the department would have enjoyed that spectacle below. He could see them now, half hiding behind their coffee cups—those smiles of sadistic glee. And Dan Pauling, his office mate and pretended friend, he wouldn't have ended up shut in this room. Or Dr. Whitman either. If they could see him now wouldn't they both say the same thing? "Paul Danvers had the Fennel papers at his fingertips and lost them."

A QUICK REVIEW

A bandoned by Camilla, Paul had gone straight to his suitcase and retrieved *A History of the State*, or as it was com-
monly called, *Whitman's History*. Here was his evidence. Yes, a
monument to scholarship—a text with the heft of authority.
Paul sat on the bed, balanced the ponderous volume on his
knees, and opened to its thirty-two-page index. He needed a
quick review of the Fennel family. And he went where the index
instructed.

Fennel, Anise. p. 21
   According to Dr. Whitman, the Spanish, angered by incur-
sions of the English, had in 1687 sent two ships up the coast
from Florida to harass the infant colony. Having sailed past the
Caladium harbor, they anchored in the mouth of the Ulacca
River where they may have received supplies and fresh water
from Captain Anise Fennel. The curious and solitary adventurer
was tending a large bonfire to warn ships of the position of the
extending shoal—an enterprise established with a Letter Patent

from James II. Whitman suggested that the unproved accusations against Anise were linked to this—"to the political intrigues of contentious settlers, those anxious to strike out at their king with whatever means available."

Fennel, Basil. pp. 71, 72

It seemed that in 1706 Basil Fennel and five others were accused of trading whiskey and firearms to the Indians in exchange for deer hides. A particularly grave charge, considering the major offensive these disgruntled natives were about to launch against the settlers. But most of the accused were prominent landowners. Even the governor's brother was involved. "Red man and white were not destined to lie down together as lion and lamb," Whitman concluded. "For this disputed frontier was neither a peaceable nor a partitionable kingdom."

Fennel, Chervil. pp. 210-12

Then in 1715, the pirates came. More powerful than the colony, they plundered at will and even seized a ship at the Caladium docks. One of these bandits, Petit Shearwater, was finally captured and brought to trial. Though this dashing and cultivated criminal admitted to no wrongdoing, he did inform the vice admiralty court that he'd often found safe haven nearby at the Ulacca River signal light. The pirate was hanged. Chervil Fennel ignored the court's summons and the matter was dropped. "A time of great turmoil," Dr. Whitman commented. "One where the legal niceties bowed before the stern master of necessity."

Fennel, Capers. p. 306, 310, 360-61

Dr. Whitman presented the the Fennels as having been full-fledged lighthouse keepers by the time of the Revolution. But whether they kept it for the colonists or the king was the question asked at the war's end. Fortunately for Capers, the daring guerrilla leader Colonel Isaac Limpkin stated in his usual modest but forceful manner that on more than one occasion he had been allowed to hide within the very confines of the Fennel light. Charges of treason were dropped. Dr. Whitman referred to Caper's accusers as "a vengeful citizenry fed by war which bred hatred and private gain." And he brushed over the fact that the lighthouse had contained a Union Jack as well as the flags of both France and Spain.

Paul paused long enough to take in a deep breath and let out a sigh. The accounts were just as he remembered them. What here could Camilla have found so offensive? It was Whitman's duty to mention the slanders against her family, but in each case he had closed in their defense. Repeatedly the historian had come down on the side of expediency—on the side of the Fennels. And this, Paul knew from his interview with the man, was not what Whitman actually believed. But then it was difficult to say exactly what Whitman's beliefs were. What mattered, though, was what was written, and *Whitman's History* was fair— more than fair. But what exactly had Whitman said about Camilla's own father—the controversial Jack Fennel? Paul yanked his way over to the final entries—an impulsive action which brought a stab of pain to the injured hand. He loosened his tie and then tightened it once more. The broken mirror above the dresser reflected his earnest search for knowledge. He touched the corner of his mustache.

Fennel, Jack. p. 521, 532, 546-49
   When the Civil War began, Captain Jack Fennel had shut off his light in accordance with Confederate directives and for several years his situation had gone unnoticed. But as the Union

blockade tightened around the more distinguished cities of Savannah, Charleston, and Wilmington, the small inlet at the Fennel light became a haven for blockade runners. The passage, which Whitman designated as the "Caladium Keyhole," proved a crucial link, for by using it and the inland waterways that connected Caladium harbor and Port Ulacca a steady stream of diplomats managed to exit into the wide world. And since several European countries still considered entering the war on the side of the Confederacy, it was essential that this open channel of communication be maintained. However, the Caladium Keyhole had been closed. Dr. Whitman wrote the following:

> The Southern command had established a garrison and battery of some two dozen pieces, these alone being adequate to defend the already treacherous inlet. Unfortunately for their Cause, however, neither men nor weaponry were to see action since a solitary shot from a Union cruiser brought a signal of surrender from the island, and a pleasantly surprised Federal force found themselves in possession of the critical passage. Three days later the desperate Confederate forces launched a heroic but futile counterattack. The Fennel light would remain in the hands of an entrenched enemy for the remainder of the war.
>
> Events surrounding the unwarranted surrender have ever since been shrouded in mystery and confused by groundless conjecture. Because the Letter Patent accorded a form of British citizenship, Captain Jack Fennel was not prosecuted by the Union, and Colonel Parker, the Confederate officer who gave up the light, would also escape interrogation for he had died, apparently of self-inflicted wounds. In any event, the Caladium Keyhole, the Confederacy's last open passage with the outside world

was closed forever, and its hope for foreign intervention dealt an irreparable blow. From that day forward the noble Southern Cause was lost.

Paul closed the book. *The unwarranted surrender*. A hint of reprimand in the final summation? Was Dr. Whitman suggesting that Jack Fennel was somehow to blame for losing the entire Civil War? That did not seem likely. But perhaps the scholar who penned the *History* had believed this in his younger days. Perhaps Camilla was right to take offense. As he did with the other Fennel lightkeepers, Whitman certainly knew far worse things about Jack than he printed. But how would Camilla know that?

Paul turned to the back flyleaf and studied Whitman's photograph. Fifteen years had passed since it was taken. The distinguished scholar wore a tweed coat and held a pipe in contemplative gesture. The forehead was high. The shock of hair already white. The slight jowls barely suggested the sag to come. In the background was a bust of Herodotus, the father of history. Far in the background and slightly out of focus. What hint there that this man would soon take over the history department in a purge still referred to as "Pink Tuesday"? Or that he would anchor his position as department head by founding "The E Zee End Zoners"?

Paul donned pajamas and once more examined his own perplexed young face in the cracked mirror.

Would he end as Dr. Whitman had?

That didn't seem likely.

The young scholar slipped clumsily into bed.

For one thing Dr. Whitman believed the entire world could be divided into State University, which he called "Terra Firma," and the rest, which he referred to as "that other place."

Paul tucked the crocheted bedspread beneath his chin.

Well, maybe the department head was right about that. Paul's twenty-six years at the university and his single evening with the Fennels certainly made it seem so. But just how firm was Terra Firma?

DAN PAULING

Paul's office at the university was a windowless concrete cubicle pinched in between the furnace and the stairwell. It was of course the worst office possible, but he was the newest and youngest member of the history faculty. And yes, his lot would improve if he persisted. Let his enemies laugh. He had faith in his own abilities, a faith shared by few others, perhaps no others; but he planned to make himself a scholar of consequence.

Gradually he would work his way up from the basement until he had laid claim to one of the prestigious corner rooms. No. Not the southeast corner. He had no illusions about that. He'd seen what that had done to Dr. Whitman, and besides, Paul didn't have the makings of a department head. He wasn't at ease around people. Not just his enemies, but anyone. And it went without saying that he had absolutely no gift for office politics — for that dirty in-fighting at which Dr. Whitman was a master. No, Paul would simply persist. His name would matter in certain small but important circles. Essays and articles would be followed by a book. *Whitman's History*, no matter how good, would eventually be replaced.

At the end of this first semester, however, Paul had been forced to plot a new strategy. Persistence would not be enough. He had been demoted. There was no change of title, no cut in pay or lessening of responsibilities, but when he returned from the Christmas break he was sharing his minuscule office with another person.

Turned to the wall, his filing cabinet was impossible to open and his bookcase had disappeared—its contents stacked on the floor. All this was to make room for another desk and chair.

Paul's enemies had been busy, but he knew that even before he'd opened the door. The typed card beneath the office number now read:

Paul T. Danvers, Ph.D.
Daniel E. Pauling, Jr., Ph.D.

The similarity of names could not be the product of chance alone. A sadistic intelligence was at work here. And it had created a sabotage so subtle even Paul was awed by the prospect of what lay ahead.

The office mates' mail would be continually confused, and people, especially the students, would be calling Paul, Pauling and Daniel, Danvers. Paul had been around the university too long not to know what misery lay in store for both men, but still he could smile to himself because growing up there on the campus gave him a definite edge over the unfortunate new arrival. His own identity was established. It would be the new man who would have to scrape and claw.

Three weeks into the next semester Paul stopped smiling, or at least trying to smile. As he'd predicted to himself he was being called Daniels and Pauling and Daning and Palvers, and not just by the students, but by faculty members, many of whom had tickled Paul in his crib. However, the real Dan Pauling was having no such trouble. No one called him anything other than Dan Pauling. The same was true of the mail. Paul received none of Dan Pauling's mail, but Dan Pauling received practically all of Paul's. And the new arrival had actually opened a letter. True, it appeared to be an honest mistake and had been apologized for quite sincerely. No damage done. A form letter from a book club. Still, Paul was shaken. Clearly, it was not enough to persist. His identity was being swallowed up, and he had little doubt that his job was in jeopardy.

But now he wasn't sure who to blame. At first he had surmised his enemies, but they could not be manipulating the entire student body and faculty of the school. If he were to admit that over ten thousand people were out to get him or that someone as obviously good-hearted as Dan Pauling was scheming to take his job, then there would be only one word to describe his state of mind.

And that word stayed with him. Whenever he was alone he began to say it out loud. He drew the syllables out, watching his lips move in the mirror. Par-a-noid. He wasn't. If he was then he would be crazy and he knew he wasn't crazy, but nevertheless he was going to lose his job and they were out to get him. With the aid of calming logic and a legal pad he examined the situation. Before, there had been one person in his office. Paul drew the numeral 1. Now there were two. Paul drew the numeral 2. That could mean just one thing. He circled the 1 and underlined it for good measure then ripped the sheet of paper into shreds. He could do that math in his head.

The humanities weren't exactly a boom field, especially at a state university still bent on its pre-Depression mission of bringing electricity to all the farm homes. "The arts suck hind tit around here," was the way Curly Whitman put it, registering a mild complaint, but at the same time indicating he was nothing more than a country boy who'd taken a wrong turn somewhere early in life. No matter how you put it there wasn't enough work or money around there for another history instructor. Tenure became an impossiblity. One of them was bound to go, and Paul had a sad feeling it would be Paul Danvers.

The facts spoke for themselves. The new man was warm and outgoing while Paul gave the unfortunate impression of being cool and reserved. The new man had graduated near the top of his class at prestigious Sewanee. Paul, despite his best efforts, had been a mediocre student right there at State. The new man had traveled everywhere in the service of either the CIA or the Episcopal church and knew from first-hand experience all the ways of the world. Paul had never been anywhere for anybody, and beyond the knowledge found in books, he knew nothing about anything. The sun rose in the east and set in the west. This he hoped was true of every culture, but even here he was guessing.

Yes, Paul Danvers, young Ph.D., had made these calculations, adding and subtracting from the mental columns countless times. If he dismissed what he was capable of doing in the future then it came down to this: he really had just one item in the plus column—his mother's old lover, Dr. Whitman.

That was probably enough for the present, but even a department head could not keep his job forever. Eventually Dr. Whitman would drop dead in that office with its case of Southern Comfort and stack of girlie magazines. When that happened, and it would be sooner than later, Paul would be out of work as well. Unless . . . unless he could publish, publish something significant.

Up until now he had published nothing. He had tried and been rejected at least a half-dozen times. He had submitted several chapters of his dissertation, "The Importance of Discovering America," done a short piece on Indian tribes east of the Mississippi, and sent in an interesting essay entitled "The Presidency." Nothing. Nothing. Nothing. And his rejections had not been encouraging. One editor commented that Paul's topics were too broad and the conclusions he drew too obvious. Six weeks later the same man turned down his "Little-known Repercussions of the Disastrous Macon County Pecan Harvest of 1897."

However, Dan Pauling, for all his ability and charm, had hardly done better. He had published one article in an obscure journal and another in the *Sewanee Review*. True, Paul was behind, but he might still be within striking distance.

It was at that point in his life, almost to the day, that Paul read the autobiographical essay of Ginny Fennel and perceived her connection with the famous Fennel family papers. And here was sweet salvation—a coup of such colossal proportions that Paul actually shook with excitement.

"What's wrong with you?" Dan Pauling asked. "You got ants in your pants?"

"What? What did you say?"

"You shake my desk when you tap your foot like that. I can't write with the top of my desk bucking around."

"Oh." Paul hadn't realized he'd been tapping his foot. "Sorry."

"You must be in love," Dan Pauling said before going back to his writing.

In his entire life no one, not his mother nor Dr. Whitman nor anyone else, had ever accused him of being in love.

"Just anticipating," Paul answered and laughed at his own cleverness.

"Well, I hope things work out for you before you make this building fall down." Dan Pauling didn't bother to look up. Just pointed his pen in the direction of Paul's foot.

The foot was still tapping. Paul grabbed the knee with both hands and pressed down. "Sorry," he said.

Dan Pauling shook his head and smiled.

Paul could not, of course, admit that he liked his office mate. To let down his guard now would prove fatal, for though he was certain Dan Pauling was not in direct collusion with the others (Paul was not paranoid) the new man could easily become their pawn. Perhaps he already had.

The only concession Paul could make was to take part in good-natured bantering, to reply in kind to whatever friendly overtures came his way. He could hardly do otherwise with their desks just inches apart.

That was how things stood between the two men when he returned to his office that fateful day to find Ginny Fennel waiting for him. She sat smiling timidly at something that bastard Dan Pauling had just said, and for the first time since they'd become office mates Paul's anxiety gave way to outright anger. Figuratively speaking, only one of them would come out of that office alive, and literally speaking, Paul intended to be that one.

Dr. Dan Pauling removed a new pipe from his mouth and grinned a cheery hello. He'd started smoking a pipe the week before. And two weeks before, he'd begun to grow a mustache. It was coming along nicely. Soon they would both smoke pipes and wear mustaches. What would Paul's life be like then? He had an inkling. Ginny Fennel stood up and spoke.

"Dr. Pauling, did you want to see me?"

"Danvers," Paul said evenly. "My name is Dr. Paul Danvers."

AN ESCAPADE

Paul couldn't relax. Not in this house. Beneath him the mattress was a sea of lumps. The bedspread smelled of mothballs. And the night was filled with noises. The wind, tree frogs, the creaking of the Fennel house, even the sound of a car horn. To sleep he needed the hum of a central heating and air unit, not this din of nature. This . . . this . . . Paul heard another sound which he realized was his own heartbeat. His hand began to throb in time to the rhythmic thumping. He should have asked for Epsom salts and warm water. But *should have* and *might have been* were the story of his hopeless life. Yes, his hand could wait, for what mattered was his coming eviction. He thought he'd spotted Ginny's bedroom on the first floor, and if he could reach it and tell her what had happened, they could make plans.

She knew how important the papers were to him, knew without him even saying. She could help him apologize in the morning or even lead him to the papers this very night. His imagination raced on and he saw the two of them loading the priceless papers into the trunk of the old Chrysler, but even he could recognize the insanity of that.

In frustration he pulled the pillow over his head and was enveloped in muffled darkness. More than his hand throbbed now. His whole body seemed to pulse and the sound of the blood pounding in his ears was far louder than any night noises imaginable. Furious with himself, Paul pressed the soft down further into place.

Only then did he hear the voices. Despite the pillow they were quite distinct. The cook, Da Bena, was speaking to someone. They were in the next room or maybe down the hall. Paul listened. Though he could make no sense of what she was saying, he heard his name repeated again and again, and there was something else—the smell of burning hair or maybe feathers.

Paul sat straight up, half expecting to find the strange black woman standing right beside him. She wasn't, and the single naked light bulb that dangled overhead left no shadow big enough to hide her. Thankful that he always slept with the light on (as a boy he'd been terrified of the dark, and so out of habit he always kept a light burning), Paul brought his feet to the floor and listened. Heard nothing. No one was repeating his name. Only the tree frogs, and far in the distance a dog barking.

He eased from the bed and tried a cautious step. The floor came up to meet him and then dropped away. Clutching the bedpost he reached out and caught the corner of the dresser. The feeling of dizziness he'd experienced earlier hadn't gone away. If anything it was worse. One final swaying step brought him to the dresser and he picked up his watch.

Twenty after twelve. It didn't seem possible that he'd lain there for over three hours. Perhaps he'd slept after all. Again he listened for Da Bena's voice. Nothing. And instead of burning hair, he smelled the familiar sweetness of the wisteria. Paul took a cautious step and stood unaided. The time had come. Once on his feet there was little point in turning back. For better or worse he would find Ginny. She was his one hope of salvaging the research project and of experiencing a future.

With surprising ease Paul stepped into the hall and closed the door behind him. But this plunged him into almost total darkness. A rush of prickly heat passed over his body. Without light he could fall and hurt himself or bump into something with his bad hand. Or bump into someone with it. Some nameless person could be waiting or even moving towards him and in this inky corridor the person could have just one name—Da Bena. Paul pushed back into his room.

At the university there were no unlit areas. His apartment, the stairwell, the parking lots, the foyers, the walks, the classrooms. Everywhere was a blaze of light, and if there was some small dark corner, Paul avoided it. In an agony of indecision he sat on the bed, hugged himself, looked about, and then sought solace in his pipe. And of course to fire the pipe he had his box of matches. A godsend. Back in the hall he struck the first match and, half bouncing off the walls, headed for the stairway. The floor, as treacherous as ever, seemed to slope downhill steeper and steeper, hurrying him along until the match burned his fingers and left him stranded. He struck another. Just as he thought, he'd been standing on the edge of a precipice. His toes hung over the top stair tread and another step would have plunged him to his death. The second match died, which was just as well, for he wanted both hands on the rail as he crept downward. And a third match wasn't needed. Light from the dining room dimly illuminated the hall and three doors that opened off it. Paul stopped to listen. He heard only the ticking of a clock. He studied the first door and then, acting on his earlier hunch, crossed to the middle one and eased it open. On the far side of the room was the dim outline of a four-poster bed. And the dark form sleeping there was surely Ginny. Paul approached, realizing as he did that the attack of vertigo had passed and that there was nothing here to fear. He shook the shoulder of the sleeping girl.

Nothing happened. He shook again but the body beneath his hand felt strange. Paul drew back but chalk-stick fingers already clutched his arm and a face like white wax came out of the shadows—a Halloween mask, the skin pulled tight across the skull, bone threatening to break through tissue.

"Martin," Camilla whispered.

Paul froze. She had spoken but still she slept. Her eyes were closed. Gently he removed her hand and backed towards the door. But he could sense the eyeballs moving behind the lids. Sunk deep in their Fennel sockets, they followed him from the room, and only when he'd reached the hall did her head return to the pillow.

Outside, Paul slumped against the wall and waited. She did not follow. And what was more, the worst that could happen had happened. Comforted by this thought, he hesitated no longer, and opening the next door found himself staring at Ginny's father.

Adam had been moved from his wheelchair to a recliner. The television was on, but without sound. It cast a metallic blue glow on the invalid—pinned him to the recliner. He blinked back at the screen where a man in a tuxedo was dancing with a girl in a bathing suit—a skimpy bathing suit with feathers attached. She was a show girl. The man stumbled and the girl laughed or seemed to. They talked and smiled and started to dance again. In this matter of seconds Paul felt himself being hypnotized—blinking at the set along with the paralyzed man.

Paul didn't own a television. There'd been none in the apartment he shared with his mother. The one in the dorm lacked a "horizontal hold" so the picture spun by in a continuous loop. Like cards and food and much else, the device held little interest for him. But still he watched as the dancing man stumbled again and the woman caught him. They kissed. Their lips touched and then they laughed again. Were they married?

Outside a car drove up. The motor cut off. Azalea. He'd forgotten about Azalea. She would be returning from bridge. The car door slammed as Paul eased out of the room and headed for the darkened stairway. She was already on the front porch. His vertigo forgotten, Paul took the steps two at a time. She entered the house. His wariness of the dark misplaced, Paul crouched in the black hallway above. Below, the sound of Azalea's movements diminished and stopped. Then, like a small nocturnal animal, Paul scurried through the night to his own room.

Wrong again. It was Ginny's room. He'd been stumbling all about the house while she was sleeping right next door.

LULLABY

No, there'd be no mistakes this time, for the room was lit bright with an unexpected moonlight. And Ginny—she slept on her back, and beneath the sheet Paul could make out the contours of her body. One leg stretched towards the foot of the bed, while the other was drawn up as far as possible. The arms, too, spread akimbo, one lost from sight as it fell beside her waist and the other emerging from the cover to deliver a thumb almost to her mouth.

Paul forgot the purpose of his visit. He leaned in to watch the breasts rise and fall. He listened for her breathing, but instead heard a quiet footfall in the hall. He stepped behind the door just as the knob turned. He shrank against the wall. With a will of its own, his mangled hand began to throb. He was staring at the back of Leroy's thick neck.

As Paul watched, Leroy crossed to the bed and pulled back the covers. Ginny was naked. Paul was amazed. Her body lay exactly as he had traced it, except Leroy's view left nothing to the imagination. The nipples were soft dark dots on moonlight-whitened mounds. The navel was a bottomless crease. The pubic hair was a pale haze. He strained to get a better view and when Leroy lowered the sheet and took an appreciative swig from the beer bottle he carried, Paul felt cheated. Disappointed the show was over. But this was his girl. He didn't have to peer over other men's shoulders, especially not her uncle's shoulders. Paul's disgust with himself turned to helpless fury, and back to disgust. He wasn't going to start a fight he couldn't win, much less one where he'd be massacred. Especially not in Ginny's room in the middle of the night and not if there was still the slightest chance to see those papers.

Gently massaging his aching palm, Paul judged the distance to the hall. Ginny hadn't cared when Leroy pawed her at supper, and his own caring hadn't helped a bit. Anyway, an uncle wouldn't hurt his niece. It was unnatural. Wasn't it unnatural? Should he go? Should he stay? Leroy turned and faced him. No more than three feet separated them, and only a parched mouth kept Paul from screaming for Azalea.

Lucky for him he didn't. After a full minute's silent confrontation Paul realized that Leroy wasn't seeing him at all. Perhaps the man was drunk. Something was wrong, for instead of acknowledging Paul's presence, Leroy left the room.

Paul waited, checked the hall, and then shut the door and locked it. At the sound of the bolt clicking the girl stirred.

"Paul?" After the harried hours of silence his own name spoken quietly boomed through the old house.

"Yes," he whispered.

This time it was Ginny herself who was holding back the covers. And Paul shrugged off his pajamas and climbed onto the bed. He did have to talk to her about Camilla and about the papers, but there'd be time for that. Beneath him her body was damp and warm. He felt her back stiffen and arch against him as he fumbled to enter her. There was no time to put into practice the romantic daydreams of the past week. There was only the painful and clumsy urgency he'd heeded at the motel, compounded now by a new expectancy.

Certainly, he was not expecting the thin black hand that appeared to dance like a tarantula before his face, and certainly he was surprised when a black arm swung like a cobra beside the pillow. Ginny's legs and arms hugged him to her, but Paul broke free, scrambled from the high bed, and stood pointing at the far side.

"It's her," he managed to whisper. The black hand and arm had withdrawn from sight, but moments before, Paul had peered over the edge of the mattress into the face of the gaunt black woman and seen the sightless white eyes staring into his own. "It's Da Bena."

"Of course it's her." Ginny's voice was thick with a lazy sexuality. "She sleeps there."

"She was watching us."

Ginny rose on her elbows and glanced down. "She's asleep."

"Her eyes are open."

"She sleeps like that. Just the whites are showing."

"Her hand was moving around in front of my face."

"She tosses like that all night. Trust me, Paul. She's asleep."

"What are you talking about? What's she doing here?"

"She sleeps on the trundle bed. She stays in here so she can keep the baby."

"Baby? What baby?"

With a matter-of-fact shake of her head, Ginny got up and, taking him by the arm, led the way to the window. In the brightest of the moonlight was a bassinet. Paul's mind raced ahead. He was ready to accept Ginny, crazy family and all. He was ready to accept her with an illegitimate child. He peered inside. What was hard to accept was the sheet stretched flat and the miniature afghan neatly folded. There was no sign of a baby.

From the direction of the bed came a strange sound.

"She's awake now," Paul insisted. The black woman would see them white and naked, standing over an empty bassinet. They would look like fools.

"She's singing in her sleep."

Again the sound came, accompanied by a thin waving arm that could only be beckoning them back.

"Singing?"

"It's a lullaby."

"Ginny?" Paul asked. There were a hundred things he was afraid to ask. The girl took his arm and gave a tug.

"Just come to bed," she said. "Don't be such a worrywart."

But Paul stumbled away, retrieving his pajamas as he went.

"My hand," he said, but that made no sense. "Sleep," he added. There was no time for him to mention the Fennel papers or the fact that Camilla had thrown him out of the house.

BROWN JACK

Paul woke to a harsh angry light of day, but nothing more. No hostile crowd of Fennels ready to escort him to the town limits. No zombie woman waiting to accuse him of the previous night's blundering. He felt renewed. Determined. True, his hand ached. It had reddened slightly and should be soaked in hot water and salts. But first he must see Ginny and get her to change her great-aunt's mind. Papers first. Then he could tend the hand and try to make sense out of the empty bassinet and the "sleep in" nurse.

Plans made, Paul struggled from the tangle of sheets and spread. The iron bed frame, the spindly dresser with broken mirror, the captain's chair. Nothing in the room matched. Unless he matched the captain's chair to the clipper ship print— which had been clipped from a calendar. Yes, the light of day now shone into the Fennel house and he realized with some satisfaction that his impressions of the night before were not due to an attack of vertigo. The floor did slope dramatically. In fact, it fell in all directions from a hump in the center. In fact, the four walls joined with anything but a right angle, and even more eccentric were the slopes of the dormer ceiling and the cock-eyed openings made by the windows and door.

Captain Jack Fennel, for all his strength and vigor, had been a very poor architect and builder. If he had run the lighthouse the way he built this house, God help the commerce of the day.

Paul dressed quickly. Then looked in vain for his shaving kit. It wasn't in the suitcase and the dresser drawers were empty. He tiptoed down a hall whose dipping floor was indeed treacherous. He stuck his head in Ginny's room. The bassinet was gone. But he hadn't imagined that either. Or Leroy either. Or anything else.

In the bathroom, which had once been a closet, Paul found his toilet articles laid out on the wicker washstand. It was a logical place for them to be. He completed his ablutions as silently as possible, straightened his tie, brushed the lint from his tweed jacket, and crept downstairs.

There was no sign of the family. He retraced his route of the night before. Leading off the wide hall was Camilla's thick-draped bedroom and next to it the room where he'd found Adam and the television. And finally the narrow parlor with the ominous portrait of Captain Jack Fennel. Yes, the house was as dark and inhospitable as it had first appeared, and a level floor or straight wall was nowhere to be found. Paul muttered, "I was born in the house my father built," and returned to the hall.

The apartment that he'd shared with his mother might have been tiny and unassuming but at least it did not threaten to tumble down around their heads. He took a cautious step into the dining room. With linen removed, the table revealed itself. Warped oaken planks pocked with scars. And above his head wires from the erratic ship's lantern were crudely stapled across the ceiling. "These people," he muttered. "These people." But

confronted with the door to the kitchen he called out a respect-
ful "hello." No answer came back. He opened it and found a
combination of hall and pantry. The exterior shutters were
closed but light filtered through their slats. Jars of preserves,
coated thickly with dust, had been stacked along shelves on each
side. He could see that the contents of many had separated.
Brushing one clean, he raised it eye-level. Embryonic-like tissue
hung in a bejeweled suspension that seemed to have more to do
with biology class than marmalade. He replaced it and fled into
the next room.

The kitchen. A low, sooted ceiling. And exceedingly dingy
walls. A scrap of curtain hung at one window and a piece of plastic was tacked across another. On the floor were several layers of
rotting linoleum. Paul gasped for breath and retreated half a step.
The heat was so intense that the air felt almost solid, and the contents of the room shimmered like a mirage. Through watering
eyes, he could make out the ever-present captain's chairs around
a square wooden table, an antique refrigerator, an enameled sink
with a pitcher pump instead of spigots, and the obvious source of
all the heat, a massive cast-iron cookstove. Paul could easily envi-
sion the black woman working over that stove—arms snaking
out for pots, face glistening with demonic sweat.

On the far wall a screen door led to the outside. He bolted
through and was once more staggered—this time by the bright
unobstructed sunlight of a spring day. Not an unpleasant sensation, actually. Bees buzzed about the wisteria that crowded up
against each side of the small back stoop. Before him stretched
an expanse of fruit trees, grape vines, and flower beds, and
beyond those a large vegetable garden, some rambling pens and
outbuildings.

He drew a deep breath and heard a distinct rasping sound.
Metal against metal. He jumped and reached for the screen door

handle. Sitting on the steps practically under his feet was a man — a man using a file to sharpen an axe. But with his back to Paul and his mind to the work, he hadn't noticed the intrusion. Paul let the screen door shut with a rap and the man turned and looked up.

The face was familiar. The same small sunken eyes and the same beak of a nose that Paul had seen on both Adam and Camilla Fennel and of course in the portrait in the sitting room. There was a slight difference, however — one previously shielded by a battered felt hat. This man was black — or rather brown — and even the most Fennel of his features had a distinct Negroid fullness. He was old, older than Da Bena, perhaps. The eyes were yellowed and bloodshot. He had a beard but it seemed worn away to a faded white nap. And the weathered skin hung loose on a frame that had shrunk to only bone and sinew. Still and all, the man was formidable.

"Morning," Paul said after the initial surprise had passed.

The man with the axe grunted and resumed his work. Paul could think of nothing else to say. He hated to go back into the house, especially if help lay in this direction.

"Have you seen Ginny Fennel this morning?" Paul asked. This time the brown man gave no sign of hearing.

A soft noise came from the kitchen and Paul glanced in. Though the rusty screen and shimmering heat were distorting the image, he was certain that a young woman had entered from the pantry. She wore a long white dress with ruffles at the neck and cuffs, and she had pulled her hair up and fastened it above her head.

"Ginny, is that you?" he called.

No answer. But a clank sounded behind him and Paul glanced back. The man at the bottom of the stair looked over his shoulder at Paul.

"Not you," Paul apologized and opened the screen door. Da Bena stepped out grinning. Startled, Paul peered around her. The kitchen was empty and now he shared the stoop with the skeletal creature who had watched him from the trundle bed the night before. He sensed the arms about to entrap him. He flinched, but the arms were raised to the sky.

"Dis a beautiful mornin', ain't 'em, Master Paul." Again Paul was struck by the incongruity of the soft guttural voice. It rose out of her chest. Came up beneath a breastbone that rippled like a washboard. She was a shade darker than this man. But her dusty skin seemed translucent—tissue thin—the bone threatening to pop through. And the clothes. Today she wore a man's sport coat—blue and white checks over a yellow sundress. The dress ended midthigh but bunched expansively at the waist and above. The hat and bandanna were replaced with a canted sailor's cap. Her feet were bare. She lowered her arms and asked, "You like these here clothes?"

"Ma'am?" he answered.

"You so polite. I just askin' 'bout this outfit?" She made a rough curtsey.

"Fine." He gave a nervous glance to the sharpener who, ignoring them both, continued to sharpen.

"Dis outfit just somethin' Bena throw on when mornin' come."

Was this a veiled reference to last night's misadventure?

"Yes, ma'am," he said.

"Do, boy. Call me Bena. Ain't have to ma'am me."

"Yes," he said. "I can. I will. But can you tell me where Ginny went to?"

"Dey send that gal to the store."

"Oh."

He would have to wait out here. There wasn't much choice.

But at least Ginny had been right. Da Bena had slept through his failed debauchery or at least she didn't care.

"Ma cha'e ran the ra, ha," the woman called suddenly to the man with the axe and, after a sinister chuckle, added, "Plum ba' go, haa."

This time Paul couldn't understand a word that was spoken but it did bring to mind the lullaby he'd heard the night before. Below, the man stood and faced them, a grin creasing his ancient face. With a precise caution he ran his thumb across the glistening edge and motioned in Paul's direction. Da Bena gave a snorting giggle, and looking at Paul, she rolled her eyes back until once again only the whites showed. And drawing a finger across her throat, she made a clucking noise.

Him? Paul? Paul who had meant no harm? Perhaps it was a joke. He tried to smile and pretend he understood, but it was useless. In truth, he knew little of black people, and most of that little he'd gotten from books. He had no black students. No blacks were on the faculty. There was a law, an unwritten law against that, but black women worked in the cafeteria. They were plump and happy women who spoke normal English and offered extra large servings, though Paul couldn't bring himself to make eye contact with them. And there were others. He had seen both black women and men when he went on vacation with his mother. They stood on the side of the road. They hauled trash and scrubbed floors. He'd seen them in Atlanta. If you left the campus they were everywhere. Still, he'd assumed that these people, occupied in their menial labor, would not notice him. He'd assumed that Da Bena was acting alone the previous night and not in concert with her entire race. But was this man a true black? Clearly Fennel blood flowed in those angry veins, which, considering the rest of the family, might explain his behavior.

Now, the woman spoke several more hurried sentences in what must have been the same African dialect, and the man with the axe nodded in agreement. And yes, Paul understood that he was the sole topic of their grim conversation. He felt himself begin to flush and tingle from an uneven mixture of guilt and terror. This was what he should have been expecting. His whole body was beginning to itch.

"Paul! You out there, Paul?" a voice called from the kitchen.

"Out here, Leroy. I'm coming."

Da Bena stepped aside, allowing Paul to surrender the stoop, and he scrambled in to join his unlikely ally. The crippling handshake and Leroy's visit to the girl's bedroom were events of the distant past.

"Who is that with the axe?" he whispered once inside.

Leroy peered out the screen.

"Brown Jack," he said.

"Who?"

"Brown Jack Simmons. Da Bena's husband. He splits firewood for this baby." Leroy slapped the shimmering cookstove with his rock-hard hand and it rang like a bell. "Come on, Miss Camilla wants to see you." He motioned towards the front of the house and Paul saw that his chance at the Fennel papers was gone. Ginny had been sent to the store so that he could be dismissed quietly. That much was clear, but he was still baffled by the couple outside.

"They were speaking African," Paul whispered as he was ushered away.

"That's Gullah. Thought a professor would know something that simple."

"They were speaking a foreign language," Paul insisted as he entered the sun-striped pantry.

"Not hardly." Leroy was behind him now. "Brown Jack don't

speak nothing. He's deaf. Been deaf since Uncle Jack Junior drug him off to dig the Panama Canal."

"What?" Paul asked.

"Just this," Leroy whispered hoarsely. Paul saw a muscular arm slipping under his chin as the small of his back exploded in pain.

"Leroy?" he gasped, sinking to his knees.

"A hundred ways to kill a man," Leroy whispered in his ear.

On the walls the jars of preserves glistened brightly and then dimmed. The door to the kitchen cracked open and Da Bena peered in.

"Help me, please," Paul gasped, twisting to look at her. She grinned back at him and shook her head no.

"Leroy! What are you doing. Let go of him right now." Azalea was standing in the dining room entrance.

"We was just playing, Sis."

The pressure on Paul's neck surged and then he was released. Free to float downward, he passed out before he struck the floor.

When Paul came to he was stretched out on the floor beside the dining room table. Azalea knelt over him mopping his brow with a greasy dishrag. Groaning, he touched a pulsing temple and drew back fingertips spotted with blood.

"It's all right," she assured him. "Just a bump."

"I know I'm not welcome here," Paul croaked. "But he almost killed me."

"Leroy? He was just playing. Don't be mad. You wouldn't think so but he's very sensitive. He was very frail as a boy."

"Frail? Sensitive!" With Azalea's help Paul sat up. Da Bena was present. "And her," he said, pointing feebly. "She just stood there and let him strangle me."

"Da Bena. Why didn't you stop Leroy?" Azalea accused.

The skeletal black removed her sailor cap and rolled her eyes back. And for the second time that morning mimicked Paul in his death throes.

"Bena ain't know what wrong with that one. She think he throw fit—catch a convulsion."

This seemed to satisfy Azalea. She smiled at the black woman and then at Paul.

"Azalea, her husband, he had an axe," Paul wailed. "An axe."

"Do, boy. That a tease. A tease." A black thin fingered hand covered in part the piano-key teeth. Mirth stifled.

"Well, see there," Azalea crooned. "A tease. Now don't say you're not welcome here, Paul. You are very welcome, and you must stay as long as you like."

THE FENNEL CURSE

Good morning, young man. I hope you slept well." Camilla
sat in a rocker and stared across the front lawn and the
endless marsh beyond.

Paul murmured a reply. Ginny he saw was not at the store.
She had pushed her father out on the bluff where the marsh
began and they too were gazing at the horizon.

The rocker gave a creaking groan. The old woman watched
him.

"That is a nasty bump," she said and returned her attention to
the landscape.

Paul wondered what his face must look like. His shirt was
spotted with blood and his tweed jacket was filthy from being
dragged through the pantry. One knee was ripped out of his best
pants. This was not the impression he'd set out to give. He nudged
the knot of his tie and addressed his answer to the porch floor.

"I just fell. Nothing." He indicated the interior of the house.
It was useless to explain. She had sent Leroy after him in the
first place.

"Paul was in the back yard," Azalea spoke up gaily. "I believe he met Brown Jack Simmons."

"Did you?" Camilla addressed the marsh.

"I saw someone."

"An exceptional Negro in every possible way." Camilla looked him squarely in the face for the first time. "He and Bena are both exceptional Negroes. Exceptions to their race, I'm afraid, but that is the one good thing to come from all that disorder we see on our television. Those few exceptions are allowed to take their rightful place in society. Not that it was necessary in this case for as I'm sure Virginia has told you Da Bena and Jack Simmons have always been like members of the Fennel family."

Actually, Ginny had never mentioned either of the blacks or her uncle Leroy. As he'd realized at last night's supper, she'd told him absolutely nothing of consequence about her family. It was easy to see why. But thinking of the girl now, he let his attention wander to the bluff, where she lay on her back in the unmowed grass. If he could just signal or call out or even run to her—do something to rescue himself. At that moment Leroy was probably loading Paul's things into the car and before Ginny knew it, he'd be gone.

Azalea beamed at him. She had just bestowed her worthless assurance that he was welcome here. If he was to have just one ally in the house why did it have to be her?

"Dr. Danvers?"

"Excuse me?" he said.

"Dr. Danvers, I asked if you didn't agree that they were exceptional Negroes?"

"Remarkable. They seem to have their own language." Paul spoke once more to the porch floor.

"Da Bena was speaking Gullah." Camilla actually laughed when she said this.

"It's a form of pigeon English that was kept here along the sea coast," Azalea added.

"It sounded more like . . . some African dialect." Yes, joke or not, the blacks had not been speaking English in any form and nothing more would be lost by stating the facts.

"That's an easy mistake to make," Azalea countered. "Gullah uses many African words and mangles most English ones. If you listen to it long enough you'd understand."

"For once I must agree with Azalea. To the untutored ear it does sound like a foreign language. Especially when spoken rapidly the way Bena would speak to Jack Simmons." Camilla cocked her head and raised the chalk-stick fingers to one ear.

"Leroy said Jack was deaf," Paul muttered.

"Since he was a young man," Azalea said.

"They communicate," Camilla interjected. "They get on very well. But now we must discuss the topic at hand. Azalea has insisted—I should say she has convinced me that because you are Virginia's suitor and because you appear to be an honorable young man you should be given access to the family papers. This is against my better judgment, but I will agree on two conditions: first, that no papers leave this house, and second, that I review all notes that are taken and approve of any article or book that is written. Some of this I suppose should be placed in writing. But if you agree to these terms we will accept your word as a gentleman and a scholar."

Paul looked at Azalea, amazed not that she would, but that she could intercede on his behalf. Nervous once more, he brushed the dirt from his pants legs before answering.

"Fine. That's fine with me. You won't be disappointed."

"I hope not." Once more Camilla addressed the marsh. "Azalea will show you around now, and after lunch she will arrange for the papers to be moved to your bedroom. I should think that would be the most convenient room for your studies."

The interview was over. Azalea opened the screen door and Paul was back inside the Fennel home.

"Every post and lintel, every door and sash of this house was gathered on the beach by Miss Camilla's father, Captain Jack Fennel. He was the keeper of the Fennel light from 1854 to 1910 and was perhaps the most illustrious of the Fennel light keepers."

Apparently there had been enough visitors to the house to bring about a codifying of the family history. Everything had been reduced to a brief, well-ordered oratory which was delivered as they stood transfixed in the parlor.

"You have seen the portrait," Azalea said. "And I believe I mentioned the particular phenomenon of its eyes."

Obediently Paul gave the portrait a sideways glance and received the same from the man above the fireplace.

"Who's this?" Paul asked. By trying to avoid the Captain he'd ended up examining the sketch of another face. It was a very familiar face. Ginny, but not quite Ginny. The hair was piled high on the girl's head—perhaps that was the only difference. The work was initialed at the bottom right corner with a very meticulous *A*.

"Captain Jack's sister, Virginia. Ginny is named for her and the sketch is thought to be by Audubon. The bird painter."

"Audubon?" Paul said in disbelief.

"Yes. He is thought to have visited the light several times before the war. It looks like Ginny, doesn't it?"

"Yes. It could be very valuable if it were really by him."

"I suppose, but Camilla would never part with that. She's had to sell many things over the years. You wouldn't know it now but when I was a girl this house was like a museum—one of those ship's museums." Azalea gestured hopelessly at the contents of the room.

Paul made an appraisal—the first open and honest one of his

visit. Yes. He was free to take stock and to realize "gathered on the beach" meant just that. The furnishings of this room were distinctly nautical. The chairs were all captain's chairs and the small desk and table were obviously companion pieces suited for cramped quarters. Even the Victorian sofa was scaled down to the confines of a captain's cabin. On the wall was not one but two barometers. The bookcase held a battered ship's model, a sextant, several pieces of scrimshaw, some oriental bric-a-brac, and a pair of large exotic seashells. Stuck away in a corner were a handsome telescope and a large ornately boxed compass, both of which Azalea cradled in his arms. Paul tipped forward and then back. He pressed the objects close, which brought a sharp pain to his injured hand. The brass sleeves of the telescope threatened to extend. The compass needle flung around wildly before steadying on the ornate *N*.

"That's north," Azalea said and pointed out a window.

"Yes," Paul answered.

"This is all that's left," Azalea said, "but the house used to be packed with these things, literally to the ceiling." She pointed towards the heavens and sighed as if in mourning.

But Paul continued to examine the oddly bowed window. Crooked, yes. But it too had probably come from a ship. The windows and doors. And this tilted flooring was actually planking and everything was framed with ship's timbers—"every post and lintel."

"He salvaged all this?"

"From 'tall ships.' Yes, everything, built and furnished from what washed ashore."

"The Dog Tooth Shoal must be very dangerous." Though he hadn't meant it to, the statement sounded like an accusation. He wanted to be free of telescope and compass but would need Azalea's help.

"It's the worst on the coast. The currents are very bad and storms are always sudden and violent." Though Azalea had spoken softly, she'd been heard on the front porch.

"But now its terror is lost," Camilla called in. "And safety and life have sprung from danger and death."

"Yes. Yes, it has," Azalea called back. And she took Paul by the overloaded arm and led him again into the old woman's presence.

"My father, Jack Fennel, had a fine mind. The finest mind of any man I've known," Camilla declared. She rocked methodically, but stopped when she saw Paul ladened with telescope and compass. "My father's glass, Dr. Danvers. Are you planning a voyage?" Camilla smiled or at least it seemed so.

"Oh, no," Azalea said. She grabbed both objects from his arms and fled to the parlor.

"A fine mind," Camilla continued. "For the life my father lived was calculated to develop the patient and enduring qualities of a man and cultivate in him a habit of self-reflection."

"He built this house," Azalea added as she rejoined them. "Every post and lintel."

Instead of scolding Azalea, Camilla echoed her. "Every post and lintel."

Paul feared that the house tour would now be repeated word for word, but Azalea pointed to the horizon. "There's the Fennel light. There. You can see it on a clear day like this."

Sighting down the woman's plump little finger, Paul was able to make out a vertical line no bigger than a pencil mark. He should have held on to the Captain's glass.

"Do you see it?"

"Yes. I think so."

"The Fennel family built, owned, and operated that lighthouse with practically no assistance from any government. They kept it because it filled a need."

"A grievous need," Camilla added. "Theirs was a high and holy service to humanity. A steadfast devotion to the interests of others. That has been the Fennel curse."

"Yes," Azalea agreed. "A curse."

"What?" Paul asked.

"This light," the younger woman began again, "is called the new light though it is hardly new. It was completed by Captain Jack's father, Heraclitus, in 1852. The light is of the first class and replaced a much older and lower light of the fourth class. The history of the light is long and complex . . . but I am sure you know that." Azalea glanced apologetically at Paul and then hurried on. "You're familiar with the history of the Fennel lighthouse. Captain Jack Fennel ran it from 1854 to 1910, and then his son Jack Junior kept it until 1943 when my husband, Adam, took over. Then Adam fell . . ." Azalea's voice trailed off and Camilla's rocker gave an emphatic groan. Apparently they had crossed the line between history and current family matters.

"It must have been lonely out there. I mean so far from everything." Without Azalea to show him, Paul could not even spot the lighthouse.

"Removed from the common-day aims and concerns of this world, let me assure you, but hardly lonely," Camilla declared. "After all, Dr. Danvers, they had for their companions the glories of the sky and the splendors of the sea."

LOVE LIES BLEEDING

Paul appreciated the view once more for the women's benefit and then Azalea led him down the front steps.

"Can you imagine? Ginny takes her father up and down that
by herself." She indicated an adjoining ramp.

Paul murmured in polite disbelief. It was steep. He would
have trouble just walking it, but where her father was concerned
Ginny was probably capable of anything.

They followed a narrow conch-lined path for a distance and
faced the house. And with his new generosity towards everything of and by the Fennels, Paul viewed the residence for the
first time as a whole and found it pretty—in a Jack Fennel crazy
sort of way. Painted a flaking white and raised a good six feet off
the ground, the building seemed to float as it rambled among
the tremendous live oaks and cedars. It was a giant shack.
Everything the Fennels did looked better from a distance.

"It's very nice," Paul said.

"You see." Azalea pointed to the bluff where Ginny lay and
Adam sat. "The workmen had only to carry the salvage from

there to there. The tin roof was added when Camilla came back from the island and there've been a few repairs along. But the original house was a gift of the sea."

Paul nodded. He was anxious to see Ginny and anxious to get to the papers, but Azalea had saved him. He was obliged to enjoy the rest of the tour and to observe.

"I think I recognize some of the building material," he said. "I mean what it once was." Which was easy. Yes. From the outside the sea-worthy influence was even more noticeable. Pieces of ships and ocean-born debris stuck out from every angle. Except for a few points resting on brick or cement blocks, the house sat on sections of masts, and these had sunk and leaned until the line of the floor and roof rolled like an ocean wave through the trees. And what Paul had taken for a porch was actually a portico like that found on antebellum mansions—only here the six columns were also cut from masts and the pediment above was embossed with three portholes.

"Keel, keelson, stempost, sternpost, floors, frames, planking, ceiling, decks, masts, and spars." Azalea recited what had been built into the structure. "It's a whole ship, really, assembled in a different way. Do you understand?"

Paul humored her by saying yes and they joined Ginny and her father on the bluff edge. The girl was lying on her back in the thick grass, and beside her in the wheelchair Adam slept, his chin resting on his chest.

"Look who's here!" Azalea cried brightly.

Ginny shielded her eyes with a hand and studied them. Her T-shirt rode up at the midriff and exposed one breast almost to the nipple.

"How'd you get that bump?"

"Roughhousing with Leroy," Azalea answered for Paul. "You know how young men are." Ginny made no reply. Paul noticed how long her hair had grown since they'd first met, how it fanned out in all directions, long auburn threads floating on a green sea of vegetation.

"Paul will be staying with us awhile," Azalea added. "He's going to start going over the papers this afternoon."

"That's nice." The girl lowered her hand and closed her eyes. The T-shirt fell back into place, but now both nipples showed through as small dark shadows. It embarrassed Paul to be standing beside her mother.

"They love it out here," Azalea explained. "As long as the weather's good and the bugs don't bite they'll stay here all day."

He barely heard Azalea. The hand which Ginny lowered had come to rest with a light possessiveness on the chrome spokes of Adam's chair. Paul was almost jealous.

"It's easy to see why," he said finally.

Azalea was patting her husband's shoulder. A nervous gesture, the kind a mother might give someone else's child. "Oh, Paul," she said. "The best is behind us."

And lecturing nonstop Azalea led him off to see the gardens. Jack Fennel this and Jack Fennel that, but when they reached the driveway she did pause long enough to show off her powder blue Plymouth station wagon. "Walter picked it out for me," she said. Paul nodded. She added, "Oh, I shouldn't say that." They were moving again. Paul nodded again. "Oh, you understand." Of course, Paul didn't, but he shook his head up and down. "You see, Paul, I'm an outside person." She smiled a not-so-crooked smile and halted. They'd reached the gardens, which turned out to be the back yard. Paul had glimpsed it already that morning from the back stoop. But the stoop was to the far side and the black couple was nowhere in sight.

"An outside person," Paul repeated.

"Now, just touch that grass," she instructed. "Isn't that the finest carpet? So rich and green. And smell the wisteria and look at that magnolia. The bees, Paul. The bees. Paul, don't you just love spring?"

"Yes," Paul said. "I love spring. I love all weather." Then he added, "I love spring especially." Which was an outright lie. He'd grown up in that apartment with only a sprouted avocado seed growing behind the sink. He didn't like what was going on outside. For him the tree-lined paths that connected the campus buildings were obstacle courses a person ran to get from one sealed room to another. The rest of nature was an outright menace. It was too late for him to change. Of course, he couldn't say any of this to Ginny's mother. Anyhow, he'd be inside soon enough, shuffling through papers to his heart's content. He touched the grass.

Azalea gave a blissful sigh and started over.

"This whole yard was planted by Captain Jack when he left the light, which gives you some idea how old the trees are. After all those years on the island where nothing but stickle burrs would grow, he just went wild. Three kinds of figs, and two kinds of grapes, and there's a pear orchard there." She pointed with a plump little finger at the gnarled vegetation. Much of it dying off at the top—but still sending up new shoots from the bases. "You see there—crab apples—and that's a plum thicket behind the pump house and these biggest trees are pecans."

"That's something." Paul still squatted on the grass. He tugged at a stubborn blade, causing his hand to throb. He studied the torn knee of the pants. Flannel couldn't be sewn. They were ruined.

"Most of these are so old now that they don't bear like they should," Azalea whispered. "But nobody here would dare cut them back. We can't use half of what grows, anyway. Bena and Camilla used to put a lot of it up, but not even that got eaten, and so they quit."

"Ah." Paul remembered the preserves from the pantry and the force of Leroy's blow. "That's something," he added, rising to his feet. He touched the bump on his forehead and checked his fingertips for blood. None.

"He did all this for his new bride, Camilla's mother, Jewel," Azalea enthused. "He built the house and planted the orchards. She loved flowers so he put in all these shrubs, the camellias, the azaleas, the mimosa, the wisteria. They're so tremendous now and so, so beautiful."

Paul shook his head up and down and pretended to sniff a nauseously sweet wisteria bloom. Its individual flowers of white and bluish purple clustered together like the short stubby fingers of some alien hand. They began to walk.

"He planted this flower garden too. It's mine now. I don't mean really mine, but it's my favorite place and I keep it up." She took Paul by the arm and veered off down yet another narrow conch-lined path to where a small clearing had been separated into portions bordered with the big shells. Well-tended patches of greenery grew in each. "There's not much left of Jewel's flowers. A few poppies, that's all. The rest of these I've planted. You wouldn't believe this place in the summer. As much color as spring and it stays so cool."

Paul continued to nod and they continued to walk and he realized the hysteria had vanished from Azalea's voice. She seemed younger, years younger. He guessed being outside had done that or maybe just getting away from Camilla. Fine for her, but he needed a bite of lunch before tackling the papers. He opened his mouth to say as much, but she'd released him to kneel before a group of spidery green leaves.

"These are summer poinsettia. By mid-July this will be nothing but a mass of white and red blooms. Guess what it's called." She watched him. Expectant.

"Forget-me-nots?"

"No!" Azalea laughed. "It's called love-lies-bleeding. Isn't that a strange name? There's such poetry in the names of flowers. I guess I think that because my name is Azalea, but still it's true, don't you think?"

Paul had never thought about it, but he agreed there was.

"I know this will sound silly, but in the winter when I can't come out here I just sit and read the seed catalogues. That's silly, isn't it? Sometimes I don't even look at the pictures, I just want to hear the names."

Paul smiled politely and wondered if Ginny's mother wasn't even more addled than he'd first suspected. Not that he could blame her, living here as she had to. She was a strange person in a house full of truly bizarre ones, but who was he to judge? Paul told himself that when the papers were done he would talk to Ginny about Azalea, and then he remembered that he needed to talk to Azalea about Ginny. Here in the garden he could risk it. He needed to know. He had a right to know and she seemed in an answering mood.

"Azalea, may I ask you something?"

The woman stood and looked up at him. She flashed the vulnerable crooked-mouth smile—her out-of-the-garden smile.

"What?"

"Did Ginny ever have a baby?"

"Why are you saying that?"

"I noticed a bassinet upstairs."

"There is no baby. I'm not sure there ever was." Azalea rubbed tears from her cheeks with chubby dirt-covered fists and turned towards the house. "Sometimes I think she and Bena just dreamed it up. I don't know." This last came out as a muffled sob, and she ran down the narrow garden path with awkward little steps.

CURLY WHITMAN

Paul didn't know much about women. His mother had been one but she wasn't the kind you could practice on. Why had he asked Azalea about the baby? That question could have waited. Waited forever if necessary. He liked Azalea, liked her very much. She'd saved him from Camilla. She'd rescued him from her brother twice. If things worked out she would be his mother-in-law. She would be his friend. He should have called out to her, but it was too late. Azalea had fled the garden, or was it gardens in the plural?

Paul kicked out at the nearest seashell. He'd seen the ocean. More than once. His mother had taken him to the beaches south of Charleston. They went on vacation and sometimes Dr. Whitman would show up. Anyway, the conch struck Paul as an admirable creature. All that hard shell to back into. And if he put one to his ear he would hear the breakers, which was really the blood pounding in your head. But he'd heard that the night before. Why had he asked Azalea about the baby? Why had she run? Love-lies-bleeding? What kind of name was that for a flower? Paul considered the dead white shell. A bug could be hiding in there. If he were to listen it would crawl in his ear and eat out his brain.

Paul Danvers had enemies. He had enemies aplenty back there in the history department. He had suspected this as a graduate student. As an instructor he was sure. He recognized them in the faculty lounge before he quit going there. They would stop talking when he entered or would lower their voices. They hid snide smiles behind their coffee cups and in their own clumsy and inept ways plotted against him. It was to be expected. Anyone who went through life made enemies. Just the same, he tried to avoid them.

By the time Ginny Fennel and Dan Pauling entered his life he was existing almost entirely in his classroom, his office, and his apartment. He had worked out routes, often circuitous, that enabled him to go from one of these places to another without having to be seen. The only problem was the library. When he went there he always found at least two or three of them. They would appear to be doing something, but it seldom concerned legitimate scholarship. They rummaged about, always watching him. He kept his eyes on his work. If they said hello, he nodded. He persisted in his efforts. It would be enough.

How naive he had been. Worrying over these people, he had allowed Dan Pauling to enter his office and to almost steal his job and personality. Then he'd met Ginny and in the excitement of making plans to examine the Fennel papers, he'd almost forgotten he had enemies. Indeed, he would have forgotten if the woman who claimed to be Robert Penn Warren's distant cousin hadn't confronted him at the faculty party.

Dan Pauling had insisted that he attend and so he'd played along. He went and had his usual miserable time. He couldn't drink. It made him sick. Late in the evening, the party wound

down and he was standing in the corner waiting for a ride home.
A drunken history professor from another state and his wife (the
woman who claimed to be the distant cousin of Robert Penn
Warren) found him there. They began to spit out ugly truths.
Paul was staggered. He had never seen these people. Surely the
conspiracy of his enemies could not be this far-flung. But these
people were very real and they seemed to know him.

They said he was a second-, third-, and finally a fifth-rate
scholar who owed his instructor's position to "the incestuous
intrigues of this jerkwater school." Didn't he realize that brilliant
young men and women with Ph.D.s were digging ditches or
even graves somewhere out there in the lonely night? Didn't he
understand it was he, and not those young people, who should
be driving cabs? At one point, the woman had actually grabbed
him by his tie, called him a "dim-witted, priggish bastard," and
filling her mouth with bourbon and water she'd pursed her lips
and sprayed it down the front of Paul's tweed jacket.

Dan Pauling had come to his rescue. "Her brother drives a
cab," he explained, mopping Paul's front with his own handker-
chief. "Just ignore them."

"That's easy for you to say," Paul snapped back, and he'd
brushed the help aside, realizing that it was Dan who angered
him most.

In a way he was glad it happened. Otherwise he would never
have gathered the courage or rather been driven to the extreme
desperation that it took to place him in the office of the department head. He'd already read over *Whitman's History* and followed
through on the meager sources suggested by the bibliography—
three earlier histories and a handful of legal documents and government reports. He'd even read the most recent articles—all of
them poor rehashings. Nothing of consequence there. Tenure
was at his fingertips.

But at the faculty party he'd seen how bold his enemies had become. Yes, a misstep at this point would be fatal. Paul went to see Dr. Whitman. He didn't have far to go. Just three stories up, and he was on familiar ground. His mother's many years as Dr. Whitman's mistress still counted for something. Of course, his enemies saw this as a joke as well. Their affair, once considered an outrage, was now ancient history in the history department, and the fact that his mother taught there a lifetime without even a BA was a laughing matter to most. Not to Paul. He knew these same scoffers resented his presence at the school. They doubted his abilities. He'd suspected this all along and after the faculty party he knew it with a diamond-hard certainty.

The next morning, he entered Dr. Whitman's reception room and received a cool greeting from the woman behind the desk. She was new on the job, so it was impossible to tell if she was against him or simply obtuse. It didn't matter. She was already assuming the position of power that department head secretaries are notorious for assuming.

She stalled him for an appropriate length of time, inquiring, in this case futilely, about the purpose of his visit and then said:

"Let me find out if he is able to see you."

This, they both knew, was a euphemism meaning exactly what it said: Let me find out if he's physically able to see you. She knocked lightly on the chairman's door and then stuck her head inside. A moment later she withdrew and gave Paul a sardonic smile. "He will see you now, Mr. Palvers."

Though the office was on the prestigious southeast corner of the building, heavy drapes kept the sunlight from entering the four large windows. At first Paul saw nothing, but as his eyes grew accustomed to the dark he began to get his bearings. The crowded bookshelves. The cluttered desk. And there in the far corner the divan where Dr. Whitman sat with his head buried in his hands.

"How's your mother, boy?"

Paul knew that in cases like this the truth never hurt.

"She died, Dr. Whitman. You remember that. Four years ago."

"Oh, yes. A wonderful woman, wonderful woman. We were always very close, you know." The shaggy head turned towards him for the first time.

"I know," Paul said. "She was very fond of you."

"A wonderful woman," the old man repeated, coughed until he was almost breathless, and then spoke again. "What do you want now? Isn't the job enough?"

Paul braced himself. These interviews had an inevitability about them, and if he remained calm he'd get what he came for.

"The Fennels. I've been reading in your book about the Fennel family who kept the lighthouse. I notice that no really extensive research has been done in this field and I'd like to give it a try."

This was greeted by an angry laugh.

"Bravo! Daning. Just what is needed. Another paper on some obscure, esoteric, and totally useless subject."

"I thought you could help me."

"Look in the bibliography."

"I did and it was a big help. Still, I was looking for something else. Something you might have come across but for some reason or other didn't include in your *History of the State*."

And having said that, Paul was struck by a curious sense of the unremembered—some hazy impression of his childhood. Dr. Whitman had left something unsaid about the Fennels. Paul had heard hints of this from his mother—sharp remarks about the Fennel family which only now had registered. What had she said? The exact words were forgotten but the tone, the seemingly unwarranted fury, had remained.

There was still no response from the divan, and as Paul

waited, his sensation of déjà vu began to fade. He had come to the room with something much more concrete in mind. He had no reason to believe that Dr. Whitman had ever had access to the Fennel papers. As far as Ginny knew no one had, but other sources of information existed. Dr. Whitman himself had told Paul that there was a history published and a history recited and that the two were often at odds. It made sense that the latter, the oral history, might never find its way beyond a family's bedroom. But sometimes it reached the kitchen or the back steps or even the neighborhood tavern. Perhaps it might even have come to the attention of Dr. Whitman, who could not repeat it in print without documentation.

"Why the Fennels?"

Paul wasn't prepared for this question.

"No reason especially. I just got interested in them. Having my degree has . . . "

"The Fennels." The voice cut off his own. "They were guilty of everything and convicted of nothing. Every charge I mentioned in my book could be substantiated at the time and yet over and over they escaped punishment and went on to commit some further atrocity."

"I think there's clear evidence . . . " Paul began.

"Stranger still," the voice went on, "were the incidences involving slavery that for one reason or another didn't reach the courts at all." The old man stopped once more to cough violently and wipe the good hand across his lips. "In 1713 Basil Fennel sold the entire Ulacca tribe into slavery by convincing them that England lay just beyond the horizon and if they would just take their dugouts and paddle over there they could trade directly with the English king. They followed his advice and the lucky ones were rounded up by the Spanish galleon that Basil had waiting off shore."

"But that isn't recorded anywhere." The old man glared. "Unless I've forgotten it," Paul added in quick apology. And possibly he had. Whitman still gave his brilliant lectures—but he read them from the yellowed transcripts. Read some of them two and three times in a row and skipped others. He didn't expect the students to listen. The tests were multiple choice. Perhaps Paul had let his mind wander for a critical moment. His own students did that. A few slept, which was preferable to the wide-awake indifference of the others. But he wanted to teach them something. Not the lesson of history that Whitman seemed to hint at—how human beings were capable of anything. Paul wanted to teach them something besides that and once tenure was gained he would. And if they failed to learn it he could flunk them with impunity.

"Chervil and Capers kept dealing in slaves," the old man continued, "and used the lighthouse island as a sort of holding pen for plantations in the Port Ulacca area. Jack Fennel's father Heraclitus kept this up, but at the same time he turned the Fennel light into a key link in the Underground Railroad. Escaped slaves were brought there from the states of the deep South, put on coastal steamers, and carried to New England or Canada. It was risky business but he was being paid by the abolitionists, and being a Fennel he had a little sideline. He sold the pick of his charges back into slavery."

The man coughed with a renewed violence. His huge body curled into a knot and quivered uncontrollably as the raw rasping sounds came from deep in his chest.

"Can I get you anything?" Paul asked. "Water?"

Whitman shook his head. "Nothing," he muttered. "It's this goddamn congestion." He brushed the shock of white hair back and braced himself, both hands on his knees. "Jack was the one. Everybody knows he was a turncoat and a rascal, but that's just the tip of the iceberg . . . just the tip. In '57 or '58 he and his sister Virginia tried to smuggle a shipload of slaves straight from Africa. They were caught. Not exactly caught—the cargo ended up in Mississippi. The next time they were luckier."

"I've never heard that."

"No. You haven't, have you? And you've never heard of Virginia marrying the commander of the Confederate garrison either. Jack performed the ceremony himself. It was legal since under the charter he was 'captain' of the lighthouse. And best of all, they loved each other. What a joke." Whitman cleared his throat and spit to the far side of the divan. He stared at Paul.

"Sir?" Paul asked.

"Love? You know about love, don't you?"

"Sir?"

"You know what a joke is, don't you?"

"I mean what happened then, sir?"

Paul had come here in search of some incidental piece of information, a clue at best, but Whitman seemed to already know it all.

"Oh, there's more," the old man laughed. "The Caladium Keyhole. Keeping that would have changed everything. And he . . . he . . . Oh, there's much more. Much much more." But he would not say what more there was.

"Sir?" Paul coaxed.

"Sir?" Whitman mimicked in a slurring whine. "Know what I say, Danvers?"

"Sir? I mean what? What, sir?"

"More power to them. The Fennels were a bunch of bastards but who cares. I sure as hell don't."

"But sir, how could you know this?"

"Ghosts." The laugh turned into a strangled cough and again Whitman spit. "That's all history is. Stories about people who are dead." Then groaning, the man stood and held his right hand up to the light. The first three fingers were missing. Some of Paul's earliest memories were of that hand—the pink-white grublike stubs wiggling in front of his face. Whitman took an unsteady step in his direction and presented the mutilation as if a present.

"Your mother was a whore, Palvers!" the voice shouted hoarsely. "A dirty stinking whore."

"Yes," Paul said. "You've told me several times."

A bottle flew past and shattered on the wall behind him.

The room filled with the sweet cough-syrup smell of Southern Comfort.

"Thank you," Paul said, letting himself out. In the reception room he stopped to brush the broken glass from his coat. The secretary stared at him with ill-concealed delight. Paul didn't care. He'd picked up the trail. Yes, Dr. Paul Danvers would unlock the mystery of the Caladium Keyhole.

THE CHICKEN YARD

And here he was at the Fennels and the papers were close at hand. Except Azalea had run off crying. Paul would apologize. The problem of the baby could be settled after the problem of the papers. That would be a busy time in his life, that moment when he finished with the Fennel papers. Using his shoe tip, he replaced the weathered conch shell, took a last look at the flower beds, and set off for the bluff. He could sit with Ginny until lunch was ready. That was his new plan, but approaching the house he spotted the girl pushing her father into the far corner of the back yard. He hesitated, and they disappeared behind one of the low rambling grape arbors.

Da Bena? Brown Jack Simmons and Da Bena?. Tease or not, he'd assigned that side of the grounds to them and hadn't planned to visit. Still, he did want to see Ginny. He followed— checking behind any plant capable of concealing an old black man and an axe. The trail was easy enough. The wheelchair left two fresh ruts. And at the end he found Adam parked in the middle of a large chicken yard.

Propped up by saplings, a dilapidated patchwork of rusty wire fencing and wooden slabs encircled the area. The ground was bare of all but droppings and a battered feeding tray. A flock of big speckled hens drifted about the enclosure, passing in and out of the open gate and in several places stepping through the wire. One sat quite at home nestled in Adam's lap. It blinked in unison with the man and squawked in outrage when Paul shooed it from its perch.

"Ginny, where are you?" he called.

"Here." The voice came from beyond a slab section of the fence which Paul now recognized as a building. "I'm in the henhouse."

A door flopped open on leather hinges and the girl approached. She cradled eggs in the pouch she'd made from her shirttail.

"What are you doing?"

"Getting eggs for Da Bena." As she spoke Ginny retrieved a carton from the recesses of the wheelchair and opened it on her father's lap. With care she began the transfer of the eggs.

"Can I help?"

"We're almost through, but Da Bena wants us to catch a hen."

"What for?"

"What do you mean 'what for'? For supper."

The idea that they would eat an animal that was at that very moment alive and running in the back yard made him uneasy.

"You thought chickens came from meat counters, didn't you?"

Paul shook his head no, but she was right—he did.

"And milk from cartons and vegetables from cans."

Maybe he did think that way, but how did she know?

These insights of hers were becoming unsettling. She seemed to understand everything about him, while he didn't have a clue to what was on her mind.

"Which chicken?" he asked.

"One of the old ones—that one'll do."

Finished with the eggs, the girl had approached the unsuspecting hen and motioned for Paul to come from the other side. He did as commanded and a second later was clutching the wildly flapping bird by the tip of one wing. He wasn't sure how this had happened. He hadn't even planned to touch it. The feathers were filthy. The beak and claws looked lethal. The furious beating of its one free wing and the frantic squawking alone were enough to make him drop it—but Ginny was beside him shouting.

"Take her feet! She can't hurt you, Paul. You're scaring the poor thing."

Paul was sure his own feet were leaving the ground. The bird was lifting them both and in another minute he would be looking down on the Fennel roof. He closed his eyes and turned his head away.

Ginny brought her hands firmly over the chicken's wings and held the body tight. "Now take her legs and hold them."

Paul did as he was told and gave a sheepish smile. He didn't think he'd done too badly. If you excluded dogs and cats this was the first live animal he could remember touching. He heard a soft guttural chuckle. There at the gate stood Da Bena. She still wore the sagging yellow sundress and the man's checkered coat and the sailor hat. But she'd slipped pink bedroom slippers onto the bare feet. And of course she held the axe that Jack Simmons had been sharpening that very morning.

"Dat very fine," she sang out. "I ain't think you been raised 'round chicken."

"I can't believe he doesn't know how to hold a chicken," Ginny said in disgust.

"Child, they is very many people on this earth, but they be only one Bena to teach them these thing."

"You didn't see him."

Ginny was angry with him. She was embarrassed by his performance. But he hardly listened. His attention was fixed on the axe the old woman held. She had seen him in bed the night before. Joke or not, she'd told Brown Jack Simmons to kill him and then stood by while Leroy almost did. And now she blocked the gate.

"I see him. I been watchin'. You hush up. And you, the young gentleman, you bring that bird here to Bena."

Paul heard this well enough. He eased towards the axe, trying to obey and still keep out of striking range.

"Lay the head right hey." She pointed to a tree stump that apparently served as a chopping block. "Hold that darlin' tight."

Paul watched the glistening edge of the axe rise above his outstretched hands. It hesitated and then descended with a flash. The chicken's head was gone and from its neck spurted a thick stream of bright red blood.

Paul released the bird and stepped back revolted. He'd never seen blood like that before. He'd never cut himself seriously or seen a person who had. There had been no blood when his mother died. Struck by a devastating attack of vertigo, he grabbed for the fence and held on.

Meanwhile the headless chicken raced back into the pen, thrashing about wildly. And before Ginny could intervene, it expired beside her father, spattering him with tiny specks of blood and droppings.

"Dat the first time the boy seen a chicken kill, child."

The girl picked up the limp carcass and, returning it to the chopping block, laid the scaly feet against the wood. The axe descended a second time and the feet came off. Then the bird was rotated and the wings followed.

"Now you goin' to smile at the young gentlemans. Crack 'em teeth."

Ginny gave Paul a half-hearted smile. Still clinging to the fence, he returned it. Stooping between them, Da Bena gathered up the feet, wings, and head of the chicken, and put them in a plastic bag, which disappeared into a pocket of the checkered coat. Noticing Paul's open-mouth stare she chuckled and explained.

"Dat for the soup."

"Oh."

"Azalea's calling you, Paul. It's time for lunch."

"What?"

"Azalea's calling you."

"Oh."

"Dat all right. You go on now with Miss Azalea. The next time we goin' to teach you some more."

Paul released the fence and backed unsteadily away from the site of the slaughter. Then he trotted off towards the kitchen and Azalea's calls—and away from the strange black woman and her assistant, Ginny Fennel.

GINNY FENNEL

Paul kept Ginny's first essay folded in his wallet, a sort of talisman that he could take out at times of stress, at times when things weren't going right. At times like these. Except it was no longer necessary for him to see the essay. He'd long since memorized it.

> she can't Think of anything to say abbout her ecept she is the great granddaughter of Captain Jack Fennel who is a war hero of the war wich was between the north and the south and the north one and her Momma is named Azalea and her daddy is Adam and he was a light house keeper and that is all she can say About her ecept she is not happy to be here

That was it. The assignment had been to "write a short history of yourself." The fact that aside from a few capital letters her paper had not a single mark of punctuation set it apart from the others, but not much apart. Paul had seen worse. A few. He scrawled "Is this a joke?" at the bottom, but then he thought better of it. The girl had tried. She'd turned in a paper. He scratched out his first note and put a brisk impersonal "You can do better than this" below it. There was no numerical grade. The paper was meant to break the ice, and he wouldn't presume to judge his students on the quality of the lives they'd been living. No, not much. Except to note the obvious fact that again this year ninety-nine percent of them did not belong in college, and Ginny Fennel was clearly not among the blessed one percent that did. She wouldn't last a semester. Certainly not two.

He'd put the paper in his "done" stack and continued grading. When he finished he sat back and lit his pipe. Only one autobiography stuck in his mind. Only one writer claimed to be the great-granddaughter of Jack Fennel. Impulsively he retrieved the girl's paper, scratched through the second note and wrote "Come see me, please." After all, the family papers of the Fennels were legendary. The chance was slim but Paul had to take it. Then, before he even met the girl, she came close to falling under the spell of his office mate.

"Danvers," Paul had repeated through clenched teeth that day he returned to the office and found her waiting with his rival. "This is Dr. Pauling you've been talking to, but he is not your instructor. I am."

The girl had said nothing. She looked briefly at Dan Pauling and shrugged. She was thin, thinner than he'd remembered from class. And she had a fever blister on her lip and her hair, cut just above the shoulder, was unwashed. And she was also lacking in the social graces. No apology was coming. She said nothing.

"I just thought we could have a little talk," Paul said.

"What do you mean?" She'd pushed a stray lock behind her ear. It stayed there.

"I like to get to know my students. Even at a school this size, teaching doesn't have to be a totally impersonal business."

"What do you mean?"

"He wants you to have a cup of coffee with him," Dan Pauling said, holding his pipe at parade rest. Paul couldn't imagine him without it or without the mustache either.

"Oh." The girl reached for her coat.

"Ginny's family is the one that kept the lighthouse all those hundreds of years. You've heard of the famous Fennel family papers? Paul. Well, those are her Fennels."

"Is that so, Ginny?" Paul asked politely.

"I guess," the girl said, biting at the fever blister as she hunched the coat over her head and shoulders. "I guess we're that family."

"That's interesting." Paul kept his back to his office mate. "The name does sound familiar."

He took her to a small coffee shop just off the campus. It was a sterile, inhospitable spot, favored by neither the faculty nor students. When Paul ate out he always came here, so it seemed a natural place to take the girl. Under all this glaring fluorescence and surrounded by enamel and chrome, who could be accused of dallying? Anyway, this choice made sense to Paul and so, seated across the booth from the freshman coed, he launched his calculated plan of seduction.

"Tell me about yourself." He pulled out his pipe and tobacco. Coffee was on the way.

"What do you mean?" She stared at him without expression. It was a look he would become quite familiar with in the following months.

"You know. What are you studying? What are your plans for the future? Where are you from? That sort of thing." He tapped the tobacco into the pipe bowl with ponderous deliberation.

"Didn't you read my paper? You wrote all over it." She pulled the folded paper from her coat pocket and slid it across the table.

"Yes, I read it." He nudged the paper back. It was difficult to contain his exasperation but lighting the pipe helped. He sucked in until it fired, and then exhaled. "I just wanted some additional background. Your paper was a little vague on some points. It was brief compared to most." Paul returned the pipe to his mouth.

"I guess I should have said I was studying pre-medicine. I just started this semester. It's Dr. Rupple's idea."

"Dr. Rupple?"

"He's our doctor."

"I see. All right. Pre-med, that's a tough one. What will you do when you finish?"

"Go back to Port Ulacca and be a doctor, I guess."

The waitress arrived with the coffee and a smile for Paul, the first he'd ever received in there. He decided to leave a dollar tip. Ginny drank her coffee black, and Paul thought it would be unmanly not to do the same.

"Port Ulacca?" he asked. The pipe was laid aside and he watched her over the lip of his cup. "That's on the coast, isn't it?"

"Yes."

"And your family kept a lighthouse?"

"Yes. I put it in my paper."

"I remember. It sounds like a romantic profession. Why don't you stay in the family business?"

"What do you mean, romantic?" She eyed him suspiciously. Paul had to set down his cup.

"Romantic. You know, lonely but exciting. You're out there with just the sea and the sky, and the big storm comes up and the ship is in distress." He had no idea what lighthouse keeping entailed, and he was beginning to think this approach was hopeless. He had the right Fennel, but if they were all like her he could start emptying his desk.

"Oh. I can't be a lighthouse keeper because the government

closed down the light after Adam's accident. They were only keeping it open 'cause of the Fennel family in the first place. They have all kind of electronics on ships now. Radar and sonar and lorans. They don't need lighthouses."

Now it was Paul's turn to say "Oh," to which he added, "Who is Adam? Someone in your family?"

"My father. It's in the paper." This time Paul took the paper back and kept it.

From there he'd gone on to ask about Captain Jack Fennel and the other members of the family. He was disappointed at the extent of Ginny's knowledge. At the time, she appeared to know little more than what was in her essay, but the existence of Camilla came as a pleasant surprise.

"You mean that Jack's daughter is still alive? She must be ancient."

"No. She's descended from the second wife. I don't think she's but sixty or seventy."

"Does she talk much about her father?"

"Sometimes." Ginny finished her coffee and declined a refill.

"I guess you have researchers coming around the house. They study everything these days."

"Sometimes. A man brought a tape recorder to the house once and recorded some of Camilla's stories. He wanted to see the papers but she wouldn't let him."

Papers. There were papers. Paul's heart leapt up. Carefully he retrieved his pipe and began once again to light it.

"What papers?" Already he was rocketing along the course of action. His enemies must be kept in the dark, and he must at all costs keep the girl away from Dan Pauling.

"Just things. Camilla has cardboard boxes full. Some of it goes back to the beginning."

"The beginning?"

"Yes. You know. When the Fennels came to Dog Tooth Shoal. But most of the stuff is my great-grandfather's."

The match burnt down until it reached Paul's fingers and he dropped it with a mild curse. Ginny, her face slightly tilted, studied him with a strange expression.

"So you want to be a doctor?" Paul asked with sudden enthusiasm.

Ginny pushed another stray lock of oily hair behind an ear.

"Not particularly," she said.

"I see."

Like Napoleon marching on Moscow, he now discovered himself in the midst of a long and bitter campaign—one in which there was no turning back. The first meeting had been a breeze compared to the months that followed. And Paul's courtship was, of course, a disaster. Time spent with Ginny gained him nothing. She remained enigmatic and withdrawn. She shrugged off his clumsy advances, which was just as well, but still the frustration added to his general anxiety. Though still plump by others' standards, he had lost weight, and Dan Pauling spoke with open concern over his haggard appearance.

The girl, on the other hand, blossomed. The fever blister went away and the pale blotchy skin gave way to robust color. She gained weight and began to wash her hair and care about her appearance. Paul's attention gave her at least a semblance of self-assurance and soon she was capable of carrying on a limited conversation—when the mood struck her.

Dogged perseverance saw Paul making progress of another kind, however. It was understood almost without asking that he would go home with Ginny at the end of the semester. And, even more importantly, she had agreed without his even asking that it would be better not to discuss the family papers with anyone else. And they did ask. At least four others in the department approached her and went away disappointed. He heard this from Ginny and he heard it from Dan Pauling who said these inquisitors were convinced that not only were there no papers, but that Ginny was simple-minded. All four thought she and Paul made a perfect couple. Dan Pauling seemed to think this particularly funny, but he couldn't explain the humor of it to Paul—who laughed anyway, safe in the knowledge that Dan Pauling knew nothing of the Fennel papers.

As far as their consummating the relationship, he had long since given up, given up with relief, in fact. When exams were finished, however, Ginny had suggested they drive to Atlanta and spend Saturday night at the Armada Inn on Peachtree Street.

Her insistence had made Paul uneasy and he almost backed out. It wasn't difficult to imagine outrageous plots concocted by unknown persons. Movie cameras behind mirrors or police raids. Things that would discredit him and cause him to lose his job. But he'd lose it anyway if he didn't get the papers, and if he couldn't trust Ginny who could he trust?

He went, not knowing what to expect, either of himself or her, but things had gone all right. They had made love, and then slept together with the light off until morning. Like other couples, they had gone down to breakfast and then driven back to school. They were just like normal everyday human beings and Ginny was happy. He hadn't imagined that.

THE STORM

It wasn't necessary to apologize. A cheerful Azalea was waiting for him with a sandwich and a glass of tea. And after today she planned to bring his lunch upstairs. That way he'd have the maximum amount of time to spend on the papers. Paul agreed. He'd have a cup of coffee for breakfast and eat the evening meal with the family. The schedule was settled. He wolfed down the sandwich and hurried off with Azalea to meet Camilla.

The old woman's bedroom appeared little different than it had the night before. Thick curtains blocked the windows. But where the sun entered, it cut a narrow swath across curlicued Victorian furniture. This room, airless and shadowed, had belonged to her parents, he was informed. She had changed nothing. The furnishings were the same and they had remained in place just as she had inherited them.

She had stored the papers beneath the canopied four-poster. Eight large cardboard containers stuffed with loose papers, records, ledgers, and books. A thick film of dust covered everything, suggesting that they had not been examined, at least not in a long time.

"The Fennel Papers," Camilla announced. "The bulk of this came to me upon my father's death, but as I mentioned to you, I've added a few things over the years."

"Looks very interesting."

"Several people have been here to the house to inquire about these papers, but I turned them away. I told you why last night, Dr. Danvers. I did not feel I could trust an outsider with the contents of these boxes."

"Yes, ma'am."

"You have treated Azalea's daughter with kindness."

"Yes. Yes, ma'am. Now, I should sort and catalogue what's here before I actually begin reading. That would be best." It might be true that he thought chickens came from meat counters, but he didn't expect to find family papers in filing cabinets. Still, he was surprised by the jumbled mess that was piled high in each of the broken-sided containers. Unless he was very lucky, this would take much longer than he'd hoped.

"That would be fine. I shall trust your judgment in these matters."

Paul had unrolled a long sheaf of paper from the top of one box. An electrical diagram of some sort. Not at all what he expected to find.

"This will be great fun for me," he said. "And perhaps in some small way I can repay you for your gracious hospitality." He had been rehearsing this statement for months. He was amazed how spontaneous it sounded.

"My only request of you is that you do not forget our conversation. Many ugly and totally false things have been written about my family. Justice must be done, Dr. Danvers."

Paul nodded. Azalea and Leroy joined them.

"That's Jack Junior's patent," Azalea said, spying the sheaf of paper that Paul still held. "Don't ask me what it means, though. Leroy's the one who understands those things around here."

"Leroy?"

"That's right, Professor. Walter got me interested. I'm going to Tech."

"Explain it to Paul." Azalea held one end of the drawing.

"Not much to explain, Sis." Leroy ran his fingers over the curious lines. "Resistance, conductors. It's about as complicated as a flashlight. On. Off. Bang!"

Camilla cleared her throat.

"Leroy, help Paul get these boxes up to his room," Azalea whispered.

Leroy gave Paul a playful punch that somehow mashed his collarbone into his ribcage. By the time they'd transferred the eight boxes to his bedroom the pain had all but gone away, and Paul was ready to start. He'd been provided with a small desk and he had the captain's chair. He had a pad and a pen. He was alone. But he couldn't just dip into this uncharted ocean of papers and come up with the secret to the Caladium Keyhole. As he'd told Camilla, he must sort and catalogue first. He must work methodically towards his goal and if by sad chance there was no final word on the mystery, he could at least submit his index as a piece of scholarly craftsmanship.

Reverently he tipped over the first box. Dust rose in the air and a mouse ran from between his feet out the open door. It had shredded a fistful of the documents for a nest and Paul brushed this aside with distaste. Two roaches scurried from beneath his fingertips. He took a deep breath and sorting began.

The first item retrieved was a scrap of lined paper. A recipe for "Port Ulacca Boat Stew" set down in a hard fine ink scrawl.

"Stir well," the writer cautioned. Next, Captain Jack Fennel had a dentist appointment on 10 A.M., December 12, 1898. A collection of rolled sheaves turned out to be coastal charts. Then a plat for marshlands adjoining the lighthouse island and a deed for a building lot in Port Ulacca. Here was a stray letter from the Lighthouse Board requesting information on the placement of a light ship, and jammed inside the same envelope was a century-old receipt for hemp line.

Paul had laid each piece out on the floor, organizing them according to date and subject matter. Now realizing there'd be many stacks, he drew a rough plan of the room, showing his bed and desk and the position and meaning of each pile. Then began again.

An hour later he found a log book from the lighthouse. It was a smallish gray volume stamped with an official United States seal and the year, 1871. Excited by the discovery, he took a hurried look through all the boxes. There were others, perhaps one for every year. Paul was tempted to abandon his cataloguing and simply search them out. But he decided instead to stay the course—and take the material as it came.

Which was probably for the best. Though the first log's entries were in a hard but legible hand and initialed *J. F.*, it contained little of interest. The date, time of day, and the weather— wind direction, barometric pressure, visibility, and a one-word description of the seas. An occasional "sail sighted" broke the monotony. "*Palmer* grounded," read a January note. "Buoy placed on *Lucinda*" occurred in July. And on December 31 the writer closed with "Randolph sick." What had gone through Jack Fennel's mind during all that time was in no way indicated, and the fate of the *Palmer*, the *Lucinda*, and Randolph was not revealed.

The next log was for the year 1888. And it was even more disappointing. Again the entries were in Jack Fennel's scrawl and most gave only the date and time. Many pages were altogether blank. On the flyleaf at the back the light keeper had scratched 6 *sheephead* and, underneath that, *9 drum*. Superimposed over this piece of information was an ancient brown ring left by a coffee cup.

After spending an hour on the first, Paul began to give the remaining logs only brief inspections. Perhaps they would give up their secrets when placed in the context of the whole but for now he was in a hurry. So it was fortunate that the 1859 volume caught his attention or rather the faded white ribbon did. A bookmark. The familiar *J.F.* was still the main contributor, but the ribbon indicated the participation of a second author. A woman with a strong neat hand. A woman who initialed her entries with a bold *V*.

Here was the legendary Virginia Fennel, and though she had hardly used the log as a diary, the few lines she had written seemed book length when compared to her brother's commentary.

February 4th—Whale washed ashore on the south end of the island.

March 2nd—Bell buoy adrift. Boat sent to secure it.

March 6th—Received a barrel of apples and six new hens. 4 goats for compound.

March 15th—Coastal freighter *Eliza Arden* sought refuge at the wharf. Were entertained by a Capt. Dowitchin at supper. He sang for us several songs as he was intoxicated. Quite drunk.

April 3rd— The garden is doing much better than usual though still very poor compared to those of the mainland.

April 4th—Two calves born.

May 19th—Steamer *The Duchess* run aground close by the island but able to back off in a light swell. Jack rowed out to offer assistance but none required.

June 24th—T. fell and broke arm which was set by myself.

June 26th—Several newcomers to the compound.

July 2nd—Received hemp cord and wicks. Baby born to Ruth. Attended by the woman Bena.

July 6th—Leaving today for the mainland.

There were no further entries by Virginia until August 22 when she began to make the daily weather notations. The weather seemed quite ordinary until the following week.

August 28th—The haze of the morning has not abated and there is a stiff breeze blowing from the east. Went to T.'s quarters and attempted to wake him, was cursed at a great length and so left, deciding he was not worth the trouble needed to rouse him. Returning to the light found the woman Bena waiting. Believe she means to tell me two of the men have not returned from fishing. She is greatly concerned about the approaching storm. Appears quite agitated but was sent back to the others with my reassurances.

August 29th—Passed the night alone in the light. Knew storm had worsened though still not prepared for the sight brought by a feeble dawn. Trees bent double and many uprooted. Water rising over island as far as rain allowed me to see. Have decided to try and reach the compound. No sign of T. who is probably still drunk and as well off drowned.

Only passed several yards from the base of the light and found water to be at my mid thigh and the current running strong. Breakers curling in many places. Was met at this point by the woman Bena bringing in the seven women, the infant, and four of the men. Each carrying a meager bundle of possessions. Will and John were indeed out fishing. They are surely lost. Bena could not be stopped from returning to the compound. Was extremely anxious that I watch the ragged parcel she brought away and could not be kept from going back. Made the others secure on the first landing before taking two men to go in search of T. Water over waist deep in many places. Were all in constant threat of being carried away. Rain often blinding us completely. Reached the house but could find no trace of T. Retraced our steps without a kind thought for the poor man.

Night 29th—No sign of the woman Bena or of T. and since the water is now over chest high I fear they are lost. Both houses breaking apart. Porches gone from each and must assume that the dock and the second skiff are gone as well. Rain and wind continue unabated. Have moved the company to the second landing. Hardly a word of English spoken, must rely on signs. Will manage somehow. They are all quite terrified and pose no threat. Fortunately the week's supplies for the light have just been stored and with careful rationing there should be sufficient to last but someway must be devised for catching and holding the rain water.

August 30th—Light maintained though difficult to imagine any vessel surviving this weather. A second dawn bringing us an even stranger sight. Only wild water as far as the eye can see. No sign of the island. All the buildings are gone. The trees, the dock, none of it remains. There is a steady pounding of surf against the light but I do not think we are in any danger. T. is certainly lost as well as John and Will and the woman Bena. T. of little use, his being here for my protection a quite laughable matter. The loss of the others more unfortunate. Though she had been with us only two short months my brother and I found Bena to be a remarkable negro and she will be greatly missed. Even now the Africans appear to be mourning her loss though they have not fully recovered from their long night of terror. I have attempted to assure them that the worst is past. We have funnelled in water through a piece of sail, and are keeping a small oil fire burning.

The water is receding rapidly and it is sad to think that all is gone. The cottages, the stock, the garden, the dock. Nothing remains but some of the masonry foundations and some twisted tree limbs. All that has been built destroyed in one night, but I have great faith in my brother and know that certainly within a year all will be returned to normal.

Morning Sept 1st—Providence provides. All has been swept away but a large lumber frigate has grounded on the southward end and the surf is thick with planking. There can be no question of salvage for all souls have undoubtedly perished and I have sent the men to collect up the lumber and begin to dismantle what remains of the ship. The women have been set to work bailing out the cisterns and the well.

Sept 2nd—Four days alone and I am happy that Jack has returned today bringing fresh supplies and good news in the form of the woman Bena. He was greatly concerned for my safety but had faith that the Fennel light could withstand whatever nature could unleash and that as long as I was within I would be unharmed. Many have died on the mainland. He thinks perhaps thousands and there is great devastation in Port Ulacca and the surrounding countryside. Much of the crops has been destroyed and there is a threat of hunger both immediate and future. Jack in good spirits despite all and busy planning the rebuilding of our small estate. The lumber frigate is to him like a toy to a young boy. He is quite taken with it and with the woman Bena who miraculously made it ashore carrying a very bedraggled stuffed monkey. A golden monkey I should add. All her brethren were overjoyed at her return and made more joyous still when she scratched through the silt of the compound area and uncovered what Jack claims is their giant petrified egg.

Though I would not say it I believe it is nothing more than a rock and hardly worth drowning for. Indeed the bundle she left in my care held nothing but a few bones, shells, and bits of glass and cloth. I will never understand these people and should by now have given up such a vain endeavor.

Assistant keeper Theodore Taylor is missing and presumed drowned.

September 3rd—Very busy. John and Will returned today but not even Jack can truly make sense of their journey. They have apparently rowed an open skiff through the great hurricane. Our other Africans do not find this tale in any way surprising, insisting that the woman Bena predicted their return.

My brother finds this quite believable. His faith must suffice for both of us, I fear.

There is a layer of silt covering everything. Before we can begin to rebuild this must be cleared away. Our other immediate need is food but as soon as coastal traffic resumes this should be no problem. In the meantime we must make do. Much rebuilding to be done. We will be busy in the days ahead.

Virginia made no more entries that year. Paul shuffled through several boxes searching for log books that might bear her mark and found none. Then he returned to the first box and spent the remaining time until supper sorting its contents. He found nothing else of importance.

A REPOSE

Paul went down to supper quite happy with the day's accomplishments. Instead of being evicted, he was in possession of the papers and he'd begun to work. True, the narrow escapes of the morning had been, at the very least, harrowing. Plus, he'd made a poor showing in the chicken yard. Still, that last was nothing to be ashamed of. He belonged inside reading and cataloguing. Ginny would have to understand that she was marrying a scholar, not a farmhand.

Already he'd uncovered the story of the hurricane, which though it wasn't of particular historic importance, spoke well of things to come. Only five short years separated these entries from Virginia's marrying of the Confederate commander and the mysterious closing of the Caladium Keyhole. Yes, and because the South's diplomatic ties had been effectively cut, the history of the world had changed on that momentous day. Paul knew the secret of "why" was waiting to be discovered in his bedroom. So he had every reason to smile at the members of the family when he took his place at the table beside Leroy. They were a little eccentric, but nice in their own way. Paul had no frame of reference, really. Maybe all families were like this. For the first time since arriving, he felt confident.

"Thought you'd died up there, Paul!" Leroy said, giving Paul's arm a punch that set everyone's tableware rattling and splashed water from glasses. There was beer on his breath.

"Hush, Leroy," Azalea said. "We're waiting on Camilla, Paul. She'll be here in just a minute."

Paul had been too busy watching out for Leroy to notice the empty seat.

"You can wait if you want. I'm hungry." Leroy began to pull in the serving dishes and heap his plate.

"Stop it!" his sister whispered sharply.

"Why should I? You pay for this. You're the only one with a job."

"Almost everything on this table was raised in this back yard."

"You know what I mean." He continued to pile his plate high.

"What do you do?" Paul asked. He hadn't realized she worked.

"She teaches school," Leroy said.

"The sixth grade." Azalea smiled a straight-lipped school teacher's smile.

"I didn't know that."

"Azalea's the only one in the house who makes money. I'm studying too, you see. And there's no money left from the patent or anything else, so Azalea pays for everything."

"Hush," Azalea whispered.

"Ah, I'm sick of all this Fennel crap. They act like we're shit just because we're Ramonas."

"Ginny's here," Azalea reminded.

"I don't mean Ginny. She don't give a damn about being a Fennel. Look at her."

Paul did look at her. She was gazing idly from Azalea to Leroy and back again. She was listening but apparently Leroy was right. She didn't care. And neither did Adam. Slack-jawed and pale-eyed, he looked straight ahead. Paul had been mistaken in thinking Adam was somehow conscious of the surroundings. Adam was elsewhere.

"You've been drinking, haven't you, Leroy?" Azalea accused. "You know you shouldn't. I begged you."

Leroy jammed his fork into his rice and gravy, but stopped short of lifting it to his lips. Camilla was taking her place and soon the dishes were being passed. Only when everyone was served did Leroy begin to eat.

Supper was the same as before, except candied sweet potatoes replaced the okra. The chicken, Paul supposed, was the one whose slaughter he'd botched so ignominiously that morning, so he waved his drumstick at Ginny and smiled. She stared at him and returned her attention to Adam.

"So, Dr. Danvers, tell us how did your research go this afternoon?" As usual Camilla picked at her small servings.

"Very well. I'm really pleased by what I've seen so far."

"I thought you might be."

"Paul's doing an excellent job. I told you you wouldn't be sorry," Azalea said.

"I've never doubted Dr. Danver's abilities and I'm sure I have a better concept of the task at hand than you can possibly realize."

"Yeah!" Leroy shouted. "That ain't no bridge game up there, is it, Professor?"

"Well, in a way it is a game. It's sort of a puzzle."

"I don't see what would be puzzling about it, Dr. Danvers. You have the facts before you." Camilla had laid down her fork.

"Organization," Paul added quickly. "I mean the chronological order."

"Of course, but the outcome of your project is inevitable. The conclusion I would assume is favorable."

"Yes ma'am."

"We could write your closing remarks now, if you like. It would help with the organization, I should think."

"I'm sure Paul can do it," Azalea volunteered.

"I know he can do it, Azalea, but let me repeat, this project is more formidable than you can imagine."

"He ain't planting no flower garden. Right, Aunt Camilla?"

"Let me tell you what I found today," Paul said and proceeded to tell the story of Virginia Fennel and the hurricane. He told it graphically, leaving out no details and trying to convey the excitement he'd felt that afternoon.

As he spoke, Leroy began to shovel in his food, pausing just long enough to spit out a bone or sip some tea. Occasionally he made a grunting sound.

Ginny fed her father. She looked at Paul from time to time. She said nothing.

Azalea smiled at Paul and made murmuring sounds of interest. Camilla picked at her food and nodded.

Paul assumed they were spellbound, but when he finished only Azalea responded. She clapped her hands together once.

"I thought Ginny would really like to hear that," Paul said, disappointed.

"Why?" It was her first word of the evening.

"Because it's a story about the first Virginia Fennel."

"I've heard it from Camilla and I've heard it from Da Bena. I can't remember how many times I've heard it."

"It's always nice to hear the old stories again," Azalea said.

"Always," Camilla agreed. "Always. Virginia Fennel was exceptional in every way."

"It's exciting for me and I'm not even a Fennel." This brought no response so Paul hurried on. "I mean here's someone else named Virginia Fennel and there's an African woman named Bena."

"Da Bena's grandmother," Azalea said, looking to the head of the table for confirmation.

Camilla nodded ascent and spoke. "There was a bad storm when I was a girl. The storm of 1918, but the one you described was the worst."

"It's called the Big Storm," Leroy said.

"A lot of people drowned," Azalea added. "And a lot more went hungry afterwards."

"The Fennels survived, however," Camilla concluded for everyone. "They took the brunt of the storm and still survived."

The kitchen door opened a notch and Da Bena's head popped through. The sailor's cap now tilted far back.

"How that supper? Y'all satisfy?"

Camilla surveyed the table and made a shooing motion with her hand. But Azalea spoke.

"Everything is perfect, Da Bena, just perfect. We were just talking about the Big Storm. Paul read Virginia Fennel's description of it."

"Oh, that a sad story," the black woman moaned. "That a very sad story. That gal get marry three time." She stuck her hand through the door frame and held up three fingers. "The first one get the fever." Down went one finger. "The next one had the wheel run over he head." Down went the next finger. "And the last one take a bullet." The last finger dropped. "Then she drown." The head and the hand vanished and the door shut.

"Virginia Fennel disappeared," Azalea corrected. "They never found her body."

"She probably ran off. They all run off," Leroy muttered.

"Leroy! What are you saying?"

"They all run off. Uncle Jack's momma ran off. Adam's momma ran off. My momma ran off."

"Leroy! Our momma is right there in Fort Lauderdale, Florida. She hasn't run off. Don't talk that way in front of Paul. What kind of ideas do you want to give him?"

Paul looked from the Ramonas to the head of the table. Camilla's small hooded eyes were still frozen on the spot that Da Bena's face had vacated. Apparently upset by what the old black woman had said, she wasn't listening to the Ramonas at all. Neither was Ginny. She continued to feed her father and wipe away the food and saliva that dripped from the corners of his mouth.

MISS CAMILLA'S ALBUM

Miss Camilla's album was bound in red Moroccan leather and hinged with a black tasseled cord. The gold inlay on its cover was faded away but the stamped impression of the word *Photographs* still lingered.

Paul gently cradled the small book. Though the old woman hadn't instructed otherwise, he didn't dare to open it. The dog-eared leaves of heavy black paper were shuffling about loose and threatened an avalanche of photos, envelopes, and even dried flowers. Perhaps there was something here, but whatever it was could have waited.

Paul had slept late to make up for sleeping poorly. No, he hadn't tried visiting Ginny and her chaperone again. He'd gone straight to bed and fallen asleep almost immediately. But he had dreams—dreams he couldn't recall but disturbing nonetheless. Waking, he took a bath in the claw-foot tub and soaked the hand which was still slightly reddened and now puffy to the touch. The bump on his head was healing and the scar, if there was one, would be small.

He put on a fresh shirt and his second-best slacks and went downstairs. Breakfast had been over for hours, but as he'd explained again to Azalea he only required a cup of coffee. This she fixed and he returned to his room to find Camilla waiting with the album. Now she'd gone off to bring more treasures and left him waiting.

Around his feet were the papers, books, and ledgers—everywhere around. He'd only gone into one box and already the floor was covered with small stacks that were supposed to mean something. He couldn't remember what and would have to refresh his memory before starting to catalogue again. Oh, yes. It was all promising and every torn and tattered piece had value, but it was the slim gray log books which seemed connected and to which Paul looked that morning with secret anticipation. One of these, he somehow sensed, held the answer.

"Lemonade, made with real lemons," Camilla announced and set down a small silver tray. "I thought you might need some refreshment, and we could go through the album together."

She poured them each a glass of pale, greenish liquid, took the album from his arms, and opened it on the desk. An aerial view of the lighthouse came first—a tall white octagonal tower with a black cupola on top, and at the base three small wooden houses surrounded by a great expanse of lawn. And circling all a picket fence and beyond that the underbrush and dunes.

"So much has changed."

"This picture? It's new?"

"Yes. It was taken fairly recently, but sometime before Adam's accident." Camilla's pale hands appeared phosphorescent against the black rag paper. A fingernail began to trace out the meaning of the landscape. "This slab is the base of the original lighthouse. My father used the brick from this to build these additional cisterns. They often had to rely on rainwater, you know. Much later, he used the same brick to construct the chimneys of this very house. Before the old light was built a fire was kept burning on the top of a large mound located here. The present tower was erected by my grandfather in 1852. My father, Jack Fennel, became the keeper in 1854."

"When he was only eighteen," Paul said on cue.

"That is correct." Camilla regarded him with the admiration due a scholar. "But he was ready to do a man's work." The fingernail tapped one of the three cottages. "This was the house he shared with his sister Virginia. It and the others were built shortly after the storm you read of. Some years later it was here that he brought Jack Junior's mother. Indeed, Jack Junior, Adam's father, was born in this house, and so were Adam and our Ginny. I was to come here to live when my father died, but as I may have mentioned Elizabeth and I traveled a great deal at that time." The nail tapped a second time. "When she chose to leave Jack Junior, it fell to me to raise their only son Adam, so I remained on the island until Adam married Azalea, at which time I returned to this house."

Paul found it impossible to keep this genealogy completely straight. Captain Jack Fennel had fathered Jack Junior, which led to Adam and then Ginny. By a second marriage Captain Jack fathered Camilla, which led here to this room. That sounded right. Anyway, one thing was certain. Camilla, for all her aristocratic airs, had not had an easy life. She had grown up without a mother, nursed her aged father until his death, and then raised her nephew Adam, by which time she was either intentionally or unintentionally an old maid.

But what of the first Virginia Fennel? Had she lost three husbands? Was she dead or disappeared? Paul wondered if Da Bena could be trusted on that or any other subject. In fact, he wondered about them all. Could you accept tales told in a madhouse?

As if on cue, the old woman straightened and addressed him in her most formal cant. "I have brought this album this morning because I fear you are forming a bad impression of my family. Please remember that the Ramonas are not Fennels and that Bena, though she may be the most faithful of retainers, is getting on in years. It would be a mistake to confuse what goes on down below with the work you are doing in this room."

Astonished by Camilla's sense of the situation, Paul shook his head no.

"Don't lie to me, Dr. Danvers."

"I'm fine. I mean they're fine."

She waved him silent. He sipped his drink. She'd forgotten the sugar. And what reached his stomach reacted violently with the morning coffee. He listened.

"At one time or another, I suppose, I have read all of what is here before us, but it was years ago, perhaps a half-century. I read a great deal when I was a girl but it is the tragedy of my life, I suppose, that I never gained a formal education. There were many books in the house, however. Though some were badly water-stained, I had crates of them to choose from. The finest thoughts of the finest minds, Dr. Danvers. I read a great deal. Are you familiar with the Romantics?"

"Yes, ma'am. Some. Somewhat, I should say."

Camilla drew herself up.

"The maiden gentle, yet at duty's call
Firm and unflinching, as the lighthouse reared
On the island-rock her lovely dwelling-place;
Or like the invisible rock itself, that braves,
Age after age, the hostile elements,
As when it guarded holy Cuthbert's cell."

Paul smiled and nodded.

"Do you recognize that, Dr. Danvers?"

"No, ma'am. I'm not sure but I think no."

"It's Wordsworth's epitaph for Grace Darling. She was the daughter of a light keeper. She saved nine lives."

"It's nice. I've never read much poetry but that sounded nice." Camilla frowned.

"It had a poetic sound to it," Paul added. "Very poetic."

"I am disappointed. I thought perhaps we could share an appreciation of the finer things. It is not important, I suppose."

Enough. Paul made a desperate frontal assault. That is, he leaned over the album and, indicating an odd series of dunes in the aerial photograph, asked with enthusiasm, "What was this?"

"Those? Those were the gun emplacements built by the Confederate government at the beginning of the war. When I was a girl there was still a powder magazine here." The ivory nail of the chalk-white finger tapped. "But it was torn down some years ago."

"I see, and what are these?" Paul pointed out a small row of markers that lay on the edge of the lawn, surrounded by a much smaller circle of picket fence.

"That is the family burial plot. Most of the Fennels are resting there. At peace at last. Beset on every side."

Not waiting for an elaboration, Paul flipped the page. An old photograph. One blistered with age. A lanky young man sat formally for the camera. He was dressed in a coat of some coarse material and this fastened with two rows of shiny buttons. On his head was a cloth cap with bright insignia above the visor. And in his hands was an unlimbered telescope. Yes. The face was familiar. Small piercing eyes stared out hypnotically from beneath heavy brows. The beaked nose fronted by a handlebar mustache.

"My father in uniform. This was taken about 1870, I believe." She pointed to the page opposite. "And this was the volunteer life-saving brigade. I'm not sure when the photograph was taken but the Captain still appears to be a young man."

The same figure stood at attention beside an open boat. Four shirtless black men stood to one side eyeing the camera with varying mixtures of suspicion, mirth, and decorum.

Camilla turned the page. A schooner was tied at the wharf and in the background stood the Fennel light. The picture was badly spotted and poorly focused. "Eighteen eighty-six. This is Mildred, Jack Junior's mother." The woman was no more than a blurred object standing on the shore. "It is the only picture of her that exists," Camilla added gravely. "My father met and married her on a single trip to Caladium. She was not meant for this kind of life. Shortly after her son was born she returned to her home for a visit and stayed there. She abandoned her son." Camilla raised the page to turn it and then stopped. "We should be astonished by this, Dr. Danvers. Persons of a certain excitable temperament might easily fall under the influence of the endlessly rolling seas and never-ceasing winds and find in such a state of blessed solitude only a deadly boredom. Such persons might soon feel a maelstrom loosened in their brains, which pulls away all control of reason and causes the mind to yield to the first impulse that strikes it. Don't you agree?"

Paul nodded. He thought he agreed or at least understood what she had just said. Leroy was right—the women did run off.

Camilla let the black rag page roll over. There was a husky young Jack Junior glaring at the camera. He was coming home from a duck-hunting trip with his father. And the dog-eared photo beside it showed a skiff being built. Camilla began to flip the pages faster. A parade of unsmiling weathered faces and nautical scenery passed by. Then a Christmas card. She stopped. Three black women stood beside a pushcart. One might be Da Bena's mother and the girl in pigtails on the edge of the wharf could be Da Bena herself. And far in the background was the lighthouse.

"No. That's not it," Camilla said. Another page turned. Two figures seen in distant silhouette. "That is not it." Another page. The framing of a building. "Dr. Danvers?"

"Ma'am?"

"Eighteen ninety-four, Dr. Danvers," she announced quietly. "A picture of this same house. See, here the oaks and cedars are noticeably smaller and the palmettos have just been set out." Paul could see the timbers of the house clearly and was again impressed by the nautical lines. It was indeed a ship that had been taken apart—and then reassembled as if by a contrary child.

"It hasn't changed much," he said.

"No, hardly at all. It's quite well preserved."

She turned the next page with a deliberate reverence. A young girl, simple, pretty, hardly in her teens. She wore a summer dress with billowing sleeves and a tightly cinched waist, and smiled at the camera with a child's shyness.

"This is my mother, Jewel. You can see she was quite young but the Captain took good care of her. He built this house, planted the gardens, and gave her as many servants as she needed. She died shortly after I was born."

Opposite was a photo he'd seen earlier in the parlor. The old man seated beside the young girl. Camilla studied it for a moment then began to flip again.

A young Camilla stood at the back steps. Camilla with a group of young people. Camilla with her father in a rocker. Then they were at the lighthouse and there was Adam with a goat cart. A wiry-haired man stood on a dune beside a grown Camilla. Dried flowers were wrapped in a newspaper clipping. Black-and-white pictures gave way to color. The hood of a car. A city street or maybe it was Port Ulacca. Paul gave up. A blur of images passed and suddenly there was Adam. Barely recognizable, he stood tall and proud beside a young fresh Azalea. He held a baby in his arms. In the background were the acres of trimmed lawn, the houses, and the bottom third of the lighthouse. It was the last picture in the book.

"Sad," the old woman said. "Such a waste."

She closed the album, tucked it under her arm, and picked up the lemonade tray.

"Adam?" Paul asked.

"Sir?"

"Nothing. I mean thank you for sharing the album."

"Say it, Dr. Danvers."

"Adam had an accident?"

"He fell from the front porch." Camilla began to thread her way through the sorted papers on the floor.

"Oh. I'm sorry."

Camilla paused at the door and fixing him with her hard small eyes, began to recite.

"Steadfast, serene, immovable, the same
Year after year, through all the silent night,
Burns on forever more that quenchless flame,
Shines on that inextinguishable light!

'Sail on!' it says, 'sail on, ye stately ships!
And with your floating bridge the ocean span;
Be mine to guard this light from all eclipse,
Be yours to bring man nearer unto man!'"

Paul nodded and smiled but said nothing.

"Longfellow, Dr. Danvers. Longfellow. I had hoped you would know that."

THE DAY'S WORK

Trying to make up for lost time, Paul hurried into the second box. And found a 1908 Sears and Roebuck catalogue, two paperbacks by Ned Buntline, plus a handful of letters written to Camilla from a woman in Syracuse, New York, during the 1930s. There were more marine charts and bills of sale. And an account ledger that listed page after page the price of bottled drinking water—fifty cents—and the cost of the guide—ten cents. Inside the flyleaf someone, certainly not Jack Fennel, had printed "Fine Hunt!" And then came four lighthouse log books—all from the 1890s and all disappointing. Virginia Fennel made no entries. Virginia Fennel who Da Bena claimed had had three husbands and then drowned. Perhaps she had drowned by this time or left the island or disappeared as Azalea said or had run off as Leroy said. In any event, her brother Captain Jack Fennel had even less to say. The log kept for 1892 didn't have a single entry and the rest dealt only with the mundane matter of weather and tides. What could Paul make of that? Or of the newspaper clippings that celebrated the 1939 World's Fair? Or the hefty stack of *Collier's* magazines?

The Fennel papers went on and on and the little stacks grew and multiplied until Paul's map of the room was a crisscross of cross references, arrows, numbers, high and low case letters of the alphabet, and question marks. Some piles now threatened to tip and Paul had closed the window to keep the quickening sea breeze from turning his cataloguing into a shambles.

Yes. It was a mess and worst of all it had no value. At least to him. Perhaps another scholar could compile a bibliography from this minutia but he needed something more dramatic. Some reference to the Civil War, to the tragic Virgina Fennel, to the mysterious closing of the Caladium Keyhole.

Azalea showed up with a chicken sandwich and glass of iced tea. Paul thanked her. She admired the stacks and he said he was making some progress. She tiptoed from the room and he ate and drank. He felt listless. He needed a nap. Idly he stuck his hand into the nearest pile, the pile coded *JF POSTWARLH*, and pulled free a bundle of letters. He'd examined them already or thought he had. But the string binding was knotted tight. It had to be broken. Letters from the Lighthouse Board to Captain Jack Fennel. Dating from the late 1860s. Just more of the same. Repairs to the buildings and boats, requests for medicines, reports on reports, replacement of glass, requests for money due, requests for information on wrecks, and advice on replacing a buoy. Yes, the letters gave a thorough picture of what being a light keeper entailed but they said nothing about who Jack Fennel was. Except the last two. They had been lashed together with a separate piece of twine. And they did deal with who Jack Fennel was.

October 14, 1870

Dear Sir:

It is my unpleasant duty to inform you of the list of charges that have been lodged against the Fennel lighthouse by Acting Inspector Guillemot and others. Due to the services rendered by your family during the recent War of Rebellion and the unique nature of the "private" Fennel light the Lighthouse Board has granted you certain liberalness in the past. We do not think we have been amiss in doing so. However, we have tried since the war to instill in our light keepers an even greater sense of responsibility for the obligations of their profession. In this respect the Fennel light has fallen behind alarmingly. The complaints that have come to our attention in the past year have been both loud and deep and I fear they must be dealt with.

We can no longer allow the use of untrained Negroes as assistant keepers. It is hardly necessary for me to point out that these men have taken no exams and hold no certificates. Therefore they are not qualified to hold the position with which you have entrusted them.

Though the Fennel light is rated as a first class light, one entire tier of reflectors is missing and a second is so poorly aligned that it fails to enhance the light at all.

There is about the light a general uncleanliness, the lens and reflectors being described as filthy and the burners are adjusted improperly causing them to burn unevenly and with an excess of smoke. There seems little excuse for this condition or for the lack of daily maintenance.

The exterior has never been whitewashed or painted and so serves poorly as a day marker.

We at the Lighthouse Board would find any one of these charges to be of a very serious nature but compounded as they are they create the deadliest of perils. I can only caution you that no ordinary light would be allowed to operate a single day under the conditions described above.

I have kept until last, however, the gravest of the complaints lodged against you and those concern the general unreliability of the Fennel light.

We hear all too frequently that the Dog Tooth Shoal is often without light in the most dangerous of weather and there are many captains who claim never to have sighted it at all under any conditions.

Even more serious are the claims that the light is allowed to burn for 3 or 4 hours at the beginning of the night and then permitted to go out leaving whatever vessel is relying on it in a much worse position than if there had been no light at all.

In conclusion we must address the most troubling reports of all, that the light ceases to rotate and sends out a constant beam which can easily be taken for another ship or for anything other than what it is intended to be, the Fennel lighthouse.

This letter and the accompanying report should in no way be misconstrued as levying a charge of criminal activities against yourself. However, a great number of vessels have gone ashore since the cessation of hostilities and we hope you will agree with us that something is indeed wrong. We ask you to cooperate fully with our investigators so that your light may be brought under the rules and regulations which govern all other lights and light stations in and of this country.

Yours,
F. K. Petral
Superintendent of Lights

May 1, 1871

Dear Sir:

We have received your reply to our letter concerning an investigation of the Fennel light. Allow me to repeat that we have in no way charged you with criminal acts and our investigation does not mean to suggest such. We at the Lighthouse Board are well aware of your family's long service to this country and of your inestimable contribution to the Federal war effort. However, the problems must be resolved.

Though our investigation is not completed, on the basis of Acting Inspector Guillemot's report and the contents of your letter the board is making the following recommendations in the hopes that these issues may be resolved without further delay.

Though your Negroes may be personally supervised they are not qualified, and we must insist that you hire attendants who are.

A want of liquid cleaner is hardly an excuse for dirty lenses.

If you find that your oil is bad and will not stay lit the entire night you should requisition for replacement. Acting Inspector Guillemot should be given a supply for testing.

If the gears to the revolving mechanisms are worn they should be replaced, but this does not seem likely since they should last a minimum of 25 years and our records show they have been installed 5.

Our final suggestions and instructions concerning these matters must wait for the District Engineer's report but it is our profound hope that even before this arrives the Fennel light can be brought up to the standards of this service. I am certain we all agree that no point on our coast is more in need.

Yours

F. K. Petral

Superintendent of Lights

Paul couldn't help but chuckle. The picture drawn here of the Captain was far different than that suggested by his daughter Camilla. Dr. Whitman was right. Anyway, he was right about Jack Fennel being a bastard. Paul started a new pile coded *JFfl?* and placed the two letters in evidence. Then, with a renewed sense of purpose, he approached the third box. The stacks of papers rose and the dust boiled. Paul read and sorted for the rest of the afternoon, finding nothing.

PORT ULACCA

The swelling in Paul's hand had increased. It ached. What's more, reading the difficult script in poor light was causing his eyes to burn. Yes, and bending over the desk had given him a distinct pain in his lower back. And if that weren't enough, working in a closed room with the dusty papers had brought an alarming tightening in his chest. He hadn't suffered from asthma since he was a teenager, but you couldn't be too careful.

Paul pushed away from the desk and lit his pipe. Actually, he shouldn't complain. Yesterday the hurricane. Today the Lighthouse Board letters. And he still had five large boxes to sort through. Puffing away he gazed about. All those piles and some were almost knee-high. All that paper, such an accumulation of documentation, yellowed, rolled, plain, printed, marked, white, inked, lined, bound, and loose. It was hard to understand how so much could have been compressed beneath Camilla's bed. Tattered pages filled past the margins with hen-scratch penmanship threatened to slide from their assigned location, and not even three or four broken-back ledgers could be trusted to stay together.

Yes. Except for the logbooks none of it wanted to belong together. But that stack of thin gray volumes had doubled, and these alone seemed to promise an orderly and sequential history of the Fennel light. Seemed to but did not.

Paul went to the window, tapped the pipe stem against the dusty glass and stared out. In his tweed jacket with the chamois patches on the elbow, he thought he must present a perfect study in reflection—pensive and yet alert, inert but poised.

From below his line of vision Ginny appeared pushing her father in his chair. They were headed in the direction of the street. Paul cracked the window and called out.

"Ginny! Wait up!"

The girl stopped and, shielding her eyes, looked up.

"Where are you going?" he added.

"I'm taking Adam to the store." Her voice held a distinct note of disinterest. In fact, the way she squinted almost suggested she'd forgotten who he was.

"Wait. I'll go with you," Paul shouted.

And stepping nimbly through the Fennel paper piles, he hurried downstairs and out of the house. She was gone but not far. Paul spied them on the sidewalk and set off at a trot along a street canopied by tremendous live oaks—harmless trees. Yes, nature here was more benign. And on each side were tall white Victorian homes. Halfway up the block he passed a newer one of brick and coming up on his right was a house trailer. Paul stopped noticing his surroundings and watched instead the long legs and round buttocks of his girl. He hadn't realized how she'd filled out in just the last few months. The denim of the jeans seemed stretched to the point of bursting. Overnight Ginny was becoming a shapely, beautiful woman. Other men would be finding her attractive. Her uncle would. He should warn Ginny about Leroy. He reached out to her.

"Ginny," he whispered hoarsely. Breathless from jogging a single block he hoped she would halt. She didn't. She looked over her shoulder and went back to wrenching her father along. Yes, wrenching, for the roots of the trees had undermined the concrete slabs of the walk until each rose and fell independently. The wheelchair rose and fell accordingly, and Adam's head flopped one way and then the other. Paul doubted the invalid could enjoy such a ride. He looked close. The Fennel eyes were open, but no sign of true life shone there. What had Paul been thinking when he first arrived—when he thought Adam watched him? This man saw nothing. Felt nothing.

"Can I do that for you?" Paul offered. "It looks like hard going."

"I can manage," the girl said.

"Are you sure?"

"I'd rather."

Paul started over. "I'm afraid I haven't seen much of you the last couple days."

"I see you all the time."

"I mean alone."

"You mean without Da Bena."

"Are you angry about something?"

"We're not alone now. Adam's here." Ginny nodded towards her father.

"I know. I see him. Hello, Adam. How are you this afternoon?" Paul hadn't meant them to, but the words came out as mocking. Ginny stopped pushing and gave him a rare look— one of bewilderment. "I'm sorry," he added quickly. "I just want to explain about the other night. I mean I wanted to come to bed with you." He hesitated.

"But you didn't," she said.

"Can I talk in front of your father? I mean he doesn't understand, does he?"

Of course, Paul knew the answer or thought he did, but the girl's questioning expression deepened into one of genuine astonishment. She seemed to be considering this for the first time in her life. She looked down the long tunnel of oaks that was a street.

From behind the house trailer a small girl on a bicycle appeared and began to circle on the lawn. She took no notice of Paul or Ginny or Adam. She may not have seen them at all, so intent was she on her riding and on her song.

"The bad guys done it,
The good guys done it,
The bad guys done it,
The good guys done it."

The circles became smaller and smaller as she continued turning inward and Paul watched hypnotized. The harder the turn the more wobbling her course became, but she continued singing and peddling. And finally the bike pitched over and threw its rider into the grass.

At once the child sat up and began to cry, but Paul could think of nothing to say or do. Ginny remained lost in contemplation. Without warning, the door of the trailer slammed open and a frazzled middle-aged woman in a house coat appeared on the stoop.

"You hush!" she screamed. "Do you hear me? If you can't ride it we'll just have to put it up. Do you hear me?"

A tiny, yipping dog, a Chihuahua Paul thought, raced by her and out across the lawn towards them. The little legs disappeared into the grass. It appeared to be propelled by nothing—a furious projectile aimed no doubt at his throat. But at the last instant it skidded to a halt, and then began to stalk him, growling and baring a set of minute but dangerously sharp teeth.

"Don't worry, he won't bite!" the woman shouted.

"Get back," Paul muttered at the animal.

The woman stood on tiptoes to get a better view of them. "Ginny, is that you?" she shouted in obvious delight. "Honey, you and Adam back together. I missed you, honey. We all have missed you."

Ginny came back from her trance and called out, "Hey!"

"Do you like school, honey?"

"Yes, ma'am. I guess."

"That's nice. Really. That is nice. Leroy told us you were coming. He came by and fixed our TV. We don't know how he did it. Just tinkered around and got an old tube out of his trunk and fixed it. Wouldn't take a penny, Ginny. Not a single penny. Doesn't seem humanly possible that a man could be as nice as your uncle Leroy."

"Yes, ma'am."

Dumbfounded by what he was hearing, Paul gazed, openmouthed, at the woman. And the dog struck from behind. It caught him just above the ankle.

"Stop!" he screamed. He kicked out, shaking the leg as hard as he could. The dog sank its teeth in further.

"Won't bite," the woman called, ignoring the fact that Paul was being bitten.

"Here, Buttons," the little girl called. She still sat on the lawn beneath the bike. "Come here, boy."

The dog dropped to the ground and backing away, resumed its yapping.

"Has that dog had a rabies shot?" Paul shouted.

"What?" the woman answered.

"Rabies?"

"There are no rabies in Port Ulacca."

"That's not the point." Paul stooped to examine the teeth marks. The cuff of his second-best pants was badly torn.

"We don't do things that way here," the woman shouted.

"But it's the law," Paul said to no one but himself.

"There's the phone, Ginny," the woman shouted. "Come by and visit real soon." She ducked inside the trailer and back outside to deliver a final message. "Give Leroy a big hug for me and tell him we want to see a show real soon." Then she was gone for good.

They began again, bumping their way down the concrete walk. A block away and the little dog was still yapping. Paul's hand had begun to ache. Hearing Leroy's name spoken had set it off. He must ask Azalea for some salts that night and also get methiolade for the dog bite. Unattended animal bites could be dangerous.

But what had he been discussing with Ginny? Something about Adam, but whatever it was was probably better left unsaid. No sooner had he reached that conclusion than she spoke.

"What you said about Adam not being able to hear us, how can you think thoughts like that?"

"What do you mean?" Paul remembered now. He knew what she meant.

"How can you think he doesn't understand?"

"I didn't say he doesn't. I was just speculating that he might not."

"I don't see how you can think such a thing."

In a way Paul was relieved. At the chicken yard the day before he had feared she could read his mind. At least some of his privacy remained. They went on in silence passing more houses and trailers. Narrow side lanes teed off and twisted out of sight. He spied the waterfront. Tin-sided buildings showed and beyond that the masts of fishing boats. Then their street widened and the trees thinned. And the dilapidated stores began, wooden buildings from the last century with false fronts and big square windows. Most were closed.

Ginny halted in front of a grocery. Larger than most, two stories, in fact, it leaned perilously forward and to the left. Paul helped to bring the wheelchair up the steps and then pushed, lifted, and kicked at the double doors until they spread. Inside were long rows of dusty shelves lined with dusty boxes, jars, and cans. Bins of tired vegetables fought against plowshares and fishing poles.

The grocer, a man with receding reddish hair and twinkling eyes, had watched their progress with no apparent interest. But when the wheelchair came to rest in front of the counter, he bounded to his feet and brushed past Paul to give Ginny a hug.

"Oh, my girl. It's so good to see you back. My wife told me you were home. We've missed you so. Let me tell you. We have missed you!"

"Yes," Ginny answered, staring down at the top of Adam's head.

"And how is Adam this fine afternoon?"

"He's . . ." Ginny hesitated. "I was going to say he's fine but Paul thinks he might not even know where he is. He says maybe Adam can't even hear us."

"This is Paul?" The grocer looked contemptuously at the only other person in the store. "He's a doctor?"

"Sort of," Ginny said.

"Ph.D.," Paul said, trying to smile. He held up open palms in a gesture of helplessness. He thought the man might be teasing but couldn't be sure.

"Ph.D. My fanny. That ain't no kind of doctor at all. I mean a real doctor. Doctor like Dr. Rupe. Not a college doctor. You come home if that's what they're teaching you up there." The grocer put his hands on both of Adam's shoulders and stuck his face down to within inches of the invalid's. "Of course, he can hear us. How you doing today, Adam?" he shouted. "Doing okay, aren't you?" Then stepping clear he told Ginny that her father was doing fine. He could tell by the way Adam's eyes were blinking and not blinking that he could hear good and understand everything. And then the man asked about Leroy, saying he hadn't seen her uncle in a couple of days and that it was too bad the world wasn't full of Leroys.

THE FUTURE

Air-conditioning. General Electric had seen the future and it was air-conditioned.

"Plastic domes over whole cities and everything underneath is air conditioned." Leroy addressed the other diners with an unbridled enthusiasm. "That's what he told us in class today."

"Who told you that?" Azalea asked. It annoyed Paul that she could show Leroy the same kind of interest she showed him.

"This young guy, Azalea. You're not listening. G. E. pays him to drive around to classes like ours and tell 'em what it's going to be like in the year 2000 cause they do studies and they know."

"I guess that made you feel pretty good."

"Well, I guess it did, Sis. You start talking about air-conditioning a whole city inside and out, you're talking big bucks. Big bucks. I mean it."

"You're studying air-conditioning at Tech?" Paul asked in feigned interest.

"That's right. Walt and me started last year. He talked me into it. He was that kind of guy, you know."

Paul agreed, though, in fact, he didn't know who Walt was.

"Always thinking about things like that. About what kind of cars people would be driving. That stuff. He could have been going around and working for G. E. right now. He could, couldn't he, Ginny?"

"I guess," the girl said. She didn't look up from Adam's plate. She was mashing his peas into a green paste.

"He could."

The girl shrugged. Paul wondered if it was a "Walt" who'd picked out Azalea's station wagon. Was that Walt or William?

"What did the man tell you about the future?" Azalea asked. She had put on her crooked frozen smile. Had Walt been her boyfriend? Her suitor even?

"Well, Sis, the future is a big place. He said that and he talked about a lot of things. Not just air-conditioning. He said we could forget about television and start thinking about holographs."

"Holographs?"

"That's right. No screen. It's just like sitting here now. You and me and Camilla and Adam and Ginny are sitting here and Paul's just this image that's projected into the room from all these different angles."

Paul poked at his food. Not since his first night had his stomach felt so unsettled, and now they were all looking at him as if he were a holograph. He didn't want to be part of Leroy's future.

"3-D!" Azalea exclaimed. "We had that ten years ago."

"Not 3-D! I mean it's like he's right here with us, talking and eating, but you can pass your hand right through him."

Paul felt the hand coming. Knew it was coming, had known when he came down the stairs to supper. Still he tried to shrink back into his chair. Leroy's extended fingers caught him hard in the solar plexus and left him breathless.

"Stop! Leroy," Azalea pleaded. "Please."

"Oh, I was just showing you. Paul ain't hurt, are you, Paul?"

Unable to speak, Paul shook his head no. He'd hoped some-how to bring the dinner conversation around to the Civil War years at the Fennel light or at least to some aspect of Jack Fennel's career. Now he'd be happy merely to get back upstairs. Yes, the more he thought about it the less happy he was with the day's accomplishments. He'd drunk lemonade with Camilla and walked with Ginny to the store. Leroy's prod was all that was needed to send him back for a late-night session with the papers.

"Why would someone want that?" Camilla asked.

"Ma'am?" Leroy responded.

"Why would someone want what you just described? What would be the purpose of having this stranger in your house? Would he come to study the papers?"

"No, no ma'am. You don't understand. It would be enter-tainment, Aunt Camilla. He could sing and dance or tell jokes."

"Like television," Azalea added. "Only it would seem real."

"An illusion." The others waited but these were the old woman's last words on the subject.

"Walt could have described it better," Leroy said in frustration.

"Walt?" Camilla asked.

"Walter," Leroy explained. "Ginny's husband. You remember Walter."

Camilla didn't answer. She resumed her meager eating. And Paul ceased his. Laid his fork down, in fact. This Walt had been married to his Ginny and no one had bothered to tell him. He was hurt. Angry. But Ginny hadn't bothered to look over. She was pushing mashed peas into Adam's mouth.

"We said we weren't going to talk about Walter," Azalea whispered.

"What's the difference?" Leroy shrugged.

"It upsets Ginny, for one thing, and it upsets me." She made a small sniffling noise and dabbed her nose with her napkin.

Ginny pushed mashed potatoes into Adam and said, "Hush, Momma. There's no reason for you to be concerned."

"I can't help it," Azalea whispered before bursting into tears.

"The unfortunate man has been dead for over a year," Camilla said.

"One year, one week, and four days," Azalea sobbed out. "And none of you care a bit."

Leroy appeared on the verge of tears himself. It should have been obvious to Azalea that at least her brother missed the departed Walter. And thinking back, Paul realized he should have guessed Walter's true identity. The clues were all there. Right out there in the driveway, in the girl's battered Chrysler Imperial. She said she'd inherited it, she just hadn't said from her husband.

Paul had no feeling for machinery, even less than he had for nature, and the more complicated the gadgetry, the more intense this lack of feeling became. Space rockets and cars were the same to him. His mother had never owned a car. Neither had he. They could walk easily to wherever they were going or ride the bus, and later when Paul was finishing school there was no money for such. Even after graduation he was paying back his student loans. Besides, he didn't have a license and didn't know how to drive.

Which is why Ginny used the Chrysler to take them to the Armada Inn in Atlanta. Paul had ridden in it a few times before but hadn't paid much attention. Packing it for the trip to Georgia, though, he'd found a metal box in the trunk—a tool box filled with greasy wrenches, sockets, screwdrivers. Paul couldn't identify more than that. Yes. It was a strange collection even for Ginny. More curious than jealous, he'd checked the glove compartment. And found a box of shotgun shells.

Under the seat were two crushed beer cans and an unopened bottle of aftershave.

A flesh-and-blood human was taking shape. All he'd needed was a face and he found that in a small plastic case on the back side of the sun visor. It held a work identification pass for the Caladium shipyard. The Polaroid snapshot was of a broad-faced young man in a yellow hard hat. The bearer was a W. T. Brant and he was born in 1942 and had brown hair and eyes and was six feet one inch tall and weighed 172 pounds. He was an American citizen and an electrician's helper.

When Ginny slipped behind the wheel to drive them away Paul had motioned to the pass and said, "Who's this?" And she'd answered, "Why do you want to know?" He couldn't say why. She was in the process of driving him to a motel room. "I inherited it," she said. She meant the car and Paul let the matter drop. He was wise to do so.

Azalea stood beside the table, tears crisscrossing through her thick makeup, and Leroy, also standing, was pleading for her to stop.

"Listen to me, Sis, please. The man said nobody would die. They're studying it right now at G. E. Cybernetics they call it. They just put you in a freezer."

Hearing this Azalea began to wail, while Camilla rose to her feet, propped a trembling hand on each side of her plate, and made a pronouncement on the future.

"I will not listen to another word of this. Everyone dies. Everyone."

"Dat's so." Suddenly Da Bena stood at the far end of the table. She wore a lavender dress with a broad lace collar. A dress quite similar to the one that Camilla wore each night to supper. But Camilla's dress was gray. They faced each other. As if combatants. And so alike. Not in the face or coloring but in their thinness. In their stance.

"We'll go to the stars," Leroy pleaded to anyone who was still listening.

"You're upsetting Adam," Ginny said. It wasn't a shout but was certainly the loudest Paul had ever heard her speak. And it did get the immediate attention of everyone at the table. There was silence.

Though Adam was still quite stationary, his eyes were blinking wildly and food dribbled down his chin onto the bib.

"Please excuse me," Camilla said, and she left the room.

"Yes," Paul said. "You're excused. I think I might turn in myself."

A sniffling Azalea called after him.

"Good night, Paul."

ANOTHER VISIT

Hey, bub."

Paul looked up from an unitemized and almost illegible account book and saw Leroy's eyes peering around the edge of the door frame. "Hey," he replied.

"How you doing, Professor?"

"Fine," Paul said. And in fact, the hand Leroy had attempted to crush was feeling better. The puffy redness remained, but the pain was gone. Still, the rest of him felt so bad, he'd decided he was coming down with something. That would explain his sleeping late for a second morning in a row and his groggy exchange with Azalea. While fixing coffee, she'd apologized for the disturbance at supper. She'd been contrite but in a disturbing crooked-smile way. He hadn't seen Ginny or anyone else. The last thing in the world he wanted was a visit from her dead husband's best friend.

"You got a minute?"

"Pretty busy," Paul mumbled.

"Azalea said not to bother you, but I didn't figure you would want to miss this. I don't give these exhibitions too often." Leroy stepped into the room. He wore an oversized pair of white pajamas tied at the middle with a purple and gold sash. He carried two short boards.

Paul sat back and retrieved his pipe. He had not accepted the inevitable. He meant to trick Leroy from the room or abandon it himself. "Judo?" he asked.

"Judo, jujitsu, Kung Fu, you name it, I know 'em all. A hundred ways to kill a man with my bare hands. I know 'em all."

That had a familiar ring. Paul was sure he'd heard that phrase somewhere before. Anyway, there was no need to caution Leroy about the stacks of material, since he approached down the narrow corridor with the grace of a dancer. Paul knocked the bowl of his pipe clean and tried his best to smile.

"Feel the edge of that," Leroy insisted, pushing his hand in Paul's face.

Paul had felt it several times, but he touched the callused skin as instructed.

"Feels like rock, doesn't it?"

Paul agreed. It felt like sandstone.

"Other hand's the same way, so are the feet. Know how they got that way? Beating bags of rice. It turns them into weapons."

"Those oriental disciplines have always been a mystery to me. The whole idea of learning a violent skill in order to lead a peaceful nonviolent existence is a difficult one for the Western mind to grasp."

"Yeah, but it's easy once you get the hang of it." Leroy had made a little clearing in the papers. Now he set up two even stacks of the lighthouse log books and bridged them with one of the boards.

"I usually do this in front of crowds. You know, supermarkets, ball games, dances, that sort of thing. I pick up a few bucks that way, but it's not really for the money, you know?"

"It's like praying, isn't it?" Paul lit his pipe. And shook the match dead with a modest vigor.

"I don't know. I guess it's a mind thing like you were saying. Let me point out to you that this is a piece of two-by-six pine and I'll be breaking it across the grain. Those shows like you see on TV they break it with the grain and it's some kind of balsa wood. What you're going to see now is the real thing."

Paul nodded. This seemed innocent enough considering it was Leroy. Still, he gazed longingly at the distant doorway.

"I'll have to ask you to remain silent." Paul started to nod again but realized Leroy was oblivious to everything in the room but the plank. With a curious gentleness, he laid the edge of the tempered hand against the wood. Then from deep in his chest came a low rumbling sound. The hand rose and descended in a slow arch as he made two practice runs and then it rose and stopped. The low rumbling continued, increased in pitch for another second and dissolved into a blood-congealing scream. The hand descended and the two-by-six piece of pine snapped in two and the ends flipped away, crashing into wall and ceiling.

"Amazing," Paul said. "Thank you for the performance."

But Leroy hadn't emerged from the trance. The second board took the place of the first and the rumbling began again. The attacker bowed slowly to the repaired altar and raised his hand. Once again the rumbling increased in pitch until it exploded into a powerful scream. This time it was Leroy's forehead that descended, but the results were the same.

Leroy jumped immediately to his feet and faced Paul. Only a slight coloration marked the forehead. Bracing against the desk, Paul eased from the chair. He tottered. It wasn't vertigo. He simply felt weak.

"Yes. Thank you. That was quite a demonstration."

Leroy didn't answer. Paul recognized on his face the glazed

uncomprehending look he'd received three night before in Ginny's bedroom—when Leroy had seen him but not seen him.

The man in the white pajamas bowed. Paul bowed in return. What now? Once more he tried to judge the distance to the hall. A sudden shout brought his attention back to ringside. The performer had changed his stance. The knees were bent. The feet turned outward. Not a paper had shifted from its proper stack. Now reaching into the folds of his pajamas Leroy withdrew three small objects and like a magician passed each before Paul's eyes for inspection. A credit card, a drinking straw, and a ballpoint pen.

Paul nodded. Words would be useless. Leroy straightened himself and took two sure steps through the stacks and addressed the window. His hand rose and then passed across the surface of the thick curtain, splitting it open for a yard. The credit card. It flipped between his fingers and was magically replaced by the drinking straw. Leroy moved from the window to a blank stretch of wall. The weapon rose above his head and descended. Four inches of hollow paper tubing was imbedded in plaster.

Not pausing, the man in the white pajamas whirled around and began to advance on his small audience. The bare feet, the edges of which had been pounded into weapons, slipped through the maze of paper. There was such grace and fluidity to the movements, and yet the potential for Paul's own destruction was undeniable. Leroy shifted the ballpoint pen from his left to his right hand and Paul instinctively brought the stem of his pipe to the fore. The low rumbling had begun once more and the hand holding the pen rose head-high. A single step separated the two men.

"Leroy!" Azalea screamed. "Leroy! What are you doing?" She rushed along the narrow paper corridor and yanked the pen from the assassin's hand. Paul realized for the first time she was

actually taller than her brother and that Paul Danvers was himself looking down on both of them.

"What do you mean?" Leroy asked. His eyes had cleared. "I
was just showing Paul my act. He asked to see it."

"Is that true?" she asked.

Paul had still not regained his power of speech. Carefully he
sought out the box of matches and with trembling fingers
struck one. The flame cavorted high above the bowl, but he
sucked frantically until smoke began to pass through his clenched
teeth. "Um!" he grunted and then exhaled. "Very interesting.
Really was."

"All right," Azalea said. "That's enough. Pick up your things
and let Paul get back to work."

A sullen Leroy began to retrieve the ends of the boards and
put the log books in their proper places.

"Paul, I'm sorry," Azalea continued. The crooked smile had
once more taken control of her face. The voice strained for an
unnatural naturalness. "He just doesn't understand how important what you're doing here is. I'll see to it that he doesn't
bother you again."

"I needed a break."

"Can you make any sense of this?" She indicated the papers,
those sorted and those still in the boxes.

"I'm starting to get a handle on it."

"That's good to hear. It should have been done years ago.
Camilla is such an eccentric. I get so exasperated sometimes I
could scream, but it's all worked out for the best."

Paul wasn't surprised when she began to cry softly and leaned
against him. He held his hands upward for an awkward moment
and then encircled her shoulders. And in another moment she
was hugging him about the waist, her flood of tears dampening
his shirt front. It didn't seem fair. He felt so bad he could hardly

stand alone and now he was propping her up. He was the one who should be crying.

A glum Leroy called from the door.

"Come on, Azalea. You're the one who's holding us up. Can't you see the man's got work to do? That's what you were just telling me, anyway."

The woman released Paul and blotted her eyes on the sleeve of her dress.

"I'm sorry. Really sorry. All I've done is apologize today. You get back to work now and I'll see that Leroy stays out of here."

She tiptoed from the room apologizing yet again. Paul stared at the empty doorway and waited. When neither returned he went to examine the drinking straw. It was quite ordinary and tore off at the wall when he gave a gentle tug. He turned next to the window. The cut in the curtain was long and clean—like a razor's slash.

"Paul?" Leroy said.

"What?" Paul snapped.

"There's one more thing I forgot to show you. Azalea said it would be all right."

"I've got to get back to the papers. Really."

"This won't take but a second." Leroy advanced on him. "It's something Azalea made. Here. See?" Paul couldn't retreat—his back was to the window. Leroy held up the ends of the purple sash. A gold crown had been embroidered on each. "Azalea made these for me. Leroy means king. That's what she told me anyway so I got purple 'cause that's royalty and she stitched on these crowns."

This Leroy was so childlike, it was hard to connect him with the screaming destruction that had stalked Paul only minutes before. But Paul managed.

"Nice. It goes well with the purple," he said and eased

towards the door. Leroy shadowed him like a friendly dog. "But aren't the belts supposed to be a certain color? A rating of some sort?"

"I guess so, but I like purple. I figured if anybody objected they could try and take it away from me."

"I see what you mean." Paul had reached the hall. He braced against the wall and with Leroy following eased towards the stairs. "Where did you learn your skills?" he asked.

"The usual places. TV, movies, the Marines. I picked up some from books."

"Pretty impressive." Paul clutched the stair rail and descended.

"Thanks. It's not something you can make a living with, though. That's why I'm studying air-conditioning."

"The domes over whole cities?" Paul was on the landing.

"That's right. I'm sorry Azalea got so upset last night, but the future really is in air-conditioning. It means job security. You understand?"

"Sure." Paul couldn't suppress a nervous laugh. He did understand about job security. And now he was in the hall and making light-footed steps for the dining room. Leroy sped up to a trot.

"I started to go in the Coast Guard—that's what my old man was in. That's how we ended up out at the lighthouse."

"I didn't realize the Ramonas were living out there too," Paul called over his shoulder.

"Sure. My old man died out there. He was killed in the accident."

"You mean Adam's accident?" Paul had to stop.

"Yep. My momma moved on to Fort Lauderdale, but mostly I stayed with Azalea. She raised me."

Paul swung open the sagging door to the dining room. Azalea sat at the table, her head buried in her arms.

"Azalea," Paul called softly. He'd come downstairs expecting to be rescued and not to act as her comforter again. "Azalea, Leroy's showing me his embroidery. It's beautiful."

"Thank you," she sniffed, not lifting her head.

"Paul didn't know Pop was in the Coast Guard."

Azalea sat up. Her plump little fists molded a tear-smudged face into a mask of the crooked smile. She pulled at the bodice of her yellow sundress.

"Leroy, I asked you not to talk about the accident," she said evenly.

"Oh, yeah. I forgot." It appeared that he might acutally pat his sister—but the door to the kitchen flew open and Da Bena appeared. In one hand she held two struggling chickens by the neck. Beneath the man's checkered coat, she wore the lavender dress with the broad lace collar.

"Do child," she crooned. "My Jack tell me he hear somebody cryin' in the house and we is all the way out in the chicken yard. And he deaf since that day the steamboat blow up on the Pana-mas Canal. Tell the truth now, Miss Azalea, has you been cryin'?"

"No," Azalea said emphatically, and shook her head back and forth.

THE PAST

Paul's greatest regret was that the papers couldn't be carried to another planet. But he had many regrets—too many to enumerate—and he'd returned to his work. Yes, better to set aside the concerns of the present and escape into the past.

The fourth box was proving to be particularly unprofitable. The same boat plans, recipes, newspaper clippings, and wedding invitations. Three log books had yielded nothing of consequence. Now he scanned a second batch of letters from the Lighthouse Board.

These covered the years 1871 to 1888 and dealt largely with the maintenance of the assistant lighthouse keepers. Someone was always being replaced. Exams were taken and certificates issued. Judging from the letters, only foreigners and drunkards had been hired by Jack Fennel. "Drunk and in uniform" was the most common complaint against his men. One correspondent closed with the comment, "I know not what philanthropy inspired you to employ this man, but I must insist on his removal. He is not fit to serve the government of the U.S. in any capacity."

No. Not much of interest, but a report from the district engineer did catch his attention. "The deviation of the lighthouse from perpendicular due to the settling brought about by the recent earthquake." The lighthouse was out of plumb twenty-seven inches and Captain Fennel was instructed to readjust his light immediately. The lighthouse tilted? Had Azalea or Camilla mentioned that? Why should he care?

Paul flipped through the remaining letters and tossed them on top of a convenient pile. He was in no condition to work. He needed sleep. He needed to be free of all this. Carelessly he ran his hands through the trash on his desk and came up with a newspaper illustration. A great ship beached and already partially stripped. The skyward ribs stuck up like the bones of a butchered whale. In the background the artist showed an octagonal lighthouse. The caption of the picture read: "Salvaging has begun on the five-masted schooner *Lily of Damascus* after all hope of refloating her is lost." And pinned to the sketch was a typewritten leaflet of some sort, a blue-ink carbon copy on fragile tissue paper that threatened to fall apart as he read it:

Murder at Large

Three times in the last twelve years the Lighthouse Board has held the infamous "Crazy" Jack Fennel by the throat and three times the lighthouse keeper has slipped through their fingers. How can this be? you ask. It is a good question when one considers the murderous indifference to human life that distinguishes the keeper of the Fennel lighthouse from the other brave and dedicated men who share his mission in life.

Ask any mariner to name the most dangerous spot on the Atlantic coast and invariably the answer comes back the same: the Dog Tooth Shoal. Dangerous currents and cross currents sweep by its sunken reefs. Freakish winds and weather batter unsuspecting vessels within its reach, and the shoal stretches out its arm like an angry giant and snatches them down to watery graves.

Ask any mariner to name the most dangerous man on the Atlantic coast and invariably you will get the same answer—"Crazy Jack Fennel."

Why these two phenomena should be allowed to unite at one time and place on the surface of the earth is one of our universe's greatest mysteries. Just as difficult to understand is how a lighthouse which is supposed to belong only to the government of the United States of America can remain in the hands of a private individual. No charter or letter patent can excuse this. No so-called legality can stand in answer to the continuous voicing of complaints the board has listened to. The investigation just closed heard the following from a commanding officer in our U.S. Navy.

> "The Fennel light has always been a poor concern but since the War its operation has much worsened. I, for my part, have so little faith in its reliability that I have guided only by soundings, without which in my opinion no vessel should pass the Dog Tooth Shoal. On the last ten passages I have spotted the light only twice. If it cannot be properly maintained I would propose abolishing it, for as it exists it is more a hazard than a help."

This testimony is laudable compared to some that was heard. Captain Elwood Edel and six others of equal reputation submitted signed affidavits stating that the light had either been put out or quit revolving while in their view and that in their qualified opinion this had been done in order to lure ships onto the treacherous shoal.

Over this evidence the lighthouse board has accepted once again the word of local pilots and acquaintances of the accused that "he's doing a good job and runs a d--n fine light."

Why the board should proclaim innocent a man who is acting in such clear and malicious disregard to his sworn duty is especially difficult to understand when one considers this committee's past record for putting the safety of sea voyagers above the interest of common politics. But to close such a report with the statement that "the light meets all the just and reasonable wants of navigation" is an outrage. To conclude "with the hope that it continues to send forth cheery rays to storm beaten mariners" is a blasphemy.

Something must be done. Crazy Jack Fennel is a murderer with the blood of countless poor souls on his hands. The light tower on the Dog Tooth Shoal is nothing more than a device for running ships aground. Concerned persons have no choice but to circumvent their government and come between the deranged man and his sinister weapon.

Paul did not know quite what to make of this incriminating document. After all, the essay was unsigned and the call for vigilante justice did seem a bit extreme. He didn't doubt that Jack Fennel was guilty of what was written. Still, his accuser was probably a crackpot. The reference to the existence of Jack and the lighthouse as "one of the greatest mysteries of our universe" was the main giveaway.

It was enough just to be examining the greatest mystery in the world's history. Paul didn't want to expand his research beyond that. He placed the paper under *T?JF* and crawled into bed.

REPAST

eroy gets mean when he's drunk," Ginny said.
"Is he drunk now?"

"I guess."

"Where's Azalea?"

"She's playing bridge. Camilla isn't feeling well."

"You mean it's just us for supper?"

Ginny shrugged and began to help Adam's plate.

"When do you eat? I always see you feeding your father."

"Sometimes before. Sometimes after. It just depends."

"Depends on what?"

"Nothing, Paul. Just how I feel."

Despite the small turnout there was the same amount of food waiting to be served. Fried chicken again. Rice and gravy. Tonight there were black-eyed peas and macaroni.

Paul took a small helping of everything. He felt better after the nap, but his hand had begun to hurt again. He might be running a fever. He didn't expect sympathy from the girl across the table.

"Leroy demonstrated his discipline for me today. He broke a

plank with his hand and one with his head, and he slashed the curtain with a credit card and drove a drinking straw into the plaster."

"I don't know why he does that. He could hurt someone."

"You really think so?" Leroy's bruising prods had become such an expected part of mealtime Paul wondered if he could eat without them.

"I just don't understand why anybody does anything," Ginny went on. "He does that. You sit upstairs and read those papers. Why do people do things like that?"

Paul wasn't sure how he'd gotten linked to Leroy or put in the position of defending them both.

"They just do," he said lamely.

"But why?" she asked, funnelling the black-eyed peas down her father's throat.

"We can't all be like Adam," Paul snapped.

"What do you mean by that?"

"Nothing." Paul wanted to ask about her husband Walter, but he didn't have the courage at that moment or any other. "Azalea cries a lot," he commented instead.

"She's always like that, but she's gotten worse since I've been gone. She likes you."

"That's good. I like her." He did like her and he was beginning to think she liked him more than Ginny did, which wasn't saying much.

"How did you do today?" It was the first time she'd ever shown an interest in his work.

"I'm not having much luck lately. There's a lot of stuff but I can't get it to fit together. And I haven't found anything about the Civil War. The Fennel light was very important at the beginning. The blockade runners were using the inlet."

"The Caladium Keyhole."

"How did you know about that?"

"I guess you told me." She puffed a cooling breath over a spoonful of macaroni.

"When?"

"You told the whole class."

"Did I?"

"You spent an hour on it. You said the fall of the Fennel light was a turning point in history."

"Are you sure?"

"Everybody in the class was looking at me and laughing. They knew I was a Fennel and they knew about us."

"About us?"

"You live in the clouds somewhere. You know that? When I'm looking up at the sky sometimes I think that. 'Paul lives up there.'" She motioned at the ceiling with the spoon.

"Are you sure? About the laughing?"

"Yes. I'm sure."

"Well, the Caladium Keyhole is a part of history. I couldn't leave it out just because your name is Fennel and we happen to know each other." Paul couldn't remember the lecture.

"It was on the exam. You said, 'Discuss the Caladium Keyhole.'"

He vaguely remembered the exam question. It had been two weeks since he asked it.

"Did you read my answer? I wrote a whole paragraph."

"Of course, I read it." Paul wasn't sure if he'd read it or not. Ginny's childlike script, the misspellings and the lack of punctuation. He could picture all of that, but he'd been in a hurry. They were about to go to the Armada Inn, and he'd had to correct all of those exams in a couple of hours.

"I wrote that Virginia made her husband surrender and then Jack shot the poor man with his own gun."

Paul was staggered. It fit. It could have happened that way and now Ginny was claiming she'd put this priceless information on a freshman history exam that he'd passed over.

"How do you know that's what happened?" he demanded.

"I don't know how. I guess I've always known."

"You were born knowing?" Paul shouted. "You were born knowing the answer to one of American history's greatest riddles? One of the world's great riddles?"

"Maybe Da Bena told me. I could ask her." Ginny rose from the table before Paul could stop her and left the room. Paul stared into Adam's blinking eyes. He didn't want to have to face the black woman, not like this. Not without Azalea. No. No matter what she had to tell him. Paul bumped his chair away from the table. But it was too late. Ginny returned and she brought Da Bena with her.

"Tell him," Ginny said.

"Certainly. Certainly," the old woman crooned. "My momma hear the story from she momma and . . ."

"How did she hear it?" Paul demanded.

"She been in the room."

"With Jack and Virginia and Virginia's husband?"

"She bring Master Jack to that room so he can remember what he done forget and that one thing be the very fact that no harm goin' to come to the Fennel light. That the Fennel light belong only to the Fennels."

"And Virginia persuaded her husband to surrender?" Paul hissed.

"Then Jack shoot him."

"And called it suicide?"

"That so. He dead sure enough."

"Then why doesn't everybody know that?"

"I ain't know."

"Maybe it's a secret?"

"Paul, are you all right?"

"Is that it? It's a secret?"

"That so. That probably so. This poor old nigger woman done run she mouth and this young gentlemans done learn the truth 'bout the Caladium Keyhole."

Dr. Whitman had coined the term "Caladium Keyhole" when he wrote his history. There was no way for this old woman to have heard it. No way. If Paul was certain of nothing else, he was certain of that.

"How do you know it's called that?" he demanded shrilly. "Where have you heard about anything called the 'Caladium Keyhole'?"

"Miss Ginny. She say you tell 'em to her. She say you tell the whole class 'bout 'em."

A LONG-AWAITED CURE

P aul went to bed immediately after supper and fell asleep at
once. The next morning he woke early and thought he was
feeling better. When he got out of bed he wasn't quite as sure.
The dizziness that had bothered him on his first night in the
house had returned, but it wasn't an attack of vertigo—he was
simply dizzy, and his hand, which had stopped hurting the day
before, was now much worse. It was badly swollen, and when
he went downstairs it was with the deliberate intention of finding some salts and calling a doctor.

Azalea, Ginny, and Camilla sat at the table, the remnants of
breakfast still in evidence. Paul said hello to everyone and accepted
his usual coffee from Azalea. Da Bena was giving Adam a shave
and Paul joined the others in watching what was apparently a family ritual. His hand did not hurt so bad that its treatment couldn't
be postponed ten minutes. He needed to catch Azalea alone. He
needed privacy for the application of medicines.

The barbering of Adam was quite professional. A sheet had
been tied at the base of the long neck and spread like a tent over

the useless body. The eyes, of course, appeared to have turned on Paul, but he was imagining this. The blinking proceeded unchecked. The straight razor flew back and forth in front of them, attached at one end to a lanky black pendulum that swung to and fro with a studied ease.

"How is you this mornin', Master Paul?" the old woman sang out as she put away the razor. "I been think the high blood troublin' you last night. Maybe the low blood too. That hand troublin' you any?"

"No," Paul said, lowering it out of sight.

"Sure now?" Using an electric clipper she began to shear Adam's head close to the scalp. The invalid blinked frantically at Paul as hair fell across his face and onto the sheet.

"Let me see," Azalea said, coming to his side.

"Are you ill?" Camilla asked.

"He's fine," Azalea said. "I know he's fine."

Ginny gave a rare smile, and he surrendered his hand to her mother.

"Paul, you should have said something. I'll get some salts and warm water, and you'll have to see a doctor."

"That ain't the thing for that." Da Bena lay down the clipper. "You wait right here now. You hear?"

She disappeared from the room for several minutes and the time during her absence was filled with testimonials to the old black's success with folk remedies. Camilla's arthritis had been miraculously cured with the bones of a black cat, a male cat, and water from the Ulacca River. And a tiny herb-filled pouch suspended around Leroy's neck had practically raised him from the dead several years before. Even Ginny agreed he was in good hands.

Da Bena returned with a single small waxy flower and placed it in the palm of Paul's injured hand. Then, curling the fingers around into a fist, she squeezed. The pain sharpened at first but gradually eased and finally stopped altogether. In fact, he felt better all over.

"It's quit hurting," Paul admitted to the circle of expectant faces.

Da Bena gave the hand a final pat and returned to finish with Adam. Placing his hands in her lap she began to trim the nails of the frail fingers.

Despite his new-found debt to the old black, Paul was still reluctant to watch. But he decided he must. Obviously this was a fact of life to the others—as crazy as they were they shared in a common humanity which escaped him. He had missed a lot growing up in that apartment, for even Camilla and Leroy seemed happy to see Adam being cleaned up. It was only Paul for whom the gesture seemed empty and absurd.

Da Bena finished. Slowly she removed the sheet, catching it on all four corners and shaking it down into a pouch that contained hair, whiskers, and fingernails. This she transferred to a plastic bag like the one that had held the chicken parts, and like the other bag, it disappeared into the folds of her yellow sundress. No one seemed surprised by this and Paul felt the exasperation of the previous night returning.

He wanted to scream, "What on earth is she doing with all that?" And the clothes. Beneath the sheet Adam now wore the familiar checkered coat. Camilla's dress was lavender. Azalea wore a pink double knit. But it was time for Paul to get back to work. He excused himself and, clutching the waxy flower in his fist, returned to his room.

A VISITATION

Of course, he now knew the secret of the Caladium Keyhole. Virginia had married the Confederate commander, a surrender had been coerced, and then to ensure silence the poor man was murdered by Captain Jack. He knew it but couldn't prove it unless the proof was in this room. And searching that morning he found absolutely none. But of course, the stacks of sorted material continued to grow. In most places they were at least knee-high, and he'd also covered the surface of his bed. How could five boxes have held it all? It didn't seem possible. Azalea brought lunch and they exchanged pleasantries. Paul said he was "fine." He lied.

Despite the flower, his hand ached dully, and an hour later the listlessness and loss of equilibrium had returned to his body—with a vengeance. His eyes ached, and both eyelids now twitched on occasion. He took up his pipe, lit it, and then set it aside. With trepidation he viewed the remaining cartons and tried to judge the odds of success. Dr. Whitman or Dan Pauling could make something of this—probably a great deal. But he would fail.

Paul loosened his tie and undid his top shirt button. His favorite possession, his coat with its chamois patches, threatened to broil him alive or suffocate him with its weight alone. The piece of clothing was in conspiracy with the cockeyed walls of the airless room. Yes. A conspiracy to keep him locked in here, when all he wanted was to be in the garden with Azalea or out on the bluff with Ginny.

A sudden rustling of papers brought his attention to the doorway. As if summoned by the thought, Ginny was crossing the room, heedlessly kicking papers as she came. He could have pointed out the weaving little path but it seemed irrelevant. Naked and dripping wet she came on until she reached the desk. Her deep navel was now eye-level, inviting him like a real keyhole to peek inside. To halt her forward movement he put a hand on her flank. Water continued to drip especially from her hair which clung close about her head and face. At her feet, the damp outlines of a pool were forming.

"Ginny," Paul whispered. "You can't come in here like this. Camilla could come in here any minute. Any of them could."

"Why did you let go?"

"What are you talking about?"

"You let go!"

"I haven't let go. I'm right here." Paul moved his hand from her flank up the curve of her hip. "But you better get back in the tub, honest."

"I wasn't in the tub. You know I've been swimming."

"Where have you been swimming?"

"Don't tease me."

"Tease you? Were you swimming in the hall?"

"No. The ocean. Where else?"

For the first time Paul realized that the flesh beneath his hand was dripping salt water, and the smell of the ocean had replaced that of the musty papers. There was salt water as close as the bluff. But she said the ocean. Paul didn't want to understand.

"You can't stay here," he insisted. Her pubic hair trapped tiny drops of moisture and turned each into a miniature prism that brought a halo of color to the soft brown curls. "Someone's going to see you." The flat plane of tanned muscle that ran from her diaphragm to the slope of her lower belly pulsed slightly as she breathed. Paul groaned as her two hands reached out and guided his face upward until each twitching eye came within an inch of a pendulous breast.

Paul could stand it no longer. He broke free, scrambled to the door, and shut it. Papers scattered everywhere and he scattered even more as he drew Ginny down into the middle of his precious cataloguing system. To hell with it all. There wasn't even time to remove his coat and tie. He pushed his pants down below his knees and entered her. Wildly they pulled at each other, thrashing their way through the few stacks that remained untouched. To hell with the Fennel papers. Paul screamed silently as he felt his insides melt and pour into the woman beneath him.

"Cunt hound," the soft musical voice said.

Paul looked over his shoulder. The door was now cracked open. Da Bena's face was high in the crack.

"What did you just say?" Paul whispered fiercely.

"Nothing. I just wonder what you young folks up to. I thought maybe you was readin' some of them old papers to that gal."

"Close that door!" Paul looked back at Ginny. Her eyes were shut tight and her face grim. Heedless of the interruption she went on and on, stretching out until she'd reached the mysterious object that had brought her to the room.

Paul didn't move. He lay still listening to her breathing in his ear and for Da Bena lurking in the hall. All his cataloguing destroyed. It was worth it. It was better than the Armada Inn. Much better.

"I've got to go, Jack. They'll be wondering what happened to me."

"What did you say?" Paul raised himself enough to look into her face. He refused to believe that Da Bena had just called him a cunt hound or that Ginny had just called him Jack. It was easier to admit that he was going deaf or even insane.

"I said I've got to get back. They'll miss me."

"No. I mean what did you call me? Who'll miss you?"

Ginny gave him a curious look, a look unlike any he'd received before. She was thinking hard of something.

"I called you Paul. That's your name, isn't it?"

"Yes."

"And the people downstairs? Are they named Camilla, Azalea, Adam, and Da Bena?"

"Yes."

"Dey ain't all downstairs," a familiar voice said behind him.

Paul didn't know whether to move or not. Lying as he did partially shielded both his and Ginny's nakedness. He decided to stay where he was and strained to look over his shoulder.

"I asked you to shut the door," he said wearily.

"I shut 'em."

"Will you leave us now?" Paul was too tired to really even argue with her. The numbness that had threatened him all day now descended in full force.

"Bena glad to see the young folks havin' a good time. They so serious in this old house sometime it just make this old nigger woman want to cry."

"Please leave us," Paul begged.

"I goin' now. I goin'. I ain't mean no interruption." Quietly she let herself out and Paul separated himself from Ginny.

"What a mess we made," the girl said, glancing about. "I hope you can straighten this out. It looks like a rat's nest."

She stood but Paul remained on his knees surveying the chaos of scattered papers. A few of the loose ones had been torn in half and nothing was left in place.

"No damage done," he said.

"Let me get out of here." Ginny bent, kissed him on the cheek and, tiptoeing through the Fennel papers, went out the door.

Paul pulled on his pants. Not bothering to tuck in his shirt or even zip up he began to kick through the papers with the tip of his shoe. Cataloguing hadn't been such a good idea. He lacked the methodical direction which he'd always assumed was his strong point. He would not persist. He would not persevere or endure either. It would be a lightning-quick victory or no victory at all.

Paul must find something in all this mess or the mess that remained in the boxes that would support or not support what he'd been told about the marriage and the murder. He must set aside all scientific manners and bulldoze through this crap until he had what he needed, a piece of historic yellow journalism that would guarantee him tenure—and he didn't have much longer either.

Paul was sick. Very sick. And even if he managed to hold up, Da Bena and her husband would murder him if Leroy didn't do it first. And Ginny was acting stranger every day. He had to get her back to school and soon.

So with a new resolve he kicked and shoved until he'd cleared a place by the desk to dump the next box. Only when this was done did he notice the errant sand dollar beside the door.

Examined closely, it proved to be gritty and damp. It smelled salty like the ocean. Paul stomped and thrashed his way to the window and pried it open. A strong fresh breeze pushed through the room stirring the papers anew. This smelled of salt as well.

No. Paul wasn't going to believe that Ginny had stepped from the beach into his room. He was sick and his senses were failing him, but he still had enough awareness to realize Da Bena had planted the sand dollar for him to find.

He sailed the small disk out the window and watched with satisfaction as it caught the wind and coasted in a gentle curve towards the front of the house. Leaning out the window he watched it go further and further until it came to rest in Brown Jack Simmons's open palm. The old black man held it up for Paul's inspection. Even at that distance the beaklike nose and the small darting eyes of the Fennel face were unmistakable.

"Master Paul, why for you throw that away? Them old sand dollar very lucky to find." The old woman stood in the doorway, grinning so broadly her piano-key teeth were exposed to their gums.

"I'm not afraid of you." Just telling this lie was the bravest thing he'd ever done.

"Bena ain't think you been afraid, 'cept then you sleeps with the light on."

"Habit. I've always slept with the light on."

"I glad to hear that. Bena just a old nigger woman. Ain't no reason to be afraid of Bena."

"What about him?" Paul pointed at the useless mess of papers. "Was he afraid of you?"

"Who that?"

"That man, Captain Jack Fennel."

Da Bena chuckled and brought a hand to her face like a flirtatious young woman.

"Dat man ain't been afraid of nothin'. I ain't never see him scare." She paused and then the hand dropped to expose the still-grinning mouth. "'Cept maybe that one time. The shake."

"The shake?"

"The big earthquakes that caught him up in the top of the

light. It throw him this way then throw him that way and maybe he scared then."

"Eighteen eighty-six? You remember that?"

"Bena been just a suckling babe but she remember and her momma tell she 'bout the captain. He run off."

"He ran away?"

"He think he goin' to die. He run out and get married to a woman he meet in the city and then bring she back here and then Jack Junior he born and she run off and my momma raise him up."

"And you want me to believe that's why there's a Fennel family today. Because Jack Fennel was caught in the lighthouse during an earthquake?" Paul shouted.

"Dat may be."

"It may be?"

"Dat so."

"I'm not afraid of you."

"Dat good. Bena just an old nigger woman. She ain't want nobody be afraid of her."

"Get out of here! I mean it. Just get out."

Bowing to him with a mock solemnity, the old woman left the room. And Paul collapsed into his captain's chair and tried to remember what he'd read and heard. He thought there was an engineer's report about the lighthouse tilting during or after the earthquake. Camilla or Azalea had told him that Jack Fennel had been married about that time. He could ask at supper.

THE MYSTERY UNRAVELED

A wearied Paul dumped the final contents of the fifth box into a small clearing he'd made and plucked out a half-dozen moth-eaten bills of sale. They were all for slaves and all made out to a Jonathan Wilcocks and "Dated at Caladium the seventh day of February in the year of our Lord one thousand eight hundred and sixty-one and in the eighty-fifth year of the Independence of the United States of America." And they were all sealed and delivered in the presence of Captain Jack Fennel.

Here was proof of sorts that Dr. Whitman had been right about the Fennels and the slave trade, but it didn't link them with the African smuggling. It was hardly a revelation. Virginia Fennel had referred to the "Africans" in her description of the hurricane, and if it wasn't a revelation then it could hardly qualify as a crime or even a sin. Worst of all, it had no direct connection to the Caladium Keyhole.

But actually, Paul's main concern was himself. His entire body pulsed and it took great effort to continue picking through this garbage. Stock certificates, handsomely printed, and embossed

shares in two railroads—the Caladium to Norfolk and the Caladium to Mobile. Paul knew that neither had ever been started,
probably because neither had ever existed except as a means of
swindling the investors like Captain Jack Fennel. Here was a bottomless pit into which the man's nefarious fortune could have
poured. Next came a ribbon-bound package—letters from a
Columbia merchant during the war years. They concerned the
purchase and transfer of salt and quoted its value in both gold and
Confederate currency. Yes, the lighthouse was occupied by the
Union, but Jack Fennel had continued black-market trading with
the Confederacy. He had taken his payment in salt which could
be easily stockpiled and sold to either side.

Paul could no longer lean over the papers. He scooped up
what remained from the fifth box and piled it on his desk. It was
hot. Unseasonably so. Even with the strong sea breeze passing
through the room it was hot. He decided to remove his tweed
coat and his tie. But that didn't seem to help and sweat continued to trickle from beneath his arm pits.

He propped his bad hand up on the corner of the desk.
Despite the flower which he still held curled in the corner of his
palm, the hand was aflame. Just pulling the coat sleeve off had
been enough to make him groan. To put the coat on would have
made him scream. In vain, he tried to concentrate. But his
vision blurred and he could read no more. He laid his head
down and slept. For how long he couldn't say but when he woke
he felt no better and his body was drenched in sweat.

And the cursed papers were still there. Under the chair, the
desk, every surface of the room was plastered with papers. He
had laid in them. They stuck to his damp arms and even clung to
the side of his face. Their meaning was lost.

Paul tried to stand but couldn't. He was stranded there,
mired down, beached. It was a fitting end, and he was about to

cry when he saw the three envelopes. They had been lying literally under his nose. All were addressed to Captain Jack Fennel and, judging from the familiar script, were written by his sister Virginia. Paul ripped at the first. It was empty. The second held a small scrap of paper which unfolded to become a poem entitled "Lines to V. F." With parched lips he read it to himself out loud. He'd been taught that poetry should be read out loud.

> "I know not why, but all this weary day,
> Suggested by no definite grief or pain,
> Sad fancies have been flitting through my brain;
> Now it has been a vessel losing way,
> Rounding a stormy headland; now a gray
> Dull waste of clouds above a wintry main;
> And then, a banner, dropping in the rain,
> And meadows beaten into bloody clay.
> Strolling at random with this shadowy woe
> At heart, I chanced to wander hither! Lo!
> A league of desolate marsh land; with its lush
> Hot grasses in a noisome, tide left bed,
> And faint, warm airs, that rustle in the hush
> Like whispers round the body of the dead!
>
> As ever,
> H. Timrod"

A verse written for Virginia by one of the South's poet laureates, Henry Timrod! Surely this belonged downstairs beside the Audubon sketch, but Paul didn't need another morbid reminder of the long-dead girl. The house was alive with them. He tossed the poem onto the floor and turned his attention to the last envelope. It contained a letter from Virginia Fennel to her brother dated February 26, 1861.

Dearest Brother,

There is still some sickness here. Each of the children has been down but all are mending. God in his infinite mercy and wisdom has seen fit to spare me but refuses to heal my ailing husband. I am told it is a test of my faith, this lingering of the fever. Every occurrence here, no matter how large or small is attributable to God. I believe this may be true of the entire mainland.

I can not tell you how much I long to return to you at Fennel light. If God has indeed been testing me then he has truly found me wanting for I am growing dizzy-headed from this continued talk of His will. There is only one other topic of conversation and that is of course the impending conflict. Everywhere there is a great chattering about secession and the brave fight ahead. If my James should be fortunate enough to recover I am told that once he regains his strength he would be expected to enlist in the regiment that is being formed.

I have already informed my dear in-laws that in the event of war we are returning to the lighthouse and that it was not my intention to kneel in sanctimonious prayer while my love lies bleeding on some distant battlefield of no importance. In short, I told them that the Fennels take no side but their own. James's father would have ordered me out of the house but his wife interfered. I say interfered for I would do well to be done of this place, with or without a husband.

I will say no more of that. It angers me so. I can tell you that we were quite fortunate to sell the bulk of our Africans even at a depressed price. I fear they would bring less today. As you write, the days of slavery in North America are numbered no matter how the war goes. And I calculate as you do, that it will go badly for the South.

You will not remember but my birthday passed on the 15th

and I am now twenty-two. When I return I will expect a birthday gift. A sail and a day spent on our beach would be splendid and cost you nothing. If it is summer, as it appears it will be before I am returned, James will be outraged to see us flying through the dunes like two savages. Perhaps we should leave him behind that day.

How strange these proper Christians would find our life at the Fennel light. I will pray to their God that they do not find out my lovely brother and that I see you again quite soon.

Your loving sister,
Virginia

Tell Bena that I look forward to seeing her once more and truly wish she could be here to tend my ailing husband. Her knowledge of such matters is far greater than any I have seen displayed by these learned doctors. I have inquired into the price of salt per your instruction and find that it is selling at $5.00 a barrel here in Port Ulacca. Whether this is good or bad I can not say and leave to your judgement.

Paul held the letter at arm's length. Of everything he'd read this was perhaps the most revealing. The relationship of brother and sister and their view of the world around them. Much was established and much foreshadowed. Still, he believed there was at least one more husband between the Confederate commander and the hapless James mentioned here. None of that mattered. The letter made no reference to the Caladium Keyhole. He returned it to the envelope which he then tossed to the floor.

He knew he was delirious. That was hardly a good reason to stop. A state of delirium was required to make sense of all this. This hodgepodge of tax notices, receipts, mortgages, the crude plans for yet another boat. All went sailing through the air and what was left was the log book for 1864.

"Now," Paul said aloud to himself alone. "Let us conclude this investigation."

The first page held the familiar weather notations of Jack Fennel. Nothing else. He turned to the next. It was stuck to the one that followed. Something had spilled on the log and a dark brown stain had practically glued it shut. Not caring if the paper ripped Paul began to pry and flip, pry and flip. The stain increased, spreading wider, obliterating the entries. But the entries were only weather notations. The tides, the wind, the sea. Paul caught the binding beneath his right elbow and yanked his way onward. And finally he arrived. There at the bottom of a page, there just beyond the edge of contamination was the firm perfect hand of Virginia Fennel. ". . . because I have found it in my heart to . . ." What came before? Nothing. All was covered over but this fragment. ". . . because I have found it in my heart to . . ." And beyond? Nothing. The next six pages had been ripped away and were missing altogether. Of course. This was the week of the surrender. The loss of the Caladium Keyhole. His search was over. He felt not disappointment but relief.

Paul tried to go on. To obediently turn his way through the pages to the end, but the remainder of the log had been soaked through and bound shut by the staining substance. He caught one corner in his teeth and yanked hard and the paper gave way.

Pressed flowers. Azalea would have loved this. All this work for three pressed flowers whose stems were like delicate yellowed bones and whose blooms were like tattered scraps of parchment or of skin. They were like fingers, Paul thought. Indeed, they *were* fingers! In the center of the matted page were the remains of three human fingers. They had been severed by a knife or some sharp instrument, for the paper beneath them was cut also. The crusted brown stain was blood!

Paul shut the log and tossed it onto the floor, onto the mountain of Fennel papers. Carefully he rose from the chair and, using it as a crutch, edged to the bed. The room pitched and swayed as if he were at sea, but he gained the bed. His head hit the pillow. He closed his eyes and tried to block out the memory of Dr. Whitman's fingerless hand.

"Knock, knock," Azalea sang out. "You missed supper so I've brought you a tray and something to show you, Paul. Something pretty." She stepped inside. "Paul, are you all right? You didn't touch your lunch. These papers look all jumbled up."

Paul opened his mouth to speak but couldn't. She approached the bed cautiously.

"Let me have a look at that hand."

He watched her through watery eyes and flinched when she uncoiled his fingers. He didn't want to lose them.

"Oh, this is looking bad. Just hold still now. I'm going to get this flower out of here. I know our Da is a good nurse but I don't see how that can be doing a bit of good."

She bent his hand completely open, removed the small bud and threw it on the floor.

"You just lie right there now. I'm going to go get some Epsom salts and some aspirin and tomorrow morning we're taking you to see Dr. Rupple."

Paul closed his eyes and tried to think about anything but the Fennels. It was impossible. There was no portion of his fevered brain that had not been permeated by the family. They danced about inside his head in a kaleidoscope of shapes and forms. Oh sweet mercy, he felt his hand being lowered into the warm salted water.

"Take these now," Azalea said, putting two aspirin to his

mouth. "And here's the water. I don't know how we let this happen. I'm ashamed of myself."

Paul choked down the aspirin and slumped backward once more. Azalea slipped a thermometer under his tongue.

"I'll sit with you awhile, and when Ginny gets back with her father she can take my place. I brought my cross-stitch samplers to show you so I'll just work on one of them and we'll read this thermometer and then you'll go to sleep."

Paul watched her retrieve the worn paper bag she'd entered with and draw the chair to his bedside. She took out the thermometer and read it.

"I thought you felt a little warm." She smiled her crooked smile to reassure him. "But you'll be okay. We'll see Dr. Rupple in the morning."

"Thank you," he whispered hoarsly.

"Hush. It's me who should be thanking you." Already her hands were working briskly with the needle and thread. "I've been so worried about my Ginny. Dr. Rupple insisted that I send her away from here. He's the one who signed her up in pre-med, and I knew he was right. I mean after all that has happened this just couldn't be a healthy place for my daughter." Azalea wasn't looking at Paul at all. Her eyes were on her work and she talked as if to herself. Perhaps she thought he was already asleep.

"I know Da Bena loves her dearly and Camilla does too in her own way, but they're both getting so old that they don't always act right, and then Adam . . . Adam is a burden. I know that's a horrible thing to say, but if I hadn't learned to admit that to myself I'd have gone crazy." She stopped work and looked up at Paul. So she did know he was still awake.

"I don't mean a burden really," she explained and then returned to her needlework. "I mean he puts an emotional strain on everyone in the family. Ginny would devote her whole life to

just cleaning up after him, but I'm not going to let her. I expect
you to help me."

As with the papers, Paul felt his delirious state was actually
helping him to understand her. Here was the reason for Azalea's
tears. Yes, she was a much stronger or at least lucid person than
anyone suspected. She continued.

"I can't worry about Leroy anymore. When they discharged
him from the Marines I knew there was nothing else I could do.
That was my last hope for my brother."

"You mean a dishonorable discharge?" Paul croaked.

"Yes," she sighed. "He killed his martial arts instructor. There's
something they're supposed to not do. They go to a certain
point and stop but Leroy didn't stop. I never really understood
what happened."

Paul could not suppress a strangled gasp of laughter.

"It's not funny, Paul." The woman looked at him once again.
"My brother's hands are registered with the state. If he kills
another man with them he'll be charged with homocide." She
began to thread another needle. She was changing colors.

"I'm sorry," Paul whispered.

"There's nothing for you to be sorry about or anybody else.
Being sorry doesn't change anything. Our lives, the ones around
me at least, are filled with tragedies and we must just make the
best of things and go on. Sometimes we think we can't, but then
something or someone will turn up when we least expect it.
Maybe God sends help, but I don't think so. Do you think you
were sent here by divine guidance?" Azalea glanced over.

Paul shook his head no. As far as he knew he'd been driven to
the Fennels by the arrival of Dan Pauling. His motive was job
security, that and maybe lust.

"No. I don't think so either." She set back to work with the
new thread. "Life is so complicated—so complex, but it all
comes down in the end to give and take. We give when we must

and we take when we can. Isn't that right?" She laid down her sewing and smiled at him—an open, ordinary smile.

"I guess," Paul whispered. He was having a hard time following her now. The aspirin had helped and he was sleepy.

"I'm right." She spoke with conviction and brought both hands into view and locked the fingers together. "Our needs interlock like this. We mustn't be afraid to give and take. I realized that when Adam was injured but it was too late."

"The fall?" Paul's voice sounded distant to his own ears.

"Adam didn't fall," Azalea said very quietly. "He jumped."

"From the front porch?"

"Of course not," Azalea said. "Who told you that?"

Paul couldn't remember. Azalea's face dissolved into a purple haze and he drifted off.

DR. RUPPLE'S

On the morning of the fifth day under the roof of the house that Captain Jack built Paul woke very early. There was no sign of Azalea or anyone else. The captain's chair had been pulled close beside the bed and on it were a glass of water and the bottle of aspirin. He reached for them with his good hand but was eluded. The water spilled and the aspirin rattled to the floor.

He still had fever and if anything felt worse. The skin of his hand was stretched taut and ominous red streaks were beginning to run up his wrist. The pain was intense. If he chanced even to brush that arm against the sheet, it increased—to the point where darkness begins. In vain he began to call. At first for Azalea and then for Ginny. Finally he called out indiscriminately for anyone. It was only then that Da Bena stuck her head in the door.

Even in his delirium Paul knew he could expect no mercy from this quarter. He managed a weak smile. A bluff.

"Dis the place? Bena hear one of her children callin'."

"No," Paul croaked. "I'm fine."

The old woman circled the room to the side of the bed and with surprising gentleness examined the hand.

"Honna best do what Bena tell 'em. This the only cure for that." Once again she produced a waxy sweet-smelling flower, put it in his palm, and curled his fingers into a fist.

Paul clenched his teeth and willed himself to remain conscious. Through tear-filled eyes he saw the rows of piano-key teeth grinning at him.

"You wear their clothes," Paul whispered. At last she was accused.

"Dis here?" The old black woman stepped back from the bed and curtsied. "This outfit come from The Good Will." And in fact, she wore what appeared to be a nurse's uniform or perhaps that of a nutritionalist or a dental hygienist. No one else in the family would wear such clothing. Except—except for the sash pulled tight about her waist. The purple sash with the embroidered gold crowns.

"Leroy's," Paul managed. "You . . . Leroy's . . ."

"Every post and lintel. Every post and lintel," the old black woman mimicked. "I watch the Captain build 'em. First he build 'em and then he send the undertaker off to find him a young wife. That a smart man, that undertaker. He know he goin' get paid two time. That a smart man that brung him Jewel. A very smart man." Her face hovered above his own. The brown skin slipped away to reveal the mocking skull. She gave his hand a final squeeze and the strange room filled with the paper flotsam of an earlier generation passed into blackness.

Rising and falling between consciousness, Paul dreamed. He was floating on his back in a languid green sea. Somewhere nearby was the sound of surf breaking but he could see nothing but the sun shining above and the hundreds of gulls that hung circling overhead. Slowly the current turned his body, but in the warm water it was motion unperceived. Only the view changed. Where there had once been sky alone, there was now a beach and dark figures moved on it, stretching in a ragged line from the surf to the dunes. In the distance looming above them the lighthouse rose higher and higher until it disappeared into the clouds. But this too was passing from view, for his eyes, following only the directions given by the ocean waves, saw just the empty beach stretching desolately to the horizon. A feather brushed his cheek and then a dirty white wing shut out the land, sea, and sky, and a sea gull's gaze met his own in questioning anticipation. *Are you dead yet?* the bird asked. Behind it now came the beating of other wings and the clamorous call to pluck out his eyes and be done with it.

"How's it going, stud?"

"What?"

"I said, how's it going, stud?" Paul could make out a shadow in the doorway.

"Sick. I'm very sick."

"Want me to get Azalea?"

Paul nodded weakly.

"Don't go away now. This could take awhile." The shadow disappeared.

Paul struggled up onto his elbows. Beneath him the mattress felt damp, perhaps soggy and there was the distinct smell of the ocean. This very mattress was wrestled up some sandy beach by shouting blacks, who, encouraged by the curses of the lone white man, left it on the dunes to dry and returned to the surf for other treasures. Offshore, corpses bobbed and sank, unattended except for the angry gulls.

And now Paul swung at the beating wings, for in each bird's face he saw the rapacious Fennel face. He heaved his feet from the bed to the floor, took two tottering steps among the papers and collapsed.

It was there that Azalea found him when Leroy brought her to the rescue. She had been on her way—had already called Dr. Rupple, in fact. But seeing him lying among the papers had given her a bad scare, and immediately she'd gone into action. Commanding her brother to put Paul in the station wagon, she then drove him herself to the doctor's office. They traveled "at breakneck speed." She told him this later when he was recovering. He remembered nothing of the drive except the squealing of brakes at one point and the curious drifting motion of the car. He had looked out the window against which his head was propped and seen the grillwork of a large truck and the larger-than-life letters GMC flashing by. But perhaps that too was a dream. Azalea had no memory of it. But she admitted readily that she could remember nothing about the race except a general harrowing urgency.

When Paul regained consciousness he found himself stretched out on an examination table staring up into several bright lights.

"He's coming around," a pretty nurse said.

"Oh, thank goodness! Thank goodness!" Azalea cried out. She was bending over from the head of the table, which meant her face was upside down. "Paul," she continued. "This is Dr. Rupple."

His attention was directed along his own arm to the old man who was examining the swollen fist. Dr. Rupple was at least seventy, perhaps much older. Wiry gray hair flew out high above the thin face and stuck from his eyebrows, nose, and ears in unruly tufts. One eye was glazed over and the other bobbed about wildly in its socket. A chewed match hung from a mouth that contained no more than three teeth. As Paul watched, the doctor cleaned an ear with the chewed match and then returned it to his mouth.

"I'm going to die," Paul said. It was the first statement born of rational thought he'd made that day—perhaps the first since arriving in Port Ulacca. "I'm going to die," he repeated.

"No, you ain't," the old doctor drawled.

"No, you won't," the upside-down Azalea insisted shrilly.

"You wait outside now, Azalea. We can handle this."

The nurse ushered the protesting woman from the room and Dr. Rupple, muttering about "them Fennels," returned to his examination of the hand. One by one he uncurled the fingers of the fist to reveal Da Bena's flower.

"What's this here for?" he asked Paul.

"Da Bena."

"Ah," the doctor said.

"What is it?" The nurse frowned suspiciously.

Dr. Rupple plucked the crushed blossom from Paul's palm and smelled it.

"Banana shrub. Some root, I reckon." He passed it to the nurse to sniff.

"You mean . . . Oh. Oh, that."

"Yep. Voodoo," the doctor said. "That old black magic." Then noticing the pure and undiluted terror that must have popped into Paul's eyes, he qualified the statement. "Don't worry, boy. I got that powerful white magic. You're in good hands now." As he spoke these words of reassurance the chewed match danced across his lips in wild accompaniment to his single good eye.

"I'm going to die," Paul repeated.

"That's what my grandpa thought," Dr. Rupple went on in bedside singsong. "And everybody thought he was going soon, even the doctors. So they sent him down the coast so they wouldn't have an embarrassing corpse on their hands."

The nurse submerged Paul's hand in a basin of warm water as the doctor prepared a hypodermic.

"So the first place he stops is the Fennel lighthouse where he falls in love with the sister of Crazy Jack Fennel."

Paul tried to raise himself. "You mean he married Virginia Fennel?"

"No, no, no," Dr. Rupple sang as he held the needle to the light. "He was engaged to her. She was already a widow. Wasn't but twenty or so. He didn't marry her. He came ashore here at Port Ulacca and married someone else instead." The nurse cleaned Paul's arm with alcohol and the doctor gave the shot. "Instead of dying like he thought he would, my grandfather had twelve sons and to show his thanks to God he named them after the twelve disciples. And out of all of them and all their off-spring I'm the only Rupple left so I guess it just shows you can't win." Dr. Rupple poked at the sky with his match to emphasize this last point.

"But what about Virginia Fennel?" Paul whispered hurriedly. A heavy numbness was spreading through his body.

"Her? Seems like she married the one that the wheel run over his head and then I don't recall who came next. Some call it 'white liver.' Them Fennel women don't have much luck with husbands."

"I noticed," Paul managed. His entire body was now without feeling and his tongue felt a mile thick.

"I was engaged to Camilla Fennel myself but that was years ago, and we just never could get around to settling on a wedding date."

"That's too bad," Paul whispered with great effort.

"Thank God for small favors, that's what I say." The doctor pointed to his good eye with the chewed match.

And an immobilized Paul watched the nurse hurry forward with the vial that had contained the injection.

"Dr. Rupple," she said quietly. "This isn't right. You can't administer that dosage."

"Why not?" The match danced across his lips.

The nurse whispered in his ear and he looked at Paul and grunted.

"We should do something," she insisted quietly.

He waved her away and, bending over the patient, rolled back an eyelid for closer inspection of the pupil. When he released it, the lid snapped shut and stayed there—locking Paul in darkness. From somewhere came the sound of a door opening and in the far distance a voice was heard.

"Martin Rupple, what do you think you're doing?"

"Come in, Camilla," a closer voice replied. "I was expecting you."

Paul slipped into unconsciousness.

Despite the overdose of the morphine substance, Paul did not go into a coma and die. He slept instead. But it was a turbulent dream-filled sleep. But still only sleep, which in some ways was preferable to being dead, but not greatly preferable, for in the one dream he would remember, he was dead. Not only dead but almost gone.

He no longer drifted on the ocean. He was on the beach, or what remained of him was on the beach. Now he was less than human, far less than human. Just a few vertebrae, three or four at the most, and a thin line of connective tissue were all that remained.

In this form he had come ashore, been washed back, come ashore again, washed back. How many times had the sea rolled him back and forth across the gritted surface of the beach? Polishing his bones, fraying the thin cord until it was no more than a thread. How long had it been since the receding tide had left him stranded high and dry? A pair of sand crabs had shown interest but gone away disappointed. There was nothing there for them. He could hear them talking, though he had no ears, and though he had no eyes he could see the rosy glow of the bonfire. The longer he lay there, the brighter it grew, until the tongues of flame began to show over the top of the dunes. And then he saw the figures dancing, bringing wood for the fire but dancing as they came. They were Africans—black Africans—screeching out the language of black Africans. There were other voices speaking his own language, and though he had no ears (his ears had gone their own way several days before) he could hear Camilla. She too was bringing wood to the fire. And Azalea was, and finally, he could not deny it, even Ginny was bringing wood to the Fennel fire. And above them all, if he listened carefully, was the woman Bena singing the lullaby he'd heard in Ginny's room. Only Brown Jack Simmons and Leroy were missing and Brown Jack Simmons was probably off digging the Canal and Leroy—Leroy was coming through the dunes just beyond the edge of the firelight. His short murderous body cast a long ema-ciated shadow across the sand, a shadow that fell on Paul now. For Leroy had come to step on him, to mash what was left deep into the beach sand. Paul could feel the immense pressure of that foot bearing down and he sat forward screaming.

He screamed in blackness, at first not knowing what to scream about. Then he screamed, "Where am I?" He screamed, "Help!" He screamed until Dr. Rupple stuck his head in the door.

"Oh, it's you," the old doctor said.

"Oh, it's you," Paul repeated dumbly.

"Ah, then we're both here." Saying that, Dr. Rupple closed the door, locking Paul once more into darkness.

THAT FENNEL THING

Dr. Rupple put Paul in quarantine for the first day of his recovery. No Fennel would be allowed to see his patient for more than one minute and from no closer than the door. The old doctor claimed that in addition to the infected broken hand, Paul suffered from what he called that Fennel thing—"a disease that attacks the brain and turns it into the human equivalent of a hog's head cheese."

Paul had announced some misgivings when he realized his doctor was not joking and meant this as an official diagnosis. No place here for Freud or any of his mealy-mouthed embellishers. When it came to mental or emotional disorders this practice dealt in hard realities. For the majority of the patients this meant ghosts and hexes only explained by magical roots, and for the rest fits and tempers that could only be explained by bad liquor or bad blood. "Just listen and then tell 'em they ain't alone," Dr. Rupple explained. "Tell 'em there's mysteries in this world they ain't meant to understand. Let 'em rest." This treatment had served well enough over the years and now there was a clinic on the highway for those in need of more up-to-date treatments.

Dr. Rupple's prescription stood. No Fennels. Which was just as well, for only Azalea and Leroy showed up the first day. Azalea brought clothing and his pipe. She shouted cheerful wishes for a speedy recovery and then went on to describe their desperate race to the doctor's office. Leroy looked in for a second and, apparently disappointed, walked away.

That was in the morning and Paul had slept much of the remaining day, waking only to have his hand soaked and dressed by the pretty nurse. Just before five Dr. Rupple came around to check the injury. He pronounced it much improved, and stayed to smoke a very poorly rolled cigarette—and of course to talk about the Fennels.

"I had it myself," he began.

"What's that?" his patient asked. Watching the doctor with his ragged cigarette had reminded him of his pipe and he began to fill it.

"That Fennel thing. That's why it was so easy for me to spot it in you. Having it myself, you know. I was engaged to Camilla so I saw enough and heard enough." Crumbs of flaming tobacco fell to the floor. The chewed match remained in the corner of his mouth.

"I guess they told you I've been going over Jack Fennel's papers." Paul chuckled. He did feel good. Not seeing the Fennels for a whole day had worked wonders.

"Used to see the Captain when I was a boy. He sat in the rocker like Camilla does. We called him Crazy Jack back then."

The doctor's good eye bounced around. Half the length of the cigarette was gummed wet.

"Why? Why'd they call him that?" Paul lit the pipe and drew in. He hadn't felt this relaxed in months, maybe years, maybe forever.

"Don't know. You seen the papers. Outside the family you probably know more about him than any human being 'cept possibly me."

"And Dr. Whitman? Curly Whitman?" Paul asked.

The doctor laughed, cleaned his ear with the chewed match, returned it to the corner of his mouth, took out the cigarette, and then spoke.

"Captain did a brisk salvage business out there. Must have made a lot of money but nobody knows what happened to it."

"Railroad bonds. They went bust."

"See there, you do know more. You just don't know you know you know it. Anyway, his boy Jack Junior was the one I was acquainted with."

"I heard of him from the family."

"He grew up out on that island real wild, but still smart. Real smart, I guess. He could read and write well enough, so when he was fourteen or so the Captain sent him off to MIT for a finishing. And he sent Brown Jack Simmons along to be his manservant. Didn't work. Jack Junior just kept going. Ended up in Panama and poor Brown Jack too, cause he'd promised the Captain he'd look after the boy. Then Brown Jack's home and nobody knows quite what happened to him."

"Da Bena claims a steamboat blew up," Paul volunteered. "I think that's why he's deaf or whatever he is."

"Might be true about the explosion, but Brown Jack Simmons ain't deaf or dumb or nothing else physical. Probably just quit listening and quit talking."

Paul liked the sound of that. At least some of it was beginning to make sense, and he decided to tell the doctor about the black woman's control over the family and how she wore their clothes. And to ask him about Ginny and her crippled father. Yes, having a lifetime of questions, he was naturally disappointed when the doctor chose that moment to excuse himself. And the nurse chose it to bring supper. With professional good humor the young woman fluffed his pillows and arranged the tray. Paul didn't know what her name was. She wore no name tag and Dr. Rupple called her "nurse." She smiled at Paul and asked if there was anything she could get him. He could think of nothing but he liked having her standing there.

"Do you live in Port Ulacca?" he asked.

"Yes. My husband's a chemical engineer. He commutes to Caladium."

"Do you like it here?" Paul poked at the whipped potatoes on the tray. Everything looked tasteless, like the food he was used to preparing for himself.

"It's all right. My husband likes to hunt and fish. I enjoy working with the doctor. He's such a character." She covered her smile with a well-manicured hand.

"Do you know the Fennels?"

"Just the name. The old families stick to themselves. You can go to the same church and still they don't speak."

"But you saw Camilla?" Paul tasted the salmon patty and the nurse folded her arms.

"That was the first time and we've lived here almost a year."

"What about Azalea?"

"I may have seen her, but I'm not sure. I know her brother Leroy, though." The young woman was suddenly animated. She clapped her hands together.

"Leroy?"

"He came by last winter and fixed our furnace. He wouldn't let us pay him but he had a few beers with my husband. They get along real well."

"That's him, all right." Paul lay back against the pillows, his appetite gone.

"Listen. When you get out of here why don't you bring Leroy by our house for a beer? We'd like that, really."

"Sounds great," Paul said and then he told her he wasn't very hungry and asked her to bring him some magazines before she locked up.

He was flipping through a four-year-old *Time* when Dr. Rupple returned, pulled up a chair, and without speaking began to roll a cigarette. A study in concentration. The eye bobbing and the chewed match dancing across his lips. One shaking hand creased the paper as the other dumped a small mountain of tobacco. Then the fingers and thumb flicked together, and with seeming skill, the craftsman licked it and produced a flat crumpled object that bore little resemblance to a cigarette. Loose tobacco rained from both ends as he held it up proudly for Paul's inspection.

"So Jack Junior runs away," Dr. Rupple said, beginning where he left off. "He goes down to Panama and when he shows back up he knows higher mathematics and before the first war he's patented a torpedo fuse. It never got in production over here, but he still made money off of it." The doctor lit the cigarette and the gummed paper appeared to melt.

"But he made money?"

"The Germans had the same fuse. Some people seemed to think he made German friends while he was down at the isthmus, but that don't seem likely to me. I mean the idea of Jack Junior having friends. German or American. He had the money, though, from somewhere and he had a wife, Elizabeth, that could spend it. She was always traveling—would stop anywhere but the Fennel light or Port Ulacca."

"And when the Captain died Camilla traveled with Jack Junior's wife?"

"Until Elizabeth slowed down enough to get pregnant with

Adam and that's when I got it, the Fennel thing. I delivered Adam. No problem, but as soon as she was fit to travel, Elizabeth did the same as Jack Junior's mother. She took off. People around here laughed and said they knew it would happen, but it wasn't funny if you was there. Camilla moved back onto the island, and she and that same Bena raised the baby. That's when I got engaged to Camilla. I would go out there and visit and I got to know Jack Junior about as well as anybody did. Guess what he was talking about at the end?" The cigarette had gone out and dangled from his lip alongside the chewed match.

"His wife leaving him?"

Dr. Rupple laughed and managed for just a moment to focus the one good eye on Paul.

"Submarines. The second war had just started up and there was a blackout, so we'd sit in the dark and he'd rave about how good the German U-boats were. I guess he quit saying that when they set up the Coast Guard base, but I was gone by then—I'd give up."

"Give up?" Paul repeated.

"On marrying Camilla. She wasn't much different than she is now. Set in her ways and her head full of poetry and the Fennel family. Besides . . ." The speaker halted and chewed on the match and the undisclosed memory. The eye? A liver? What had he said earlier concerning Camilla? The cigarette was relit but that subject was closed.

"What about Adam?" Paul asked.

"What about him?"

"I meant about his . . . the shape he's in?"

"He's in remarkable shape considering the distance he traveled."

"From the front porch?" Paul couldn't remember who told him this.

"From the top of the lighthouse."

"Oh."

"I guess Mr. Ramona broke his fall. He was waiting at the bottom. I had to look at both of them. Worst mess I've ever seen."

It was Azalea who said Adam jumped but maybe that was a family secret. Best not to mention it.

"It's a miracle he lived," Paul said.

"Had nothing to do with my skill as a surgeon."

"Ginny stays with him all the time." Paul couldn't hide the complaint in his voice.

"She was just born. Bena and Camilla had delivered her out there at the light."

"Azalea said you sent her to the university."

"After she lost her baby, I thought she should get away for a while."

So there had been a baby. Da Bena and Ginny hadn't invented it. And what of the witch doctoring and the insistent ghost of the original Virginia Fennel? Just how much had he dreamed? How much was hallucination?

"Voodoo?" Paul asked. "And possession? What about that?"

The old doctor stood and ground the remnants of his cigarette out on the formica surface of the bedside table. "Fifty-six years I been practicing medicine here. Ghosts, hexes, roots, juju, mojo. I can't imagine a curse or a cure I haven't come across." He stopped to interlock his fingers the same way Azalea had done to express people's intertwining needs. "White magic," he said of one set of fingers. "Black magic," he said of the other. "When you get my age it don't mean squat."

It wasn't the kind of reassurance Paul had been seeking, but it would have to do.

"When I get out of here I'm taking Ginny back to the university," he said.

"You ain't staying to finish Camilla's papers?" Both the old man's eyes widened in mock surprise.

"No. I've seen enough." Paul realized he no longer cared if he finished with the papers or not. He could survive at the university for at least another year, and in the meantime he'd be with Ginny and she would be safe.

"Good luck," the old doctor said. He pointed at his sightless eye with a chewed match. The stationary bluish ball contrasted sharply with its lively neighbor. "Them Fennel women . . ." But he left this thought incomplete or at least modified it into a final piece of advise. "You don't ever really get over it. You could always have a relapse. No warning, just . . ." He snapped his fingers together and cut off the room's overhead fixture at the same time. With the light from his reading lamp Paul could still make out the wild comical face of his advisor.

"What? What are you talking about?" the young man pleaded.

"That Fennel thing. That god-awful Fennel thing."

ON THE MEND

Azalea arrived early the following morning. She brought him a day-old newspaper and a batch of Da Bena's home-made cookies. Paul had no use for either but he was glad to see Azalea.

She pulled up a chair beside his bed and took out her cross-stitch from the worn paper bag. It appeared to be the same piece she'd been working on in his room three days before.

"Paul?" She said this at once. "Paul, there's something that I want to ask you and I know I can trust you to tell me the truth, can't I?"

This was exactly what he was about to say to her. Only there were many questions he had to ask.

"Sure," he said, trying to give the single word the freight of frankness and sincerity. Azalea glanced back at the door and then leaned in and whispered. Her lips were no more than two inches from his ear.

"Do you think I'm fat?"

"Ma'am?"

"Do you . . . when you look at me do you think of me as being overweight?" She still leaned forward.

Paul looked at Azalea and tried to give an unbiased appraisal. She was heavier than her daughter and she did seem a little plump around the middle and in the face and hands. But he couldn't see what that had to do with Leroy trying to kill him or Da Bena's grip on the family.

"I'd say that's about the right weight for your build."

"It is. You're right and I should have told Leroy. He said I was fat."

"You're not."

"I believe that is the ugliest thing you can say to a person— to tell them that."

Paul wondered what had happened to the other Azalea, the one who had found him delirious in his room and lectured to him so eloquently on helping other people—and on helping yourself.

"I brought this picture for you to see." She retrieved the newspaper from his bedside and, folding it to the desired page, laid it on his lap. "That's the movie actress Cally Miller, the one in the middle." Paul studied the grainy picture and nodded. "Do you think she's fat?"

Paul pushed the paper to one side.

"Listen, Azalea, we've got to talk."

"I'm not any fatter than she is." The woman beamed like a trial lawyer who had just made the case.

"No. No, you're not, but we've got to talk about your family. About what's happening back at the house."

"Yes. All right, but will you do me one last favor?"

"Anything."

"Don't tell Ginny I asked you about whether I was fat or not."

"Azalea!" he shouted. "What's wrong with you? When I was sick in the room, you told me we had to rescue your daughter. I didn't dream that, did I?"

Azalea was packing up her cross-stitch and she was taking her movie star picture with her.

"I'm sorry," Paul called out. "I didn't mean to shout."

But Azalea was gone.

Two hours later Ginny appeared. She had pushed her father all the way there and left him in the care of Dr. Rupple and the pretty nurse. She had nothing to say to Paul except "Hello" but she answered his polite inquiries about the others.

"How's Leroy?"

"Fine."

"How's Brown Jack?"

"Fine."

"How's Da Bena?"

"Fine."

"How's Adam?"

"Fine, I guess."

"Ginny, your mother told me about Adam's accident. When I was in bed back at the house we had a long talk and she told me your father jumped." Best to say it. Get it out.

"He didn't exactly jump. I was watching."

"You were just born."

"Bena was holding me. We'd all gone up to the top."

"You couldn't remember all that if you were just born."

Ginny shrugged and stared at the radiator.

"Da Bena must have told you."

She didn't even shrug at this suggestion.

"He's lucky to be alive at all. I mean falling on Mr. Ramona was almost a miracle."

"Yes. He had come out in the yard to watch Adam circle. Then when Adam started to fall he just stood there. We thought he would move for sure but he didn't."

"Circle?" Paul asked.

Ginny stood. She appeared to be leaving. Paul raced on.

"Dr. Rupple told me you lost your baby. You could have told me that, Ginny. There's no reason to keep it a secret." The girl said nothing. "That's what your mother told me when I was sick. She said people have to help each other out. I love you and I want to help you."

Still the girl was silent but Paul could see she was thinking this over and would reply.

"I don't know what you're talking about," she said finally.

"I just mean you could have told me."

"I could be pregnant now."

Now? She'd visited his room three days before. But she must have been referring to their night in the Armada Inn.

"You mean you're pregnant now?" Paul was amazed. Frightened. Delighted.

"No. I'm not. I just mean I could have been."

"And you would know already?" Was he truly disappointed?

"I would have known when I sent you for the paper."

"What paper?" All he could think of was the nightmare papers he'd left behind in the Fennel house.

"The Sunday paper. I might have been pregnant then but I wasn't."

Yes. He remembered. The morning after at the Armada Inn. He'd crossed busy Peachtree Street to buy her a newspaper— the Caladium newspaper—and maybe she was saying she could have known then.

"At the Armada Inn, Ginny? Then?"

"Or now. I would know now if I was going to have a baby."

"My baby? You might be having my baby now but you're not."

"No," Ginny answered emphatically. "The baby would be Bena's." She left the room and an infuriated Paul rose to follow her—only to find his path blocked.

Camilla's visit was short, sweet, and to the point. Marching into the room, she took up a station at the foot of the bed and seized the metal rail. She addressed him fiercely.

"Azalea's brother Leroy informed me that your intentions towards Virginia are not honorable. He says that he suspected this from the start and is almost certain that he saw you enter her room on at least one occasion. I confronted Virginia with these suspicions and she readily confirmed my worst possible thoughts. Obviously you have taken advantage of a young girl's troubled emotional state to gratify your own animal hungers and you have taken advantage of the Fennels' hospitality as well."

"Miss Camilla?" Paul registered a feeble protest.

"It was Leroy's further contention that you were not actually examining the family papers at all. He claims to have observed you many times and never saw you do anything other than smoke your pipe and mutter to yourself. It was his suspicion that you were a fraud that led me to call the university and to my horror I have discovered you are not employed there and never have been."

"I taught Ginny," Paul broke in at last. "It's a mistake. My name's gotten confused with someone else's." They hadn't gotten around to giving him next year's contract, but that was only a formality. Dr. Whitman would protect him and, anyway, how could they claim he'd never taught there?

"Yes, there's a mistake, Mr. Daning, and you made it."

"Danvers," Paul interjected.

"Danvers, Paulvers, Pauldan. I do not care what you call yourself, you are no longer welcome under the Fennel roof."

Her voice cracked, but she went on. "This is the kind of behavior one expects from the Ramonas, but one never doubted that they were summer people. You, however, I took to be a gentleman and a scholar. Obviously you are neither."

She turned on her heel and left the room.

Paul went at once to the doctor's phone and called the university's registrar. It was true. Paul Danvers was not employed by the history department and there was no one of a similar name except perhaps his office mate Dr. Daniel Pauling. Paul begged the woman to double check and when she returned to the phone a hint of success sounded in her voice. The previous semester the department had employed a Dr. Pauling Daniel, but he went without leaving a forwarding address. Paul grasped hungrily at this crumb of an identity and begged the woman for one last favor. Was Dr. Curly Whitman still alive? He was. Paul thanked her profusely and hung up.

DA BENA

G ood afternoon, gentlemens," Da Bena said as she pounced
her way into Paul's room. The pretty nurse slipped by her
like a flushed quail.

"Good afternoon to you, doctor," Dr. Rupple said.

"Oh, doctor, why you always call me doctor? You know I ain't
no doctor." She was quite pleased to be called doctor.

"Why, you're a doctor same as me," the old practitioner
insisted.

"Hush now." Da Bena giggled like a young girl and Paul
remembered the photo in Camilla's album—the laughing girl
child. Something else was oddly familiar or unfamiliar. She wore
a faded brown dress of absolutely no shape or design. A hanging sack and the shoes were Sunday best but of cracked leather.
Yes, these were her clothes. This was the real her. She had lost
the power to frighten him. "Jack. Listen here, Jack," the black
woman called over her shoulder. "Does you know what they saying about me?"

Brown Jack Simmons appeared. Somehow his shrunken

frame managed to fill up the doorway behind her. He carried his sweat-stained felt hat in both hands. He wore a dark suit of a threadbare material. He glanced about nervously and nodded to the two men.

"Jack has been asking about you every day since you been gone. So this morning I just says come on, we going down there to Dr. Rupple's place and see the boy ourselves. Ain't that so, Jack?"

Brown Jack looked down at his feet.

"The hand's much better, Jack!" Dr. Rupple shouted. "We just finished changing the dressing and tomorrow morning we're going to put it in a cast—then I'm sending Paul home for you and Bena to look after."

Brown Jack continued to stare downward. He scratched the top of his slightly balding nappy head.

"Jack is mighty glad to hear that," Da Bena said. "We be happy to take care of Master Paul."

"Good, good," Dr. Rupple said. The nurse's pretty face appeared, bobbing over the black man's shoulders.

"Dr. Rupple," she called. "We've got a little emergency here."

The doctor laid a hand on Paul's shoulder. "Just ring the buzzer if you need anything."

Paul was alone with his visitors. Da Bena sat down in the chair. Brown Jack moved forward to the foot of the bed. They smiled at him and then the black woman spoke.

She spoke African, of course. A long unintelligible discourse punctuated by the usual rolling of eyes and gesturing in Paul's direction. Occasionally Brown Jack would grunt in response.

After a full minute of this the patient unclipped his buzzer from the pillow and held it in front of him, thumb over the button.

"If you don't speak English I'm going to ring this and have you thrown out of here."

Da Bena was brought up short. She stopped in midsentence, possibly midword, and Paul had to congratulate himself. These three days out of the Fennel house had done wonders for him. Before Dr. Rupple's cure he couldn't possibly have come up with such a simple solution to this or any other of life's problems.

"I just been tellin' Jack there what a fine, fine fella you is and that Ginny is the luckiest gal in the whole wide world."

Paul couldn't help but laugh. She was teasing him. The woman's insincerity was so obvious, she hadn't expected him to believe her. She had never expected him to. They were enemies and mortal ones at that. He threatened her control over Ginny—over all the Fennels. It was so clear now and should have been from the very start.

"I'm leaving tomorrow," Paul said. "And I'm taking Ginny with me."

"Dat a very sad thing." Da Bena was not smiling.

"It's what Dr. Rupple wants. He has strong white magic and he wants her to study his kind of medicine at the university so we have to go now." That was true in a way, though the doctor hadn't mentioned summer school for the girl. Anyway, it got Da Bena shifting nervously in the chair. Brown Jack studied the brim of the hat he held. "Do you understand what I'm telling you? No more voodoo. No more roots for Ginny. You can practice on the rest of the Fennels to your heart's content but she's leaving with me." A brief silence followed. Then she bowed her head.

"Bena just a poor old nigger woman. She don't know nothin' 'bout no root medicine and no voodoo." The bowed head rocked to and fro. "Bena a good woman and she very happy to see her child goin' to that university and study medicine. Education a wonderful thing. That why we have this here integration."

Paul relaxed his grip on the buzzer. He didn't believe a word the old she-devil was saying but he sensed somehow that she was pleased by the idea of Ginny's studying medicine—she was indeed in awe of Dr. Rupple's white magic.

"I'm glad that's settled." Paul made an awkward attempt to retrieve his pipe and tobacco from the bedside table.

"Dis what you goin' for?" Da Bena's arm snaked out and delivered them to him.

"Thanks," Paul said, knocking the bowl clean. And he decided to risk a single solitary question. Not about the baby who might have been conceived at the Armada Inn and wasn't? Or about the baby that might have been conceived here and wasn't? Of course, all this concerned him, but he chose to ask her something else—something simpler.

"Ginny was in here a little earlier and we were talking about Adam. About how he jumped from the top of the lighthouse."

The old woman nodded. Paul filled his pipe.

"And she said you were there."

"Dat may be."

"She said 'he circled.'" Paul said this casually.

"Yes. Dat may be so."

"What did she mean by that? Circled?" He put the pipe in his mouth and groped about for matches.

"Circlin'. Circlin' like the bird circles in the air."

"You mean flying?" Paul spoke around the pipe stem.

"Yes, that what he be doin'."

"Adam was flying?" Paul had expected a lie. Half expected one anyway—but nothing this bizarre.

"I tell 'em how to do it."

"You told Adam how to fly?"

"Bena can't show 'em. She can't fly sheself but she can tell 'em how."

"And he believed you?"

"I tell 'em how and then take 'em up to the top of the lighthouse."

"And you carried Ginny?"

"I cradlin' that baby in my arms." Da Bena made a cradle with her lanky forearms.

"Then Adam flew?"

"I tell 'em to spread he arms and jump."

Paul felt suddenly numb. Perhaps there was a truth here. A truth in some form. Da Bena pointed a long finger at the ceiling in a pantomime of scolding.

"Don't look down, I say. Don't look down. That what I tell 'em and sure enough he fly like a bird. He circlin' round and round way up there. Sometimes he even come over my head." Da Bena looked at the ceiling and so did Brown Jack, and their heads moved about in a slow clockwise motion. "Then Adam say, 'This sure is fine, Bena, this flyin' like a bird, but I still going to do what I say. I goin' send you off this island and I ain't goin' let you put your hand on that new baby of mine.'" She looked straight at Paul and so did Brown Jack. "Then what you think happen?"

Paul stared back dumbly.

"He look down. I tell 'em, Adam, don't look down, but he look and that when he fall and hit poor Mr. Ramona."

Da Bena's mournful cast gave way to one of open mirth and Brown Jack too was laughing after a fashion. Suddenly the bowl of Paul's pipe burst into flame and he dropped it onto the bed sheet.

"That the true tellin'," the old woman concluded gleefully as Paul beat out the burning linen with his one good hand. "I tell 'em, Adam, don't look down, but you can't tell that boy nothin'. Same as when he be in that garden. He just go on and do what he goin' do."

BOOK TWO

The Fennel Light—

Dog Tooth Shoal, South Carolina, 1963

THE HOMECOMING

The angry redness of Paul's hand had faded to its former natural sweaty pink and the pain was reduced to a dull and distant ache. The swelling too had almost disappeared and Dr. Rupple was satisfied that the broken bone could be set. In a matter of hours his patient would be free to leave. Maybe.

"Can't be too careful," the doctor muttered as he kneaded the sensitive flesh. "Can't be too careful." He plunged his thumb deep and yanked, causing Paul to howl.

"That didn't hurt, now did it?" said the pretty nurse who still insisted that he bring Leroy by for a beer. "It never hurts like we expect it to." Statements like this had suddenly begun to strike Paul as funny but he didn't laugh.

"I wasn't expecting it to hurt at all," he said.

"Got to hurt some. If we don't feel pain we don't know whether we're alive," Dr. Rupple remarked.

"I guess." The patient didn't need homey maxims. He needed to discuss the visitors of the preceding day, but the emergency that allowed these visitors to torment him had kept Dr. Rupple away overnight. Since then the office had been crowded with patients, but at last Paul's turn had come. He sat now on the examination table with an X-ray of his injury pinned to a lamp stand.

"Not much to look at," the good doctor explained. "Hardly broke but it was already starting to knit crooked. That's why we had to snap it back into place."

The pretty nurse used her perfectly manicured nail to indicate the break in the miniscule bone. But Paul barely listened. He couldn't look at the image without thinking of Dr. Whitman's three fingers, and curiously enough, he could not think about them without smiling. He wasn't sure why this struck him as funny, and he felt guilty just for thinking it was. Many things had begun to strike him this way since the combined visits of Azalea, Ginny, Camilla, and Da Bena. Things that were once annoying were now amusing. Things that were frightening were now hilarious.

He wanted to confess as much to Dr. Rupple, but they had not been alone at all and the old man himself, with the chewed match in his ear and the missing teeth and eye, was a perfect example of what now struck him as comical. It would be hard to have the conversation without bursting into laughter, and the fear he wished to enunciate was that he was always on the verge of bursting into laughter.

It was useless. All the calming insight he'd gained from the "cure" had dissolved into this new lunacy and into an accompanying anger. The anger, that was something he could talk about with Dr. Rupple. Perhaps the anger was part of "the Fennel thing" in its more virulent form. He had relapsed, he speculated, just as the old man had warned him, and now he would once more be at the mercy of the family.

"This'll fix you up, young fella," Dr. Rupple said. "Now hold that arm out here."

Paul did as he was told and the pretty nurse wrapped his arm from the fingertips to the elbow in a layer of gauze. Then the doctor lapped each side of the distance with two small pieces of stainless-steel angle and she tapped these into place. Finally layers of plaster and gauze were applied to the outside and allowed to harden. The finished product was as hard as rock and added about twenty-five pounds to the weight of the arm. Paul was outfitted with a sling.

As they'd worked, the pretty nurse described the fishing trip her husband had just returned from. He and a friend from his office caught sixteen fish. The combined weight of the fish was 246 pounds. They caught them using cut mullet and squid and fishing around the clock for forty-eight hours with eight rods and reels apiece. When she finished he began to laugh and didn't stop until she'd become very annoyed.

Before he could get out a complete apology Azalea showed up to fetch him. There was no time now to discuss his problems with Dr. Rupple. The plaster had barely hardened.

"Everyone has missed him so," Azalea said. "Paul's only been with us a few days but the house seems empty without him. It's almost like we're all ghosts and he's just imagined us." Every sentence Azalea uttered was a joke. "Have you ever felt that way, Dr. Rupple?" the woman asked.

"Nope." The chewed match disappeared into the ear, a sure sign the truth would be spoken. "And you can just relax, Azalea. There's nothing realer on the face of this earth than you and the people in that house." Paul hooted to himself, choking on his own silent merriment. They thanked the old doctor and the pretty nurse. Then they got into the powder blue Plymouth station wagon and drove away.

Despite an outward friendliness, Azalea made no attempt to honestly communicate on the short ride home. Perhaps she sensed his new perspective, but he doubted this. The frozen crooked smile was still in place, and she was talking a great deal—mostly about the bridge game of the previous night. She had bid six no trump and made it despite the fact that her partner thought they were in Goren not Blackwood. Of course, she didn't have the cards. Of course not, but she had finessed twice and the rest fell into place.

"Once in a lifetime a thrill like that comes along, so I guess there's not much left for me to look forward to," she concluded.

"You're probably right," he agreed. "Why don't you give the game up and go into a nunnery?"

"You're joking, aren't you, Paul?" she asked, pulling into the drive. "You really don't think I should give up bridge?"

"Yes," he said. "And the flower garden and the seed catalogues, the cross-stitch. Give it all up."

"Why are you saying that? You're teasing me, aren't you?"

Paul didn't know why he was saying it or even if he was teasing. There seemed little point in trying to reestablish their earlier closeness. He would be leaving in a few minutes and he doubted if he would ever see this strange woman or any of the Fennels again. If he did, it wouldn't be in Port Ulacca. He was certain of that. Ginny could come here to visit or the family could visit her at school or wherever the two of them ended up but he was not coming back here.

"I am teasing. I'm sorry. Thanks for the ride." Paul meant none of it. He saw the girl waiting for him. She had pushed her father out to "their" spot on the bluff so that he could spend another day staring either at the light or off into infinity.

It was beautiful here, Paul had to admit as he crossed the lawn with purposeful strides. The cool shadows beneath the giant oaks, the gentle ripple of marsh grass brushed by fresh ocean-born air, and the rich dark smell of the mud-banked creek. These were enough to slow if not stop his momentum.

Adam was sleeping. His long neck curved far back and the head lolled against the back rest. A lone bumblebee circled the invalid's open mouth. It had been attracted to the flowers, to the sprigs of wisteria that Ginny had twisted into the spokes of her father's chariot.

Great. Paul applauded any attempt to beautify Adam's condition. He could appreciate it now. After spending years slumped in the wheelchair, the trunk of the man's body had collapsed and settled until the various organs and rolls of fat bulged beneath his shirt like the contents of a beanbag. It was good, necessary, and proper that he be decorated like a May Day float. Paul cheered and clapped but not where anyone could see or hear.

And Ginny. The incredibly desirable Ginny lay on her back in the uncut grass. Once again her shirt had ridden up, exposing a healthy section of midriff to the noonday sun. Paul knelt beside her. From this position he could look far down the front of her jeans to where the flaring hips tapered into darkness.

"Ginny," he whispered.

The girl opened her eyes on the clear blue sky.

"Ginny, I think it's time to head back to school."

"Fine," she answered.

"There's no great rush, but I'd like to leave today, tonight at the latest."

"All right."

"I know you'll miss your father."

"Why should I?"

"Once you're back at school . . . it'll be like leaving home for the first time. That's what I meant."

She tilted her face in order to see him. She took no notice of the cast or the sling.

"I'm not going back to school. Leroy has asked me to marry him."

Paul had a difficult time assimilating this information, and he realized at last that there was a limit to what he could find funny. In a way this was disappointing.

"Ginny, let's just put aside the fact that I love you and that I want to marry you. We won't even talk about that, okay?" The girl focused on the sky. "You can't marry Leroy because he's your uncle."

"Only by marriage." She spoke slowly to Paul as if he were simpleminded.

"What are you talking about? Leroy is your mother's brother. Your children would be monsters. There are probably even laws against it." Paul dropped to all fours. He was ready to eat grass with the wild beast of the field, or more exactly to paw and trample the grass underfoot.

"You're just trying to confuse me. I'm not going back to school with you."

"It's incest. You can't stay here with Leroy."

"I'll stay here alone, then, but I'm not going back."

"Has Da Bena been talking to you? Is that what this is all about?" Paul couldn't believe the sound of anger in his own voice.

Ginny looked over at him again.

"No. Da Bena said it would be wonderful for me to go to school and be a doctor. She said I could be anything I wanted and Azalea said so too. It's my decision and I'm not going to change my mind."

"And you're not going to tell me why?"

"Paul, what are you talking about?"

"It's me, isn't it?"

"You? This isn't any of your business."

Paul stood clumsily. "I'll see you before I leave. Think about it this afternoon. Maybe you'll change your mind."

"I'm going camping in a few minutes. Leroy's taking me out to the lighthouse."

"Camping?"

"Yes, Paul. Camping."

"No one cares if you go out there like that with him?"

"I went all the time with Leroy and Walter."

"I see. Good-bye then." Paul headed for the house.

"Are you mad at me?" she called after him.

Paul couldn't stop to answer. He might cry or laugh or curse. He didn't know what he might do.

His room had been straightened. His bags were packed and waiting in the doorway. And the eight paper-filled boxes were stacked against the wall. All evidence of his cataloguing had disappeared along with his contribution to the world of scholarship. The enigma of the Caladium Keyhole was unresolved and his chance for tenure gone. And his rendezvous with Ginny? That seemed like years ago, not days. His coat and tie had been packed. He could drag them out, but appearances no longer mattered. He lit his pipe and lay back on the bed without removing his shoes.

What the girl had said, did it make sense? Of course not. But he shouldn't have expected logic. That had been his mistake with the Fennel papers. To assume some moral order. To look for a rational explanation to one "of the universe's greatest mysteries." Unlimited greed and lust—the base light of a crazed self-interest beaming out from the beginning of time. Dr. Whitman knew. That was man's true nature. But the mild relapse that Paul had enjoyed under Dr. Rupple's care had made him forget this fundamental law of the Fennels. By thinking he was somehow in control, he'd lost Ginny to her uncle Leroy or to Adam or Da Bena or to them all. Maybe she'd been swallowed up like Camilla by some all-consuming worship of the family Fennel. It was hard to imagine Ginny at seventy, locked in some sunless room that smelled of mothballs and dusting powder. But perhaps she would end so—guarding the papers of the family as if the reputation at stake was somehow her own. She would be sleeping above these same boxes and dreaming again her great-aunt's dreams. It was hard to imagine, but harder still to imagine her down at the bowling alley with Leroy. It was uncharitable, but he would much prefer seeing Leroy dead and Ginny asleep in Camilla's virginal four-poster.

But it wasn't up to him to decide. The girl had just said it was none of his business. His time was up. Paul rose from the bed and after stowing away the pipe—that last vestige of his old life—he hefted the bags. Yes. Even with one arm he could make it to the grocery store and catch a bus from there.

A resigned Paul Danvers descended the stairs. Azalea met him at the bottom.

"How's the hand feeling now?" she asked.

"Fine. Perfect." He tapped the newel post with the edge of the cast. He hadn't meant to do damage but there was a satisfying sound of splintering and a strip of wood fell to the floor.

"Don't worry about that," an aghast Azalea whispered.

"I'm not. I'm leaving."

"You've talked to Ginny? You know her plans?"

"To marry Leroy."

"She's not going to marry her own uncle. I mean about not going back to school."

"She mentioned it."

"And she hasn't changed her mind?"

"She's a Fennel through and through."

Azalea caught hold of the suitcase handle. "No! She's not. She's my daughter and I'm not going to let this happen. We're both outsiders, Paul, so we can see what's going on."

Paul pushed by the woman. "Speak for yourself, Azalea. I may be an outsider but I'll be damned if I can understand what's going on."

"My daughter's being overwhelmed. She's being taken over by . . ."

"Da Bena."

"Yes, by her. By her and by the first Virginia Fennel."

Paul didn't know why he was shocked to hear this or why he could find it so hilariously funny. It was something he'd known himself for days and yet hearing it spoken aloud by another supposedly rational human being gave it a concreteness it had lacked. He laughed in Azalea's face.

"Stop it! It's not funny!" she screamed, trying to pull the suitcase from his hands. "You've got to stop them."

"Me? I can't stay here if Camilla doesn't want me here and your daughter doesn't either. I can't make Ginny come."

Azalea had both hands knotted into the plastic of the suit bag. Tears poured down the pancake makeup and stained her polyester blouse.

"They took my husband. I'm not going to let them have my only child and you're not going to either."

Before this final maternal onslaught Paul collapsed. He released the baggage and it slipped through the woman's hands and crashed to the floor. "You know they're camping," he said. "She and Leroy—out to the lighthouse."

"Go with them. Don't let them go alone."

"Azalea, I haven't wanted to say anything about this because you're his sister, and I didn't think it necessary to mention it, but Leroy is a homicidal maniac. If I go out there with him there's a good chance he'll kill me."

"I know you're right. He is what you say but I promise he won't kill you."

"Why won't he?"

"Because I'll ask him not to."

"Why don't you just ask him not to take Ginny, then?"

"I already did."

"Well, what did he say?"

"He said if I didn't shut up he'd kill me."

TO THE LIGHTHOUSE

Paul barely had time to snatch up a blanket—and have a word with Da Bena. The old hobgoblin caught up with him on the front lawn. She hailed him and then approached with the gait of a hurrying praying mantis. But at least the mantis wore her own clothing—a tattered shift of gray sacking.

"I ain't know you going camping, Master Paul. I done pack these thing for you."

Paul eyed the greasy paper bag suspiciously, though he couldn't think why. By agreeing to go he'd already forfeited his life and there was little else that Da Bena could do to him.

"What's in there?" he asked.

"Just some thing I fix up."

"Eye of toad? Gravestone moss? Bena, if there's human flesh in this bag I'm not going to eat it."

"Hush your mouth, boy," the old woman squealed with glee. "Ain't nothin' in that bag but ham biscuit and orange soda."

Carefully, Paul opened the neck of the bag. Ham biscuits and an orange soda.

"You didn't have to do this."

"Ain't nothin' where you goin'. Bena been born and raise on that old hammock and she know. Ham biscuit and soda goin' look mighty fine when that evenin' sun a-settin'."

Paul smiled into the big bulging eyes and piano-key teeth.

"You've got to know I'm not going to touch this stuff. Why are you giving it to me?"

"What you mean? Ain't nothin' but ham biscuit and orange soda. You a peculiar actin' fella. You know that? Smokin' that pipe and readin' them old paper and then I find you rollin' around on the floor with my darlin' Ginny. And now you say that I know somethin' to be a fact, that I ain't know be a fact at all."

"What happened to Captain Jack's sister, the first Virginia Fennel? How do you know she drowned if no one else does?" If Azalea could speak of ghosts then so could he.

"Dat gal drown." Da Bena spoke solemnly now, intoning the words. "I know cause my grandmomma the one that find 'em on the beach and she the one to bury 'em. She bury 'em proper so the poor gal can look into this world from the next. And then she tell her daughter who be named Bena and that be my momma. And my momma tell me."

"Come on, Paul!" Azalea shouted from the bluff. "He says he's leaving you." Paul hesitated. What else would the old black woman tell him if he stayed? But the outboard engine raced wildly. He took the greasy paper bag and ran.

Only Azalea and Adam were there to see them off. Camilla had decided to stay locked in her bedroom until Paul had vacated the premises. Azalea hugged him and whispered, "It's Walter's boat." Adam blinked. Da Bena waved from afar. Paul scrambled into the boat and found a seat in the back. Neither Leroy nor this Virginia acknowledged his presence and before he was even settled the outboard shot down the tiny creek with a roar. Behind them walls of spray crashed over the mud banks and flooded the marsh beyond.

"So this was your husband's boat!" Paul shouted.

"She gave it to me when Walter died!" Leroy snarled.

"It's nice."

"How would you know?"

Paul didn't know. It was big and fast and shiny red. But for him the boat was just a noisy way to float him out over his head. With this cast on he couldn't swim a stroke, but he couldn't do more than dog paddle before. That hardly mattered. Drowning would deprive Leroy of the pleasure gained by using his bare hands to pound Paul to oblivion. "Just making conversation," he said.

"Shut up!" Leroy called back. The creek widened and then entered an even wider body of water. The Port Ulacca River. It curved off ahead of them in the general direction of the lighthouse. Leroy pushed down a lever and the boat leapt forward again—leaving the water, it seemed.

"How fast are we going?" Paul shouted.

"Thirty-eight, thirty-nine knots."

The wind made Paul's eyes water and so he faced backwards. The marsh shores and mud banks flew by in reverse. A large blue bird made a ponderous rise above the marsh. A brown one hovered high and then with a collapse of wings crashed upon it's prey. A pelican? A smaller pair girdled the air with lazy spirals. Gulls. Definitely gulls. But all were being left quickly behind. They were now rushing to meet the future in Walter's vehicle made of spun glass and fiberglass resin, driven forward by the combustion of fossil fuels at speeds approaching that of light. The domed cities with their holographs and deep freeze lockers could not be far in the future but he'd miss out on that too.

"There's Brown Jack!" Ginny shouted and waved to a figure on the distant shore. The figure waved back.

"How can you tell that's him at this distance?" Paul shouted. The figure was no more than a dot.

"She just can!"

"What's he doing?"

"Oystering. The same thing he's done for the last fifty years."

"Oh!" In his ignorance Paul had assumed the black man's sole occupation was haunting the Fennel house. "Don't other people ever come out here?" They had seen no other human beings since leaving the bluff.

"Only on the weekend. During the week it's deserted."

Paul considered the miles of lonely marsh land. Ahead of them the lighthouse loomed larger. He could make out the windows and the glass at the top.

"Give me a beer!" Leroy ordered.

Paul opened the ice chest and passed a beer forward. Ginny declined without actually having to speak to him. He settled back and pulled the orange soda from Da Bena's greasy bag. Just as an experiment he popped the top off. The foam bubbled angrily over his hand, but it didn't burn. It even smelled and felt like orange soda. Paul didn't taste it. He tossed the bottle over the side and it sent up a gusher of water not unlike a small depth charge—but maybe he imagined that. He was ready to toss the ham biscuits over as well when Leroy stopped him.

"What's that?"

"Ham biscuits. Da Bena made them for me."

"Give 'em here!"

Paul passed the bag forward with no regrets and Leroy quickly bit into one of the little sandwiches. Paul watched the ears twitch on the thick neck as the jaw muscles moved. Leroy ate two more of Bena's treats and finished the beer.

The Fennel light protruded far above the low greenery of the island. Paul could see the dock and the roofs of the buildings.

Suddenly the motor sputtered, coughed, and stopped dead. The boat settled in the water, coasted a few yards, and stopped. The lighthouse dock was a hundred yards ahead.

"What now?" Leroy demanded of the boat's dash and ground the ignition uselessly. The motor refused to start. With a lurch the driver moved back to the stern, checked the gas tanks, and then removed the engine hood. He tinkered for a few minutes. Then announced in a thick-tongued slobber that he had spark and gas and he didn't know why the fucking thing wouldn't run. He crawled forward, laid his head on the steering wheel, and passed out.

Paul picked up the paddle with his good hand and began to work awkwardly towards the dock. At least the current was with them. At the very least.

"What's wrong with Leroy?" he asked.

"He acts like he's drunk. He and Walter used to do this all the time but all I saw him drink was that one beer. He wasn't nipping along, was he?"

"I don't know. I was facing the rear, the stern that is. He could have been. He probably was."

"Leave Leroy alone." She had crawled over the windshield and settled herself on the bow. "And leave me alone too."

"Don't worry. I like the quiet. It's just us and the marsh and that probably hasn't changed appreciably in the last ten thousand years. I mean this is just how Captain Jack and his sister Virginia would have come here." Paul indicated the light with the tip of his paddle. The fading white paint on the structure's octagonal sides was visible and he could make out the copper and iron fittings of the cupola. The dock was now fifty yards away. But they were drifting not to it but by it. And the current was running much stronger. "Nothing's changed in the last century. It's just like we were going back in time."

"Shut up." Ginny sulked, her arms wrapped tightly about her knees.

"Still planning to marry your uncle?"

"I never told him yes. I just said I wasn't going back with you. You know I didn't invite you to go on this camping trip in the first place."

"Paddle yourself then. You probably haven't noticed but your uncle broke my hand when he shook it." Paul tossed the paddle over the windshield and it slid into the water. Ginny made a grab but was too late. She turned on him in a rage and screamed, "You son of a bitch!"

"I don't care if we're swept out to sea," Paul said with a Gallic shrug. At last he was seeing what lay behind that expressionless gaze. A great deal, it seemed.

Ginny's angry face dissolved and Paul was treated to a parade of emotions. She smiled feebly, looked grave, puzzled, anguished, and finally terrified.

"I can't swim," she whimpered.

"I thought you'd been swimming that day you came into my bedroom."

"What day?"

"The day you dripped water onto everything and we rolled around in the family papers."

"I don't know what you're talking about. You're crazy." She crawled back across the windshield and began to shake Leroy frantically.

"Is he dead?" Paul queried.

"Just shut up," she wailed. "That white water is the ocean. Don't you understand what's happening?"

"No," Paul said. "And I'm sorry if I've given that impression. Is that the famous Caladium Keyhole?"

The breaking water was still a considerable distance, but they were hurtling along. A swirling tide now pulled one way—then another.

"Give me a life jacket," Ginny demanded.

Paul looked about his feet and under the seats. "They're none here."

"I put them in myself! And where's the anchor?"

Paul should have been alarmed at their situation but all he could do was laugh. After so many months of total inscrutability she was now unraveling.

"Why did we have to go to the Armada Inn on Peachtree Street on that particular night?"

"Shut up, you bastard!" she screeched. But instead of slapping him as he expected, she grabbed out for his good hand and held it in an iron grip. Paul felt the nails cut deep into his wrist. She was hysterical and he was only using his new clinical detachment to torture her.

"Ginny, listen . . ." he began, trying to comfort her with his cast-impacted arm.

The boat gave a sudden lurch and then bumped to a halt.

Paul eased free and slipped his hand overboard. The water was three inches deep and, judging from the direction of the rippling water, this bar ran straight to the lighthouse island.

Thirty minutes later he waded ashore at the spot where the dock began. He was covered with mud and water and exhausted from pulling the boat—and from all else in his life. But Ginny caught him about the waist—not to help but just to hold on. When he tried to pry himself free she kissed him with a strangely eager and pliable mouth.

"Just tie the boat off," she said, "and bring the basket."

"What about Leroy?"

"Who?"

"Your uncle Leroy."

"I don't have an uncle named Leroy. Stop teasing me and come on." She headed towards the light.

GOING UP

Nothing was as Paul had imagined it. No perfectly laid out compound surrounded by neatly trimmed lawn and that white mile of picket fence. No. Only thick, head-high shrubs through which a narrow winding path was worn. Much had changed since Adam's accident, but the light had always been changing.

"It's leaning," Paul said when he caught up with the girl. "I guess that's from the earthquake."

"Earthquake?"

"There's a definite tilt to the tower. I didn't notice from the boat. But see. Twenty inches off true perpendicular. I think that's what the engineer's report said."

"It isn't leaning. There hasn't been any earthquake."

"Ginny? You can't see that?" The tower showed clearly through the treetops and he set down the basket to point. "It's tilted a good fifteen degrees."

"There's nothing to see. What has Bena been doing to you?" And she hurried surefootedly down the narrow alleyway. "I can't believe how this place has grown up. I've been gone five months and I find a jungle when I come back. That's fine for them, Jack, but it's not fitting for a white man."

Paul let out a weary sigh.

"Why don't you have them cut it back?"

"That's a good question," he said.

The wicker basket beat against his leg and he had to break his way at times with the arm in the sling. Ahead of him Ginny moved with relative ease and hummed an unfamiliar tune.

No use denying it. She was more attractive to him now than she had ever been. Maybe Leroy was attempting incest, but wasn't Paul contemplating congress with the ghostly? In fact, he'd already committed it back at the house. And he wasn't above doing it here and they *were* here—at last—the Fennel light. Ginny gave a loud yelp of delight. Paul craned his head. The sides of the brick octagonal were so close they blocked his entire vision at first and then shrank as they rose dizzily. The top was crowned by the round walkway of the metal cupola.

He stepped from the trail and joined the girl on a large expanse of cracked and broken concrete. Everywhere about their feet was the trash left behind by a decade of visitors, the bulk of it beer cans. Whatever bottles had been brought along had either been broken on the spot or carried to the top and dropped. In the first case the glass was in the usual scraps and slivers. In the latter, it was shattered, often powdered.

What's more, the heavy entrance door had been lifted from its hinges and a fire started in its center. All that remained were the charred butt ends and planks and a small pile of twisted bolts and iron straps. And littered over these were the oyster shell remnants of a past roast.

"Look at this!" She didn't wait for an answer but slipped into the shadowy doorway. A dull booming came from the interior.

Cautiously Paul stuck his head inside. It was dark and musty with a stubby green moss covering the walls. And at his feet a gigantic circular stairway of triangular iron steps rose in an ever-diminishing spiral. Here was the source of the noise. Ginny was running, and the lighthouse acted as a gigantic resonating chamber for her charge to the top.

Paul gave one final look to the flat and secure earth and began the ascent. Animal droppings and rust were thick on the steps and the brick was damp to the touch, but at least there was the promise of sunlight and fresh air from above. A dozen steps higher the walls were drier and they had once been white-washed. Graffiti began. Scratched and painted, it started as a few scattered names and thickened as he went. There was a heart with a swastika chiseled inside and here a skull and bones superimposed on an American flag. Paul read as he climbed, for it seemed all of humanity had passed this way either singly or in pairs. He had already spotted LEROY and WALTER LOVES GINNY. If he got to the top he could put CAPT. JACK AND VIRGINIA. If he got there. At the first landing he stopped to catch his breath and to peer through the thick masonry slit of the window. A fine view of the dock and the river but the trees hid the boat. Paul judged the distance down at perhaps thirty feet. This wasn't so bad. He hadn't experienced his usual mind-numbing attack of vertigo or the accompanying nausea. Still, several stairways on the campus were this high and he'd made cautious use of them without ill effects.

The drumming of Ginny's feet stopped and from far above came a long echoing call of "Jack! Jack! Jack!"

Paul set off.

BOB + MARY JAN. 2, 1959 HARRY HATES JESSICA KILROY WAS HERE KNIFE THE KNIFE LEROY MEANS KING BEAT THE DOLPHINS BO ANNETTE SISSY DOES IT LOVE IT OR LEAVE IT TERRI'S PAL

The steps seemed steeper. The walls of the cylinder more confining. Paul reached the next window and surveyed the opposite side of the island. He could see the roofs of the two buildings and beyond them miles of empty beach and the gently curling surf. And to the left. Paul was looking down on the Caladium Keyhole. And beyond that inlet he could make out a line of white water that headed towards the horizon. The treacherous Dog Tooth Shoal, the angry giant waiting to snatch out its mighty arm. Far off to the right Paul spied an unsuspecting trawler. Perhaps its crew had been lulled by a false serenity. Up here there was a definite breeze blowing—one that wasn't felt at all on the ground level. Again Ginny called. This time not a name but another childlike yelp of joy.

FEBRUARY 14, 1956 YOUR VALENTINE PORT ULACCA GATORS LEROY MEANS KING NO SWEAT SHAYNE BETH MEANS CHEVY FREEDOM LEROY WALTER LOVES GINNY KILROY

The next window gave a view of the dock and now Paul could see the outboard. It looked like a toy left at the edge of some gigantic children's pool, and behind the wheel Paul spied a tiny toy Leroy still sleeping off his ham biscuits. Paul owed himself a round of applause. He had outsmarted the old she-devil at least this once. It was Leroy who slept while he followed Ginny to the top of the winding stairs. Yes, he would probably pay later, but that was better than paying now. "Jack! Jack! Jack!"

Paul deserted his view and trudged on. He needed more rest. Far more.

FAIRLANE BEAT THE DOLPHINS LEROY WAS HERE WALTER CAME THROUGH GATOR BAIT LEROY LEROY KILROY LEROY KILROY ELVIS

Paul reached the next landing and sank to his knees. His breath came in shallow gasps. The ocean looked larger, the

other objects—the rooftops, the beach, the distant trawler—
had all shrunk. The wind was brisk. He could no longer call it a
breeze, for it rushed through, forcing air into his lungs. At least
he wasn't sick. He had come a mile high, it seemed, but there
was still no sign of dizziness. Other than being exhausted he felt
fine, even clear-headed. Maybe this was what they called a second wind. He stood. From above, the sound of Ginny's feet had
stopped. She must be at the top. He put his foot on the next
step. It was no more than three feet across. The walls were
pinching together.

LEROY IS THE TOUGHEST SAYS WHO SAYS ME LEROY EATS SHIT WHO
WROTE THIS CAUSE THEY WILL BE SORRY WHEN I CATCH UP WITH
THEM WALTER LOVES GINNY KILROY WALTER LOVES GINNY WALTER
LOVES GINNY VIRGINIA LOVES JACK

Paul halted in his weary tracks. This last message had been
scratched in only moments before. The dust of the brick came
off on his fingertips along with some loose flakes of whitewash.
Just above him was a framed opening. He could see a heavy iron
door hinged to one side and, beyond that, machinery and the
shining white haze of brass-bound prisms. "Ginny?" he called
before taking the last few steps.

"What's wrong with you? Don't tell me you've got the fever
too?" She sounded close.

"I guess I'm over that." Paul climbed into the small room.
Overhead was an elaborate set of gears that had once revolved,
but no other trace of the Fennels' first-class light. There was no
trace of Ginny either.

THE COMING DOWN

Paul peered through an oval-shaped doorway and found Ginny on the narrow iron catwalk that circled the super-structure. She looked to the sea. And with her lips sealed and eyes shielded by a delicate palm the girl could have served as an illustration. The Victorian heroine Paul knew only from his reading. From his studies. From his daydreams. And from a few days before in the bedroom. Anyway it was time to act.

Braced with his cast to the wall and good hand to the rail, Paul edged crabwise towards her. Left foot trailed by right. Again. Again. Stretching before him were the majestic breaking waves of the Dog Tooth Shoal. Blue water, white water. Blue. White. Actually, the entire Atlantic Ocean was on display and it too was picture perfect. The trawler that he'd spotted made a bright focal point but now it traveled in the opposite direction. A strand of the girl's windblown hair whipped by his face and Paul looked down.

Instantly his hand froze on the railing. The beach, the rooftops, the green jungle directly below had sunk away from beneath his feet, and he had the immediate sensation that not he, but the entire lighthouse was wobbling. He closed his eyes and pulled back, trying to weld himself somehow to the warm iron at his back.

He had never experienced anything like this overwhelming sense of disorientation and terror. He felt the prickle of hairs rising all over his body and then the rush of heat. He began to itch everywhere at once. His bowels were starting to move. He would soil himself. Paul opened his mouth to scream and vomited instead. The yellow slime spewed out and was blown back into his face, across his clothes, the sling, the cast, and the sides of the building. Again it came, and again. He was covered now in the stinking wetness but he couldn't move. To do so he would have to release his grip on the railing. To move he would have to move and that was unthinkable. He continued to gag until his stomach was empty and could only heave and convulse without result. Ginny turned to look at him at last and he tried to smile. His nostrils were clogged and his throat burned.

"What's wrong with you, Jack?" she asked. "You look so funny. Are you sick?"

Paul nodded that he was.

"It's James, isn't it?" She put a hand on his extended sleeve, one of the few portions of his person that hadn't been putrefied.

Paul agreed that it was James.

"He's dead and he's been buried for three weeks, so that's the end of it. He's better off dead, believe me. He suffered so those last days that I believe even his parents began to doubt in the Almighty's infinite mercy."

Paul opened his eyes onto the distant breakers of the shoal. He couldn't afford to look down again.

"James was your husband, wasn't he?" Paul whispered, trying to recall the letter he'd read in his earlier delirium.

"You think I should have brought him back here to be buried, don't you? Well, they wouldn't let me and so it's done."

"Did you marry someone else?" He had to croak the question, his throat ached so. He closed his eyes.

"Who on earth would I marry?"

"The one who had his head run over by the wheel?"

"Jack, stop teasing me. Ever since I've gotten back you've been teasing me and I'm getting tired of it."

"I'm sorry. I get confused." Paul opened his eyes. Once more the girl was staring out to sea, her arms folded deliberately.

He tried to calculate what month and year it was. The girl ducked under his arm and disappeared inside. Paul had to follow. His eyes closed, his hand sliding on the rail, his feet moving in the crabwise shuffle, he took a step. His head began to spin and he could feel a second black envelope slipping behind his already closed eyelids. He stepped again and again and fell backwards through the open door onto the interior floor of the cupola.

"What's wrong with you?"

Paul tried to focus on her. He had hit hard on the iron plate and the noise it made still vibrated inside his head.

"What's wrong with you, Paul?" The voice came from above. Ginny was sitting high in the machinery of the light. "You've puked all over yourself. I hope you know that. Where's Leroy?"

"He's passed out in the boat."

"You two are beautiful, really beautiful. You make me miss Walter and I haven't thought about him in months."

"I've been under a lot of strain. Could we go down now?"

Ignoring a narrow access ladder, the girl swung from a brass tie rod, hung with her feet a yard above the floor, and dropped gracefully. She missed his head by several inches. Before Paul could move she was through the trapdoor and clattering down the stairs. He cleaned his nose on his shirt sleeve and took in a deep breath of fresh sea air. From inside, things weren't so bad. Carefully he set out after the girl, hugging the interior walls and stopping at each window to rest. He had lost all interest in the graffiti and the view. His attention was focused on one thing alone—getting down.

Ginny was waiting at the bottom. Or at least Virginia was. There was a different manner, a different posture. Paul thought he could tell them apart now. Virginia was older. She was poised. She had a sense of presence, even of command. Ginny. Well, she was just Ginny.

But neither one was his immediate concern. The gray expanse of concrete held firm beneath his feet. He took a timid step, then a bolder one, and knelt before the wicker basket he'd brought from the boat. And found salvation in the form of a warm Coke. He rinsed his mouth and drank down the remainder of the bottle. His stomach felt better, but still not settled. The basket also held a vinyl tablecloth—an orange flower-print tablecloth. Only Azalea would have packed such. Thank you, Azalea. Despite the thick cast, Paul managed to strip off his shirt and use the clean corners of it to mop his body. Then he draped the cool orange plastic over his shoulders like a shawl and knotted it at the throat. He still felt stinking but this was better.

"Are you ready now?" The girl looked on with folded arms.

Paul said he was and they set off for the house. There were a lot of things to catch up on. She began to speak steadily about people he'd never heard of and give him news from the mainland that was a century old. Of course Fort Sumter had been fired on and the country was preparing for war. Soon, perhaps within weeks, a garrison would be sent to protect the lighthouse. Hadn't he received the notices? The new inspector for coastal defenses had visited the island. He had come twice, hadn't he? She had seen their old tutor at her husband's funeral and he sent his regards. They were putting a ferry crossing in at Ten Miles. Patricia had another baby. Even Hester had a baby. Everyone was having babies except Virginia. Did he see much of the Africans that remained on the island? How often did he visit the compound? Her in-laws were impossible. She would never marry again.

Paul pulled the plastic tablecloth shawl tight about his neck as a meager defense against this ongoing barrage. Often she glanced back, impatient with his replies. And once she stopped altogether and demanded to know why he was acting so strange. Paul could only shake his head and mumble a response. He truly didn't know and was thankful when they reached the front steps of one of the abandoned houses.

"Bena!" she called. "Bena! Where are you?" She had entered at a lope.

A more hesitant Paul crossed the porch floor. Timber creaked and threatened to give. He leapt inside. Rat signs everywhere. And the second floor had rotted out in places. Blue sky filled the holes left by missing shingles. Ginny stood on the far side of the litter-strewn living room.

"She's not here. You told her I was coming and she's not here to meet me. Jack, I've been gone five months and she's not here to even say hello."

The girl moved on to the back of the house. Paul followed, stepping over crushed beer cans and rusted window screens in order to peek into what must have been the kitchen. Yes, ragged pipes coming through the floor and the familiar soot-stained ceiling.

"I don't like this room," the girl said. "I mean, just stepping back here after all this time away . . . look at all these . . . things. They don't belong in a kitchen. Jack, you humor her with all these magic potions and superstitions. It's getting out of hand. It's supposed to be a kitchen, not the hut of some cannibal queen."

"Bena's a cannibal?"

"You know what I mean. It doesn't matter, not on my first day back. I'm going down to the beach. You do what you want."

Nimbly, she slipped by him and disappeared down the front steps. A resigned Paul trudged after her. His orange vinyl shawl had slipped to the front and tangled with his sling. He shifted everything into place and took a last look at another house Captain Jack had built. Bena? He was tempted to call out but she would probably answer him.

The path leading to the beach had almost disappeared into the surrounding thicket of briars but the sound of the surf came through. It increased as he traveled—as he prodded and poked at the relentless vegetation—and finally the dunes were in view. But where was the girl? Behind him. She was off to one side standing silently in front of a gravestone.

Paul tried to recall the picture from Camilla's album. The circle of lawn with its picket fence and the smaller circle of fence that meshed like a smaller gear. Something had changed. The shifting dunes were obliterating the fence and all that it contained.

"I thought there was a new grave," Ginny said. She turned accusing eyes on him. "When I ran by I realized there was a strange stone here, but when I stopped to look it was gone." She indicated a piece of rosette marble that marked the final resting place of her grandfather—the unfortunate Mr. Ramona.

"Just shadows playing tricks," Paul suggested.

She accepted this and moved on to the next stone. Paul couldn't tell whose it was, for the windblown sand had cut deeply into the face of this one—and all the rest. Still, Ginny was having no trouble. She passed by, attaching names and dates to each one. There was Anise and his wife and the small stones were their children. So many died young. Then came Chervil and Hester and her—that is Virginia's—own father Heraclitus.

She stooped here to brush the sand away. "That's better. It's disgraceful the way you've let things go around here. The gravestones. Jack, after all, this is our family."

"Let the dead bury the dead," Paul suggested with all the cheerfulness he could muster.

The face she turned up to him was the one of terror—the one he'd seen when they drifted towards the breakers.

"Don't say things like that." She came to her feet. "Those last days with James made me realize . . . just how frightened I was. I was glad when it was over."

Paul took her by the arm, for she meant to bolt.

"Frightened of death?" Paul asked.

"Of Bena." She broke from his grip and ran towards the ocean. Following, Paul arrived in time to see her run naked into the surf, plunge forward, and disappear. Her jeans, shirt, and underclothes lay in a ragged pile at his feet. Paul raced into the breakers, not stopping until he was waist-deep in the freezing water. There was no sign of the girl and for a panicked instant he saw himself explaining to Azalea what had happened. "I tormented your demented daughter with questions about death until she threw herself in the ocean and drowned." It had the ring of truth. Frantically scanning the surface of the waves, he played the sentence over in his mind, giving stress to different words and wondering what would sound gentlest to the grief-stricken mother. What did it matter? Leroy would kill him before he had a chance to utter it.

Far out beyond the breakers a slick head popped up and an arm shot out of the water, beckoning him deeper. Ginny Fennel couldn't swim but the drowned Virginia could.

"I can't," Paul shouted. "Besides, I've got a cast on my arm and Dr. Rupple told me not to get it wet."

"I can't hear you," the windborne voice carried his way and the girl began to swim parallel to the beach, gliding with steady powerful strokes.

Paul watched mesmerized as a large wave rolled up from the deep and thundered down on him. Holding the cast above his head he attempted to scramble ashore, was knocked off balance, and collapsed into the chilling turbulence. But the cast was saved. And the last of the vomit was washed off. After a couple of unpleasant squishing steps he removed his shoes and socks and rolled his pants to the knee. Adjusting his cape and sling, he set off down the beach in pursuit of the swimming girl.

The midafternoon sun was still high enough to warm his chest, and the deserted beach was the pleasantest of surroundings. Not the place of his recent nightmares. The place where the Fennel bonfire was fed. Suddenly Paul had a rush of childhood memories—of days spent beside the ocean. Paul left alone with bucket and pail. Paul outside in a bright safe place.

Ahead tiny birds raced back and forth at water's edge. Sandpipers? Probably sandpipers. But there'd be no test at the end of the day. This was all his to enjoy. Him here, now. Only the silhouette of the lighthouse to the landward. Only a single vapor trail in the clear blue sky above. And only the picturesque trawler marking the horizon. Modest enough intrusions. He could be almost happy except for the fact that Leroy was on the island too. And Ginny was completely out of her mind. Plus he'd left his pipe in his suitcase at the Fennel house.

Thirty minutes later the girl waded from the ocean and joined him.

"Why didn't you come in?"

"Too cold."

"Cold? Look at me. I'm not cold."

"You should be." Her blue shivering body was covered with goose bumps and her nipples had shrunk to tiny purple dots.

"Well, I'm not," she said, slipping a wet arm around his waist and working his own arm over her shoulder. "If you won't swim with me, I'll have to walk with you, dear brother. Anyway, I want to tell you a story so that you might begin to understand something about our cook. Bena told me this story, Jack, not long after the storm."

"I'm listening."

"You see, the very first man lived on the bottom of the sea." She indicated the expanse she'd just abandoned. "But he wasn't satisfied so he told God he must live on the surface of the earth even though it was a sad and barren place. God agreed and the man came up from the sea and he started to complain about how desolate everything was. So God gave him a young woman but told him not to touch her. She was to be his sister. His companion in all things."

"What kind of story is this?"

"It's an African account of creation. Like our Adam and Eve."

"I guess he touches her, then."

"He does. He touches her with his finger and during the night she gives birth to trees and bushes and all the earth is covered. God is angry and takes the woman away, but the man complains and she's returned. 'Don't touch her,' God says and again the man disobeys. So this time she gives birth to chickens and sheep and goats. Again God tells him to stop but instead the man puts a door on his hut and they hide. His woman gives birth to lions and leopards and serpents and scorpions. She was patient, now wasn't she?"

"I'd say so."

"Yes. But God wasn't. Next she gives birth to daughters and

sons. God knows that he can't let this go on forever. The man wants all of it. All of creation. So God sends death to get him, but the man's too proud and he won't go. He and all his animals chase death but it gets away and hides in an old woman." Ginny stopped walking. "I had the feeling that Bena was talking about us, Jack. I mean the story doesn't exactly fit but still she was talking about us dying. Do you understand?"

"I understand. I can see a parallel of sorts to the Fennel family but I'm not Jack."

"Who are you, then?"

"My name is Paul Danvers."

"I see. So Mr. Danvers. Is it Mister? There are a lot of colonels and lieutenants around today."

"Ph.D. History."

"All right, Dr. Danvers. Could you explain it to my brother Jack?"

"I don't think so. He died in the 1920s."

"In the next century. So he lived to be an old man?"

"Yes."

"What about me? What about his sister Virginia?"

"I don't know about her. I don't know."

"I think you're lying."

"No, I'm not. Honest."

"I don't think you're Dr. Danvers. I think you're my brother Jack and you just don't want to hear the end of the story."

"You're right. I am him. I am Jack. How does it end?"

"It ends here." They were standing on a thin peninsula of sand. The beach had melted away into an inlet. She put her other arm around him and rested her head against his chest. Paul had the uneasy feeling she was listening to his heart beat.

"Where's Leroy?" she asked. "And where are my clothes? I'm freezing."

Paul held her at arm's length. Was this better or worse? Either way she had to be answered.

"He's in the outboard. Remember? And your clothes are on the beach where the path comes out by the cemetery."

"Well, give me that ridiculous tablecloth. I'm freezing."

Paul slipped the garment over his head. She dropped it over her own and pulled the edges tight.

"Look at that flab." She poked a finger into his bare stomach. "You've got no muscle tone at all. You know that, Paul? If Leroy wanted to he could pound you into this beach until you disappeared." She made a burrowing motion with her big toe.

"Thanks, Ginny." The image was familiar.

"It's just a fact. I'm telling you a fact."

"Well, it doesn't give me much to look forward to. Do we have to go back?"

"Of course, we do. It'll be dark soon and all the gear's in the boat."

A FALLING OUT

When they returned to their starting point Paul discovered that his shoes had been carried by the rising tide. And searching in vain for them he made a second discovery. The distant trawler was no longer distant. *Sweet Mama*. Paul could read the name painted on the bow. The bright white hull was streaked with thin brown stains.

"They aren't working," Ginny said. "See, those are the doors on the end of the outriggers and the nets are whipped up."

Wooden rectangles hung from the metal booms and great triangles of webbing caught the breeze. The boat rose lazily over a swell and dipped partially behind another.

"What are they doing?"

"Shrimping."

"I mean what are they doing there? Right now?"

"Watching us." She pointed out the two men who stood in the doorways. Paul spotted the shiny lenses of a pair of binoculars.

"They're looking at you. Cover up."

"I'm wearing this tablecloth." She had wrapped the vinyl around her waist like a skirt and tucked it in.

"They can see your breasts."

"So what?"

"Ginny, cover up. Put your clothes on for me."

Shaking her head the girl collected her clothes and disappeared into the dunes.

Paul glared angrily out to sea. The glasses had come down and in another moment the boat swung from the beach. He was tired. Weary beyond belief. The sand had worked deep inside his cast and his stomach hadn't recovered from its violent spasms. Crossing over the dunes to join the girl he stepped on a cactus.

"Hurry," she called from the edge of the trees. "It'll be dark soon."

He thought she'd leave him but she didn't. She waited by the cemetery to show him something.

"See. Watch the sun setting through the prisms up there."

The light blazed from the tower's top and if he hadn't known better he would have thought it operational.

"We used to call that the ghost of Virginia Fennel. Happens every time there's a good sunset."

"Spooky. It looks real."

"You afraid of ghosts, too? You're afraid of everything else." He didn't bother to answer, for she was slipping off into the darkening jungle.

Without shoes the trip was a nightmare. Everywhere on the path were thorns and jagged sticks and more cactus. He bumbled along, crashing through the denser places and yelping. The girl would stop and wait. Even when he couldn't see her he could hear her laughing at him.

When they reached the abandoned house, the waning sun

was brightening its few window panes, making it too appear in use. But except for Paul's yelps of agony they passed in silence. No calls for "Bena" from Ginny and no replies from inside.

The remaining distance was the worst. He could only step wrong, and by the time they reached the concrete skirt of the lighthouse Dr. Paul Danvers barely stood erect. Still, he managed to slice open both feet on the scattered broken glass. And he howled.

"A hundred ways, asshole," said a familiar voice.

"Leroy!" Ginny snapped. "Where is everything? You don't even have a fire going!"

"I'm not your slave," her uncle said, rising from the shadows. He held a pint bottle of some clear alcohol.

"Stay here, Paul. I'm going to the boat and bring the stuff. When I get back we can look at those cuts." She disappeared down the dark path and Leroy stepped closer until his face was only inches away. Vodka. Paul caught a vaporous trace when Leroy opened his mouth to curse him.

"Bleed, motherfucker. Bleed."

"I won't disappoint you." Paul attempted a laugh. But he felt it already. A warm oozing between his toes.

"You think it's funny getting your rocks off out there in the dunes while you got me passed out in the boat. I think you're forgetting something, Paul. That's my fiancée and no jury in the world would convict me if I was to kill you right now with my bare hands."

Paul sensed the tension in the other's body. The toy man he'd seen in the toy boat had had its spring wound tight and the tiniest jolt would set it unwinding. Paul chose his next words carefully.

"She's your niece."

"Only by marriage!" Leroy spit this out, but Paul was still alive.

"We both want the same thing for Ginny. We both want her to be happy, and I haven't been getting my rocks off. We just went for a walk on the beach."

The shiny vodka bottle appeared below the white rage-filled eyes and Leroy took a long drink.

"I'm not going to kill you. You know why?"

"Because you promised Azalea you wouldn't?"

"Get serious."

"Because you know Ginny wouldn't marry you if you did?" It seemed like the wildest possible guess.

"You're not as dumb as you look, Paulo." Leroy drained the bottle, smashed the empty at Paul's feet, and then stuck his fingers into the scholar's belly. "You're just a sack a shit. You know that?"

"I've got no muscle tone," Paul volunteered quietly.

"That's right. You know what I could do if I felt like it?"

"Stomp me into the sand."

"That's right. I could. That's right." Satisfied, Leroy squatted in the shadows once more. Paul heard the cap turn on a second bottle. He sat down himself and began to wipe the blood, sand, and glass from the bottom of one foot.

"When you and Walter used to bring Ginny out here did she ever act strange? Like she was somebody else?" Paul tried to sound friendly—like a pollster.

"Sure. All the time. She liked to pretend the Civil War was going on and she would call Walter Jack."

"What did she call you?"

Leroy hesitated. Then said, "Nothing. She just pretended I wasn't here."

"Didn't Walter mind being called Jack?"

"He didn't care what she called him. He didn't bring her out here to carry on a conversation."

"Sounds like a fine fella."

"He was ten times the man you'll ever be." Leroy said this with surprisingly little anger.

"I don't doubt it," Paul agreed amiably.

Coming through the night was a flashlight beam. Help had arrived. With Ginny there Paul had a chance of surviving—a slim one, anyway.

The girl stepped from the night carrying only the flashlight and the first aid kit. The rest of the supplies were coming—carried by two men.

Leroy stood up. Paul remained seated. The flashlight beam reflected a bright pool of blood.

"Paul, look at that," she scolded and then motioned over her shoulder. "This is Captain Edel."

"Hello, thar," said the first man, sticking out a hand to Leroy. "Elwood Edel here and this sorry excuse behind me is what's known as Trisbee."

"Leroy," Leroy grunted, but he didn't shake the hand. "That's Paul and that's my fiancée, Ginny."

"Her," Elwood laughed. "We met her already down at the dock. We even seen her on the beach this afternoon." It was the crew of the *Sweet Mama*. They had made it through the treacherous Caladium Keyhole.

The second man snickered and then spoke.

" 'At 'ere one is cut all to pieces on the bottom of his feet. Got a broke arm too." He was a much smaller man than the first.

"Shut up, Trisbee. We just come ashore so I wouldn't have to listen to you."

"Hold still," Ginny said. She'd already washed Paul's feet with drinking water and now used a towel to pat them dry. "There's broken glass all around here," she said to the newcomers.

"We'll be careful," Elwood said. "I don't need no more cutting done on me. Trisbee ain't nearly as pretty a nurse as her."

"Leroy, why don't you light the lantern and start a fire," Ginny said.

"We'll light the fire for her, Leroy. 'At 'eres the least we can do."

Ginny's uncle didn't move at first but when the other men began to gather firewood he went to work on the gasoline lantern. He muttered under his breath.

Still laboring in the beam of the flashlight, Ginny put the finishing touches on Paul's bandages and cleared a spot for him against the wall.

"Want a shirt?" she asked.

"I'm cold."

She started to rummage in the knapsack.

"Don't give him one of my shirts. Let him get his own fucking shirts."

Ginny tossed the bag aside and found the blanket Paul had brought.

"Wrap this around you. They'll have a fire in a minute."

Kindling was being stuck under the remains of the door and a match struck. At almost the same instant the gasoline lantern burst forth with a bright white light and Leroy hung it on a nail in the lighthouse door frame.

Paul had his first clear view of the visitors. Elwood was big. As tall as him and as heavy but it was all toned muscle. A thick stock of curly black hair fell across his forehead. The nose had been broken at least twice. Like Leroy he wore only a white T-shirt, but his was ripped and dingy. The pants were salt-stained and rolled a turn at the bottom and his broken shoes were worn without socks or laces. As he walked and talked his eyes followed Ginny, and Leroy's eyes followed him.

Trisbee wasn't as threatening. He was dressed the same, but here the similarity ended, for he was hardly bigger than Ginny.

Chopped to a short white stubble, his hair melted into a week's growth of beard. He was well into his sixties. Yes, and noting Paul's interest the little man circled the fire and squatted beside him. The flat blue eyes were ringed in red and bloodshot through the middle. When he smiled, as he now did at Paul, sun-split lips parted to reveal two gold teeth among a mouth full of rotten stubs.

"I ain't proud of it," he said in introduction, "but I kilt a man once. Served time for it."

Before Paul could respond appropriately, Elwood called across the fire. "Don't believe anything the old fart says. I been on the boat with him for two weeks and he like to drove me crazy."

Leroy emptied another bottle and smashed it in the shadows. Elwood Edel glanced at him and then spoke low to Ginny.

"What did you just say?" Leroy shouted.

"I asked her if there was anything I could do for her before I went to have a drink with you."

"Is that what he said, Ginny?"

"I don't know what he said. I wasn't listening to him." The girl settled a cooking pot onto the edge of the flames.

Elwood opened the ice chest he'd toted and brought out a fifth. "Jack Daniels," he said, showing off the label and then taking a healthy swallow. "Try some."

Leroy snatched the offered bottle and drank off a third of the contents before coming up for air.

"You're a thirsty fella." Elwood retrieved his gift and circled the fire to Paul. "Here you go, skippy. You look like you could stand a taste."

Paul took a gulp. The bourbon burned its way down into the pit of his empty stomach and settled there with a warm comfortable glow. He was about to take another when Trisbee grabbed the bottle and jammed its neck down past the gold and rotten teeth.

"Don't let him have that," Elwood yelled, yanking the bottle back. "Just a drop and he goes fool—starts trying to kill people. I been hiding this damn liquor all the way from Key West and he still drank all the hair tonic and the compass fluid." Shaking his head in disgust, the captain went off to squat between Leroy and Ginny.

"I raised that 'ar boy," the little man said to Paul with a gilded smile. "Found him wandering in the Jacksonville bus station and carried him on the *Happy Trails* with me."

"Shut up, old man, or I'll tell 'em how I found you in the station and it wasn't wandering neither. He bored him a hole in the side of one of them toilet stalls and he'd scratched 'stick your prick in here' on the other side!" After shouting this across the fire, Elwood addressed a discreet "Pardon me, ma'am" to Ginny.

"That's a goddamn lie!" Trisbee shouted back. "I had me a good job at the ice plant and you got me drunk and dragged me off here and we ain't caught a mess in two weeks. I'm getting off en her the first time we come to a piling."

"You'll be getting off her right here if you don't shut your mouth. Me and the *Sweet Mama* had all we want of you." Elwood passed the bottle to Leroy and spoke quietly. Leroy answered in kind. Paul watched as the conversation continued. Somehow he felt safer when people were shouting. Maybe they were discussing him. They certainly wouldn't be discussing Ginny. Elwood wasn't going to mention the view he and his crew had of her that afternoon. But clearly that was never far from the man's mind. Yes. Yes indeed.

Paul watched the smoke ascend the side of the lighthouse and disappear into the night. There was no place to escape to. If Leroy got too drunk to kill Paul then he would be too drunk to defend Ginny. Paul settled against the wall and pulled his blanket tight. Ginny had abandoned her stew. She picked up a duffle and entered the lighthouse. If she had any sense she'd stay out of sight.

Trisbee leaned in and whispered low. "I ain't the only one here who kilt a man. Him too." He motioned towards Elwood. "Kilt a man in Brunswick. Did it with his bare fist. His hands is registered with the state. He kills another one it's murder in the first degree."

Paul took in a deep breath and exhaled slowly. He was the only one here who hadn't "kilt" a man. His right hand was in a cast and his feet were shredded. Da Bena would be in ecstasy if she only knew. She probably did know. She'd probably arranged it all and was now watching. That sounded about right and Paul began to search the shadows for the gleam of those piano-key teeth.

. . . OVER THE FENNEL LIGHT

"The Fennel light!" Elwood shouted, and gave a derogatory laugh. "This here weren't no kind of light at all. Sorriest light on the coast—always was."

Leroy sprang to his feet and so did the boat captain.

"What you talking about?" Leroy snarled. He raised his own lethal hands but in a graceless manner.

"I'm talking about this same lighthouse here. My daddy and his daddy and his daddy before him always said the same thing. Can't cross by Dog Tooth Shoal without a lead. You go trusting that light and you're a dead man."

"You know who you're talking to?" The words came slurred. Leroy rocked on his heels.

"Don't matter who I'm talking to. Truth don't change nary a bit. In its best day the light was so weak you couldn't see it flashing till you was in the breakers, and a hundred years ago when that Crazy Fennel run it, it was the same as suicide just to look for it."

"You're talking about my fiancée's great-grandfather." Leroy

motioned vaguely in the direction of the doorway. To his dismay
Paul found that Ginny had returned. Her hair was piled high and
pinned, and she'd changed from blue jeans into a white flannel
nightgown that clung to her breasts and hips. He'd seen her this
way before. This was the girl he'd glimpsed that first morning in
the Fennel kitchen.

Paul pulled himself to his feet and so did Trisbee. The four
men watched in silence as she approached the fire and lit a long
white candle. Cradling its flame with her palm, she then stared
into the faces around the fire, turned and disappeared once
more into the bowels of the lighthouse.

Elwood wet his lips. "Well, she's pretty enough, I'll say that,
but it don't change the facts and the facts is known by anybody
who's worked this coast. Jack Fennel would cut off the light
whenever a storm came up or, worse than that, he'd stop her
from flashing so ships would think she was another ship and
they'd go right on and pile up on the shoals. The next morning
he'd come out with his crew of wild Africans and pick up what
was left. And I know that's so cause my own granddaddy testi-
fied to it in a court of inquiry."

The low hum had begun in Leroy's chest. But this time the
hum was missing a beat or two.

"I don't want to fight with you." Elwood squatted and began
to poke at the fire. "Leastwise not over something like that, but
it's the true telling of the matter. If you don't believe me, ask
him." He pointed through the flames to the slack-jawed Trisbee.

"I ain't asking him nothing." Leroy spit to one side. "I'm just
asking you to stand up."

Elwood stood up. He stood up very fast, and he brought a
burning plank from the door with him. Before Leroy had closed
his mouth, he was slapped hard on the forehead.

Paul wasn't surprised to see the plank snap while its intended victim went unshaken. He'd seen the show before. What surprised him was the sharp pain that came to his own chest. He looked down to where Trisbee had tried to jab an ice pick into his heart. It had passed through two folds of the blanket, the sling, and his flesh before being stopped by his breastbone. Abandoned now, the weapon hung limply from the folds of the material. Speechless, Paul watched his assailant slip off into the night.

On the far side of the fire Elwood went tumbling over the concrete. But he ended up on his feet clasping a large open knife. The big man beckoned Leroy forward. Humming away, Leroy advanced.

Paul pulled the ice pick free and tossed it aside. It was a surprisingly painless operation, but puncture wounds, like dog bites, could be dangerous. Slowly he took down the gas lantern and entered the lighthouse. From outside came the angry grunts and curses of the captain, punctuated by the kamikaze shrieks from Leroy.

Paul ran up the steps at first, taking two at a time.

But when each bandaged foot came down he felt the cuts opening, and by the time he reached the first landing his bandages were caked in blood, animal droppings, and rust. He was out of breath as well. At that pace he wouldn't make it at all. But he wouldn't make it at all, anyway.

From below came an ominous quiet. Paul held the lantern high and saw the steps spiraling out of sight in an endless blend of shadows and light. He placed a foot on the first step and began again.

To no avail. Paul was caught before he reached the second landing. Caught but hardly taken by surprise. He'd heard his pursuer hit the first step and the iron crescendo had increased steadily from that point on. He had set the lantern down on the step above and turned to face whoever came. He was expecting Ginny's uncle and he wasn't disappointed.

"Leroy!" he shouted as the deranged face appeared around the corner. That was all he got out before the iron plate of a stair tread caught him just below the shoulder blades. Leroy's knee was in Paul's guts and the cutting edge of an already bloody hand was coming down. It struck the cast with its stainless steel reinforcing and went no further, and a puzzled expression passed across the striker's face. But in an instant Paul felt his hair being yanked from his scalp and a thumb being slipped into his eye socket. An incredible flash of pain followed and he was blinded by a searing scarlet explosion in his temple.

Instinctively, he beat the heavy cast into the side of Leroy's head, letting it rise and fall until it succeeded where the burning plank had just failed. The thumb slipped out and the knee left his groin. Paul pulled clear and focused on his tormentor. Leroy had not fallen. He stood a single step below, his forehead bloodied. He seemed dazed, but the hum resumed. There would be no second chance. Paul picked up the gas lantern and swung it with all his might. The glass shattered and there was a hiss of escaping fumes. The light dimmed and then Leroy's shoulder burst into flame.

Paul kicked outward, knocking the torchlike obstacle over backwards, and it tumbled down the stairs and out of sight. Only then, falling, did it make a noise, a long piercing scream that melted off into night-filled quiet. From somewhere below came the faint glow of a still-burning fire.

A victorious Paul began to crawl up the iron stairs on all fours. At the windows he found rectangular patches of starlight, but other than these, he spiraled up in darkness. His own harsh breathing was all he heard.

Just short of the light structure he caught up with Ginny. She was taking each step with a slow deliberation, holding the candle before her. A thick coat of wax covered her hand. Her high-pinned hair was beginning to unravel.

"Jack," she said when he clutched the hem of her gown. "You didn't have to come. I can tend this alone."

Then from below came the distinct sound of thundering pursuit. Paul could not speak. Hoarse and gasping he shoved her up into the cupola, dropped the hatch, and threw its massive bolt. In the next instant this iron sheet shook beneath the first of many hammering blows.

Gingerly he felt his injured eye. From the intensity of the pain he'd expected it to be dangling by the optic nerve from his head. It wasn't. It was swollen and sore to the touch but the ball remained in place.

Consoled by the knowledge that he was blinded but not disfigured and that Leroy's fist could not dent the impenetrable hatch, Paul turned his attention to Ginny. She had climbed high into the machinery once more, but this time she was holding the candle. The light shone a hard blue-white on the inside of the prisms and bounced eerily against her white nightgown.

"What are you doing up there?" Paul croaked.

"Bena sent me to trim the wick and light it. She says the Fennel light should never be allowed to fail. She says there are many ships in the ocean filled with slaves and it would be a great tragedy if one of these were to strike the Dog Tooth Shoal."

"Ginny," he pleaded.

"Bena says, 'You is to light the lamps every evenin' at the sun settin' and keep them constant burnin', bright and clear, 'til the sun come up.'"

"Ginny, please."

"Bena says it's my duty."

"Your duty?"

"The duty of all Fennel women to tend the flame."

"Fine," Paul said. "That's just about perfect."

At least they were safe. Leroy's poundings were coming less often and with noticeably less force. They could not be touched—not unless Leroy exited through a window, scaled over twenty feet of vertical masonry, and then leapt outward— no that was impossible. The cupola was sealed off from the out- side world—and from all it contained. With what he assumed was his last ounce of strength, Paul crawled through the oval catwalk door and stuck his nose and one good eye over the edge of the iron rim. Far below was the campfire and its orange tongues. It seemed so strange from this perspective. A minia- ture sun with flames flickering outward, it lit the octagonal sides of the tower and much of the slab area. There was no evidence of the banished Elwood Edel.

The iron felt cool on his chest and the side of his face. Stars above and a faint breeze. Paul wondered if he would ever move again. Lying flat like this he was free of the vertigo and nausea. No one could get him. He was safe and what was more he'd saved Ginny. One hundred and fifty feet below, the tiny orange tongues of flame flicked about harmlessly.

He blinked his eye. Another eye blinked back. Another nose rubbed against his nose and Leroy's hand came out of the empti- ness and grabbed at the lowest rung of the rail.

Paul slid backward on his belly into the cupola.

He screamed a warning to Ginny and slammed the oval door on a face that was singed and distorted almost beyond recogni- tion. He yanked down its two watertight latches. Once again the rain of blows began, but Paul did not bother to add his weight to the door.

He slumped against the wall, closed his remaining eye, and tried to remember some time when he hadn't known about the

Fennels. He drew a blank. They had always been there and he'd always been shrinking before them.

The pounding stopped. The silence was much more sinister.

"A hundred ways, do you hear me?" the muffled voice called out from the catwalk. "A hundred ways to kill a man with my bare hands and I hadn't tried but a couple on you."

More silence and then Paul heard the hum begin. It rose and swelled into a scream as the fist descended on the door. The entire light structure shook but the latches held firm.

Outside he could hear Leroy mumbling to himself. Then a rattling crash was delivered to the prisms. Another and another. But the glass held firm. Paul thought he could make out a shadow working its way over the perpendicular surface of the lenses— but that was impossible. That Leroy had even reached the cat-walk was impossible.

The possible had long since been breached, and there was now an infinite number of probabilities. He'd reached the same conclusion about the Fennel papers and he should have known it would hold true for the light as well.

Far above him a bloody hand and arm shot through a hole left by a missing prism and tore the side from Ginny's nightgown. The scrap of garment was sucked away as if into a hungry mouth, and then the hand returned for more. The girl hadn't moved. She continued to hold the candle high in the dome. Her uncle's hand snatched about at her feet but there was nothing there left to grab. Paul studied the long exposed flank and, almost lost in the shadows, the dark pubic triangle. There was nothing else. Again and again the bloodied hand closed on empty air. Paul shut his one good eye and went to sleep.

VIRGINIA, OR INTO THE UNIVERSE

Paul dreamed his dream once more, the dream on the beach. Leroy had won, of course, and Paul was pulverized. Ginny's uncle ground the few remaining vertebrae underfoot until they were indistinguishable from sand. It was surprisingly painless.

Nothing of Paul remained and the tide rose once more and carried this nothing, this disembodied Paul, far out from shore. He drifted on the gentle surface of the ocean and waited for the slow sweep of the revolving Fennel beam. Darkness to light, darkness to light, darkness to light. Paul felt the light. He even smelled it.

He half woke to the familiar smell of burning hair. This was the smell he associated with his first night at the Fennel house. He had covered his head with the pillow and thought he heard his name called. He listened now but heard nothing.

His good eye opened onto a flickering candle flame. It was his own eyebrows being singed—and his mustache. The candle had been fastened in its wax beside his face. Ginny knelt watching him. He saw no sign of Leroy.

"Why did you let go, Jack?"

At last Paul had an answer and he knew he would have no peace until he gave it.

"I had to. You remember?"

"We were running before the squall but you said we were safe. You laughed at me for being frightened.

"We almost made it, didn't we?"

"I could see Bena waiting on the wharf. She waved to us, Jack."

"And the skiff went over and we were carried out to sea." A guess was as good as knowing.

"Yes, but you held me."

"I held you."

"You said when the tide turned we would reach shore."

Paul leaned forward to blow out the candle but found he didn't have the breath. Instead he brushed it over and swatted out the flame.

"So dark," Ginny whispered. "But we could see the Fennel light flashing. You promised me you wouldn't let go."

"Bena made me. You weren't going to let her stay on the island much longer. I had to let go."

Ginny lay down beside him in the dark. He could hear her breathing and feel the rise and fall of her chest in the close space. With his good hand he touched her arm.

"She's free to go. The slaves have been freed."

"But she likes it here."

"She frightens me, Jack. I'm frightened all the time now. I wanted children. Yours, anybody's. I didn't care."

"And she stopped you?"

"Talk to her, Jack. She'll listen to you."

"I've tried."

"I told you she was death. I tried to warn you."

"She's more than death, Ginny. It all comes back to her. Not just evil but the little bit of good. She gives pleasure not just pain. Life. Death. Nothing's left to chance."

"Bena's not evil. You shouldn't say that."

"I know she's isn't evil. She's not even death. Not really." Somehow Paul had to put his dream into words. He had to explain to Virginia or Ginny or to himself. "She's none of those things. Maybe she's not even Bena. Maybe she's just part of some creative-destructive force that pulsates at the very heart of the universe."

"Maybe you're crazy, Paul. I mean it, really. If you keep talking like that you're going to get locked up." The girl beside him was coming back to life.

"Maybe so."

"Maybe nothing! You never talk sense anymore."

"We're lying here now because Bena wants us to be."

"No, we're not," Ginny insisted quietly. "And I can't imagine why you would think that."

PARANOID

When Paul woke again it was morning, late morning, judging from the luminous glow of the prisms. Ginny slept at his side. Gently he attempted to tuck the remnants of her nightgown over the exposed areas of flesh, but even this small movement brought pain. And the pain spread. His gouged eye, his ice-picked chest, his slashed feet, and his broken hand. Every part of his body cried out for special consideration.

Pressing against the wall, he stood. The bandages on his feet were thickly caked with dried blood and filth, and now the added pressure caused spots of fresh crimson. The sling was gone and the cast-thick arm dangled heavily at his side. He twisted his head about, scanning the surface of the glass with his good eye. He was certain he would find Leroy still plastered to the outside like a leech. But there was no shadow. That could only mean he was waiting on the catwalk or below the hatch or perhaps at the entrance to the lighthouse. There was no escaping. Paul understood this and wasn't frightened. Whatever was going to happen had been foreordained by Da Bena and her predecessors.

Following the curve of the wall, he slipped by the sleeping girl. He turned the latches on the oval door and looked out. Leroy wasn't waiting, but his T-shirt, or at least the unburnt half, was draped over the catwalk railing. Paul eased onto the narrow deck. Another beautiful day. Not a cloud in the sky and just the suggestion of a breeze. The surf had run down during the night and appeared now as a fringe of white suds stretching along the beach. Paul took all this in at a glance and then peered over the edge, hoping to see Leroy's body splattered on the concrete below. It wasn't, but at least the act of looking had brought no staggering attack of vertigo and nausea.

But Leroy could be approaching him from behind. Paul spun. No. No Leroy. But there were bloody handprints across the glass where Ginny's uncle Leroy Ramona had worked his way up to the missing prism. Yes. The time had come to test the new-found courage. Paul took hold of the railing and began a tortuous circumvention of the catwalk. Leroy could well be waiting — waiting unseen around this endless corner. Or he could be coming up on Paul from the opposite direction. Or crouched on the roof of the cupola. The possibilities for destruction were still infinite. Anything under the sun was ordainable, and the rising of the sun altered nothing that Bena had ordained. It just put Paul one day closer to the grave.

He reached the far side of the walk and peered over the rail again. No sign of Leroy below, but he was relieved to see the *Sweet Mama* was gone. Walter Brant's already useless outboard had sunk, but off towards the mainland he spied a small rectangular barge plowing towards them. Perhaps help was on the way. Perhaps not. He completed the circle and stood again at the door. Unless Leroy had been creeping ahead of him or somehow perched on the very peak, he wasn't up here. So that left only the question of how he had gotten down—or more to the point, how he'd gotten up in the first place.

Of course, Da Bena's story of Adam's flight came readily to mind. The night before, Paul had taken it for granted that Leroy flew or crawled up the masonry exterior. He was still ready to accept either of these theories, but he leaned far over the rail to check. Thirty feet down to the highest window, but there beside the opening was a lightning rod. It began at the base and rose through a hole in the catwalk and went on to end somewhere above him. Was it humanly possible for someone to climb this and then swing over the edge of the catwalk and climb up? Leroy. Leroy could have come and gone this way.

Paul gazed in pure wonderment and then withdrew. And as he did a hand settled on his shoulder. He screamed and lurched forward. But the rail caught him and he bounced back into his attacker.

"Paul!" Ginny shouted as she jumped clear. "What's wrong with you?" Paul lowered himself until he sat propped against the wall. "Look at you!" she continued. "What's happened to your eye? Your eyebrows have been singed off, do you know that? And those bandages. Paul, why is there blood splattered all over you?"

Why was she asking him these questions? Why wasn't she wondering what she was doing up here with half her nightgown torn off?

He opened his mouth to answer but found that he could only sob. He realized that he'd wet his pants when she surprised him.

"I don't belong here," he managed to gasp before burying his head in his one good arm.

"What have you done to Leroy?"

Paul shook his head. He couldn't answer that. He didn't look up and it was several minutes before he realized she was gone. She'd opened the hatch and descended. Paul buried his head once more. All the hard-earned courage of the night before was literally drained from his body. If Bena was expecting something else from him she would have to come up on this ledge herself and drag him off of it.

A scuffing noise sounded beside him and Paul looked up. A tall gaunt man in a suit and cap of coarse blue flannel stood at the rail scanning the horizon with the handsome brass telescope.

Paul gave a low moan and the scanning ended. The weathered face of Captain Jack Fennel turned on him, the small hooded eyes already demanding.

"What are you doing here, Pauling?" the apparition asked.

"Danvers," Paul said. "My name is Paul Danvers, not Dan Pauling."

"Then that must be Pauling down at the dock. You shouldn't be up here. You're supposed to be on your way down there to meet him."

"I haven't reached the point where I'm going to be bullied by figments of my own imagination," Paul said, shaking his head.

"Shut up, Danvers! You reached that long ago." A heavy work-shoe kicked out and caught Paul a hard blow on the shin. "Now you got a man's part to play." Another kick was coming but Paul was already staggering to his feet and whimpering to get inside. There was no argument left in him. It was pointless to go down but he couldn't stay here. He put a shaky foot on the top step and for the last time began to negotiate the Fennel spiral. The way up and the way down were always the same.

Leroy wasn't waiting on the stairway but Paul did find a reminder of the night's struggle. The broken and burned lantern and a sooted section of wall.

Outside on the concrete apron the camping gear lay scattered about. Most had been flung there during the fight, but it appeared that animals had come afterwards, combing for edibles. He found a thermos of water and drank it all.

He wasn't sure of his next move. He craned his neck and tried to see if Jack Fennel's ghost was commanding the battlements above. It was impossible to tell. Maybe he should look for Ginny who was probably still searching for Leroy. But that made little sense. The captain had said he was to meet Dan Pauling at the dock. That made even less sense but Paul did remember the little barge that had been heading their way. His earlier and meager hope of rescue.

He headed down the trail—his feet were beyond hurting, his entire body beyond hurting. Perhaps it was this new sense of endurance that made the path seem even longer and more treacherous. He lurched ahead, beating at the brush with the cast, stumbling, falling, and forgetting at times which way he was headed. And then when he'd decided to stop entirely—the island ended and the dock appeared.

But no one waited for him. Not Dan Pauling, whom he hadn't truly expected, or anyone else. He limped over and collapsed on the wooden planking. He'd be rescued here or he'd die here.

"Hello there. Is that you, Paul?" Paul rolled his head to one side. A man was approaching along the marsh edge. But how had he gotten there and why? And who could possibly know his name?

"God, Paul! You look like you've been through a meat grinder. What's happened to you and where's Ginny and her uncle?"

The man approaching was about Paul's height and build and he also wore a mustache. He'd removed his shirt and tied it around his waist and his pants were rolled up to his knees. He carried his shoes in one hand and his pipe in the other.

"Who?" Paul asked.

"Paul! Don't you recognize me? It's Dan. Dan Pauling, from the university. We're office mates."

Paul could think of no reply. No immortal words of greeting came to mind. "What are you doing here?" he managed to scream.

"Jesus. Don't get so upset. Ginny invited me down, but when I got here they said you were all out camping."

"How did you get here? To this island? To the Fennel light?"

"Relax, Paul. Brown Jack brought me. You know? Brown Jack Simmons. He's deaf and dumb. Anyway, when I couldn't find anybody up at your campsite and I saw how everything looked I thought I should try and signal him to return. But I was too late."

Paul lay over on the dock and groaned. Death was preferable to this existence. The thick sweet smell of pipe tobacco hung in the air, and when Dan Pauling spoke again it was through a blue haze of smoke.

"I think we've got to get you off this island as soon as possible. Where's the boat you came in?"

"It's right behind you. Sunk."

Just the tip of the bow broke water now, but Dan Pauling gave it a respectable pursed-lip attention and then continued.

"Listen. I'm going up to the lighthouse and pick up that first-aid kit I saw. Should I look for Ginny and her uncle, Paul?"

"What do you mean?"

"I mean are they alive?"

"Alive? They're fucking indestructible. And don't worry about looking for them. If they want you they'll find you."

"I see," Dan said rather stiffly. "Well, hang in there. I'll be right back."

"No," Paul said. "I'm not going to let you leave me here alone."

Returning to the light, Paul gave an abbreviated version of only the last day and night. *The motor stopped and Leroy passed out from eating a ham biscuit and then Ginny was possessed by the ghost of Virginia Fennel and she thought it was 1861. He lost his shoes and Leroy fought a shrimper named Elwood, and Trisbee stuck him with an ice pick. Da Bena arranged it all. They spent the night locked in the top of the lighthouse and Captain Jack Fennel had just kicked him and told him that Dan Pauling was waiting.*

As they walked, Dan Pauling listened to all this without comment. And when Paul finished he said, "I see," and nothing more.

"You don't believe me?" Paul grabbed the man and made him stop.

"Why would you say that?"

"Because of the way you said 'I see.'"

"I see." Dan Pauling sucked on his pipe.

"You think I'm crazy."

His office mate avoided his eyes. He gazed on the Fennel light instead. "No, no, Paul. I'm sure you've just left out some of the story or you're confused about a few things."

"That's everything and I'm not confused at all."

"I see. Let's find Ginny and that first-aid kit."

"Listen, it's the Fennels who are crazy, not me."

Dan Pauling had broken free and was striding down the path well ahead. "I spent the night at the house last night. I'm not trying to argue with you, Paul. That Bena woman does have the evil eye and Ginny's mother is a little batty too, but who wouldn't be after living with Adam and Camilla? What did you do to the old girl? She's really on your case, you know. She wants me to have a look at the family papers. There actually are Fennel family papers but you know that because you were reading them. What happened?"

"I don't know."

"Anyway, with a family like that it's amazing Ginny turned out so normal."

"It's a miracle," Paul agreed.

They reached the lighthouse clearing and there, not ten feet away, stood Leroy. Beside him was Ginny. She had her arm around Leroy's waist and his arm crossed her shoulder.

"Listen," Paul said.

"Dan!" she shouted. "What are you doing here?"

"You invited me, Gin. Don't you remember?"

"Oh, yes." She slapped her forehead with an open palm. It was a gesture that Paul had never seen her use. "Sometimes my mind just goes totally blank."

"Oh, Gin," Dan said. "Don't apologize."

"Listen, you son of a bitch." Paul screamed this at Leroy. And even managed a step in his direction.

Ginny had changed into fresh jeans and a shirt but her uncle wore only the tattered remnants of the battle. A large part of his shoulder had been burned raw and a small part of his neck and cheek were reddened. An ointment had been spread over this, and a clean bandage graced his temple. Still, he looked bad. But not nearly so disfigured as he'd appeared the night before on the catwalk. Which was a disappointment. Paul realized he was no longer afraid, and he definitely wanted Ginny to take her arm from around the man's waist. Paul raised his cast-encrusted arm.

"Gin!" Leroy cried.

"Have you been fucking her?" Paul screamed.

"Make him leave me alone." Leroy stepped behind his niece but he still he touched her.

"Paul, leave him alone," Ginny snapped.

"I thought he was your uncle," Dan Pauling said.

"Only by marriage," Paul shouted.

"Well, he hasn't been fucking me and I don't know why you would say that except you think everybody is out to get you and everybody else if they can. I found Leroy in the house. He was in there hiding, Paul, and he was crying. He says you set fire to him."

"He did," Leroy insisted. "And he kicked me down the stairs."

"Those are burns all right," Dan Pauling said, lowering his pipe enough to give Paul an accusing glance.

"He was gouging out my eye. He was going to rape Ginny. Look at this. Look at my eye!" Paul pointed at his face and then at the top of the light. "He was hanging on the outside of that glass trying to rip her nightgown off. He was trying to kill me. He knows a hundred ways to kill a man with his bare hands, Dan. His hands are registered with the state. He pounds the edge of his feet with bags of rice."

"Just relax now, Paul. Everything's going to be okay. Trust me." Paul's office mate had edged his way between them and was laying down a thick smoke screen. "Why don't we just forget all that for now."

"Forget that he wanted to rape my girl?" Paul shouted.

"She's my fiancée!" Leroy shouted back.

"Make them shut up," Ginny said.

"Both you men need medical attention. Why don't we call a truce." The smoke billowed.

"I will if he will," Leroy said.

"That puts the ball in your court, Paul."

"The ball in my court? He was gouging out my eye! His thumb was down in my eye socket. Do you know what that feels like?"

"No. I admit that I don't."

"Your eye's not all that bad, Paul," Ginny said. "Why don't you just hold still and let me put a compress on it. I can go over the rest of you too if you'll just shut up."

"You hear the lady, Paul?"

Paul nodded. He was beaten. This time he was truly beaten.

"Good," Ginny said.

"Now our main problem is getting off this island," Dan Pauling said.

"I could probably signal somebody from the top of the lighthouse," Leroy volunteered. His voice had already regained much of its former arrogance.

"That sounds good."

"Why don't you do that," Ginny agreed. "Take this." She handed him the remains of her nightgown. Paul's evidence.

Leroy gave them a jaunty high sign and disappeared inside the tower. Ginny dipped a folded rag into the ice chest and pressed it against Paul's eye. Dan Pauling stood and watched and smoked his pipe.

"Sit down and I'll dress your feet again." Paul did as he was told. She knelt and began to unwind the blood-caked mess of gauzes.

"That little one stabbed me with an ice pick."

"I'll look at that next."

"You don't remember them fighting over you, do you?"

"I wasn't there. Leroy said the fight was over something that Captain Edel said about the Fennel light."

"How can you take Leroy's side? Don't you know that I love you? That I want to marry you? That's got to mean something to you."

Instead of moving away, Dan Pauling squatted beside them.

"Can I help?" he asked.

Ginny shook her head. "I'm not marrying anybody. I'm going to medical school and learn to be a doctor." One foot was clear and she started on the other.

"Try to be serious. You won't have the kind of grades it takes to do that."

"I made four Cs and a B+."

"I gave you the B+."

"I bet she deserved it," Dan Pauling said pleasantly.

"You can't be a doctor."

"Bena says I can. It's what I want and it's what she wants too." Ginny sponged the second foot clean.

"Bena wants? It's a game. Bena wants people dead!"

"No she doesn't, and you're crazy to think that." She dried both feet.

"I'm crazy?"

"I'm going to be a doctor. I'm not marrying anybody." She began to apply Merthiolate.

"What about me?" Dan Pauling asked.

"Not even you."

"When did you ask her?" Paul cried. Dan Pauling was just out of his reach. "You don't even know her."

"The first time I saw her, that time she was waiting for you in our office. I told her I believed in love at first sight and asked her to marry me." He gave Ginny a proprietary pat on the shoulder.

"Is that true?" Paul asked Ginny.

"I don't remember. It's possible."

"Yes, it's true. I said marry me and she said no because . . ."

"Because why?" Paul demanded. The new bandages were almost in place and soon he would be able to grab his office mate by the neck.

"Because," Dan Pauling said hesitantly, "her husband of one day had been killed in a hit-and-run accident in Atlanta and she wasn't ready to go through that again."

"On Peachtree Street?" Paul screamed at the girl.

"Yes." She didn't bother to look up from the dressing.

"Crossing the street on Sunday morning to buy a newspaper?"

"Yes. How'd you know that?" There was apparent surprise in her voice.

"I crossed that same street to get you a newspaper. Your husband was killed at that same spot exactly a year before, going to get you a paper."

"So what?"

"I could have been killed. If I'm right about Bena—if death follows creation like it did for Jewel and Walter—Ginny, if you'd been pregnant then I would be dead."

"You think everybody is trying to kill you, Paul. Show me the ice pick hole." Paul pointed to the small red pucker above his heart. "You think everybody's trying to kill you or hurt you in some way. How can you have any fun?" She dabbed his chest with alcohol.

"Fun? I could have been killed."

"But you weren't. What's the word for that, Dan? When you think everybody's against you?"

"Paranoid." Dan Pauling stood up finally and stepped away.

"That's it. You're a paranoid."

"I see, and Leroy didn't try to gouge my eye out last night and he wasn't planning to attack you if he got inside?"

"Paul, there's no reason for him to attack me. We grew up together. He's my uncle."

"Your uncle . . . All right. Paranoid. Whatever you say."

"And jealous. Leroy said you were jealous. He told me this morning and now I believe him."

"Believe him? Ginny!"

"You've got to relax and try to enjoy life. When I used to come out here with Walter we had a good time. It was never like this." She reviewed the carnage with an open hand.

"Hey, you two, look at this." Dan Pauling pointed with his pipe stem. "What's he doing up there?"

Leroy was waving from the top of the lighthouse. He was waving the nightgown, but he was doing it as he balanced on the top rung of the handrail.

"He's just showing off," Ginny said. "He and Walter used to chase each other around and around on that railing."

"You're kidding," Dan Pauling said.

"No, I'm not. Sometimes Leroy would climb the lightning rod all the way to the top. See, he's doing it now. I guess he'll wave from up there."

Ginny got to her feet and Paul struggled to his.

"Make him come down," Dan Pauling said. "The last thing we need now is for him to fall."

"He'll be okay."

"No. Bring him down."

Ginny put her hands to her mouth megaphone fashion and yelled. "Come down, Leroy!"

Paul doubted that her voice could travel that far, but it must have because Leroy turned. Ginny signaled with her arm. Obediently, he dropped to his knees on the rail and grabbed with one hand. Then as he went to jump to the catwalk the nightgown twisted between his feet. He tottered for a moment and fell outward. The one hand held its awkward grip for a helpless moment and then he plunged towards the ground.

"Fly! Fly!" Ginny screamed even before the hand had slipped, and the plummeting figure began to straighten itself and spread its arms. Less than a third of the way down Leroy's fall slowed to a stop and then he began to rise, carried aloft by the steady ocean breeze.

"Oh, God," Dan Pauling moaned. "I'm not really seeing this."

Leroy hung high above them, head thrown back, arms spread and feet together. His powerful torso drifted through the air with the grace of a gull. A slight flapping of one arm and he glided out of sight around the far corner of the tower and reappeared on the opposite side.

"Do you see that?" Dan Pauling whispered. "It's not just me. This isn't some elaborate hoax?" he demanded of Ginny. She gave him an uncomprehending glance and returned her attention to her uncle.

Leroy had swung wide of the lighthouse now and was gradually circling lower. Soon, Paul realized, he would be standing once again among them and he would be a hero.

"Don't look down, Leroy!" Paul shouted at the top of his lungs. "Don't look down!"

Above them Leroy's neck contracted as if in slow motion and he looked directly down. When he did, the rigid body collapsed and he fell straight and fast into the underbrush.

But Leroy had been low and he hadn't fallen on the concrete. There was a good chance he'd survived. Ahead of him Ginny and Dan Pauling raced to the site. A reluctant Paul hobbled behind. By the time he arrived it was all over. Leroy was dead. Not mangled or badly twisted, but dead nevertheless.

"He flew," Dan Pauling said over the body as if he were delivering an epitaph. "He flew and we saw it."

Ginny knelt beside her uncle and said nothing.

"He fell," Paul said, gazing with no particular interest at the body. Was it murder? Certainly he was no more guilty than Da Bena.

"He flew, Paul," Dan Pauling said.

"No, Dan. He fell."

"What are you talking about?"

"Jack Fennel's ghost pushed him over the rail. He fell like a stone and popped like a melon."

"You saw him fly!" Dan Pauling had turned on Paul and for the first time since they met he was angry. "You saw him and he didn't pop like a melon. There's hardly a mark on him."

"Oh, excuse me. I've only got one eye. You see, he gouged the other one out so it's hard for me to get a sense of perspective."

"It's not a joke, Paul. We saw a man fly here today. He circled the lighthouse."

"He shouldn't have looked down," Ginny said, standing at last and wiping her hands on her jeans.

"I warned him not to," Paul said.

"Yes, I heard you," Dan Pauling agreed.

"I guess he really did fly. There's no use denying it," Paul said.

"We've got to deny it." Dan Pauling looked at each of them gravely. "We can't go back to the mainland and say we saw somebody fly. We'd be branded as crackpots. It would ruin our careers."

"But he flew," Paul insisted. "When we get back I'm going to have to tell Dr. Whitman that you saw Leroy Ramona fly and won't admit it. He knows the Fennels. He'll believe me."

"Shut up, Paul. This isn't a joke."

"Have it your way."

"I'll have to tell Da Bena." Ginny shielded her eyes to study the lighthouse.

"She knows by now," Paul said.

"How can she?" Dan Pauling asked.

"She made it happen," Paul replied.

"Don't listen to him, Dan. He talks crazy all the time."

Help didn't arrive until late in the day. Brown Jack Simmons had a premonition that there was something wrong out at the lighthouse. When he relayed this to Da Bena she sent him off to look.

Plowing slowly through the creeks, the old flat-sided oyster bateau served as a funeral barge for Leroy. It was well after dark before they reached the Fennel house.

LEROY'S FUNERAL

Paul was mending. He'd been given a new cast and by the time they buried Leroy the vision in his injured eye had improved remarkably. He would have to see a specialist but Dr. Rupple said things looked good and insisted that he attend the funeral. A limousine carried them to the Port Ulacca cemetery. A beautiful spot, but the minister was nowhere to be found. "Modern, modern," Camilla muttered. She went off to search for him, and most of the party drifted into the surrounding crowd.

Paul was surprised by the turnout. He understood that the young man was well liked, but hundreds of people were in attendance. And since this was hundreds more than would have shown up for his own, he asked the good doctor to identify the mourners—at least by groups.

The majority were Fennels. A mainland branch of the family, it turned out, had divided off from their outlaw cousins centuries before. They chose to make contact only at times such as these. With just a slight dour-faced family resemblance, they

now approached Azalea and Ginny, offering their condolences
and at the same time attempting to project a land-bound sense
of stability and proprietorship. This, after all, was their burial
plot. Yes, far more Fennels were buried here beneath the spreading oaks than on that sandy ocean hammock.

The Ramonas, too, had a few relatives in the area and even
friends from when Azalea and Leroy's father had been stationed
here in the Coast Guard. They crowded around to console Mrs.
Ramona who had flown in from Florida. A heavy, aging woman
with too much makeup and a too-bright dress, she cried hysterically one moment and laughed hysterically the next. Paul
looked in vain for some resemblance to Ginny. Perhaps Azalea
had borne the full brunt of this inheritance, for she too was crying and laughing in turn. On every side the other twelve members of the bridge club reached out to embrace her.

There really was a bridge club. How could Paul have ever
doubted?

And how could he have doubted Leroy's popularity? Here
were his friends. Numbers didn't lie.

Dozens of workers from the Caladium Shipyard had arrived,
many bringing their wives and children. They had come to pay
their respects, but the Leroy they knew had nothing to do with
all this. He'd been Walter Brant's friend and a young uncle to the
crazy Fennel girl Walter had married. Now she'd taken up with
some history professor. And in some kind of weird way this new
boyfriend had been responsible for Leroy's death.

Where could they have gotten such an idea? From Walter
Brant's father, for one. The mild, balding little man had ridden
in the funeral limousine, declaring the entire way that after Walter's death Leroy had been like a son to him. He had expected
great things from that boy, great things. Now he was left with
nothing—a childless widower. "Why?" he had asked, leaning

over Ginny to grab Paul in a clawlike grasp. "Why should the ones with so much life in them—with so much to do and give and be—why should these die while the others, the weak, dreamy-eyed, do-nothing pencil-pushers go on living? Why?" he asked Paul through angry tears.

"God's will," Paul answered, freeing himself from the man's grip and trying to straighten the twisted tweed fabric of his coat sleeve.

Apparently that hadn't been a satisfactory answer, for when they reached the cemetery Mr. Brant bolted from the car and joined the group of shipworkers. Speaking with tear-studded animosity and pointing every minute or so at Paul, he had told them something. Something bad—about Paul.

Beside the casket stood six pallbearers. These, it turned out, were all members of Leroy's air-conditioning class. They didn't need Mr. Brant to tell them that Paul was a grade A, number one asshole. Leroy had told them himself in the week just before he died. Paul could see this in their eyes. They stared at him as one man, in open hatred. When the dome over the city was completed and the air-conditioning turned on, Paul could rest assured he would not be invited inside.

Then again, maybe he was just being paranoid. After all, this was Leroy's day, not his. Ginny had told him he must relax and enjoy himself. In another hour he would be leaving Port Ulacca and taking Ginny and Azalea with him.

The exodus, needless to say, was Bena's idea. Ginny was going to medical school. Azalea would get her master's in education and Paul would become head of the history department. Bena had faith in all of them.

Paul searched the crowd for the old woman—which should have been easy. She'd appeared at the door of the limousine wearing a wig of some red nylon material. She swore it was her own and appeared truly hurt by Paul's teasing. This unexpected show of vanity had caught him off guard, more so even than the tears flowing from those bulging chocolate eyes. Da Bena crying—when the limousine loaded they were all crying—Azalea, Ginny, Mrs. Ramona, Dr. Rupple, Mr. Brant. Even Brown Jack cried. He was to remain behind and tend Adam. Adam was too upset to attend. His rapidly blinking eyes had produced copious tears. Only Camilla and Paul could not find it in their hearts to shed a tear over the death of one so young and vigorous.

And there came Camilla now. She had the minister in tow. A handsome man with rakish sideburns, he kissed Azalea on the cheek and made a short apology. Dr. Rupple led the way, escorting Camilla, under the funeral parlor awning. Paul took Ginny. They sat in folding chairs. The air-conditioning repairmen delivered the remains of their fallen comrade to the graveside.

Paul remembered the letter from Virginia Fennel to her brother. No tolerance for this religion there, and now, glancing down the row, he saw not a flicker of interest on the face of Camilla. But Azalea was enraptured. And a rare smile played on the corner of Ginny's lips. The minister closed the Bible and spread his arms for the eulogy.

"I didn't know Leroy Ramona," he began. "I'd seen him, of course, driving by or with a group of his friends, but I'd never actually spoken to him, or even seen him do his karate. This isn't unusual, you know, for religion and thoughts of mortality are often far from our minds at that age and I'm sure that given time this young man would have found his way into my congregation and taken his place in the pew beside his sister Azalea. She assures me of this, and given the Ramonas' long association with our church, I am certain she is right. 'Leroy feared God,' she further assured me, but she told me something even more important than that—she told me something that brought home the tragedy of this passing. She told me, 'Leroy loved people.' Yes, that's right. Leroy loved people! He was a little wild, still a young boy in many ways, and mischievous like all young boys are, but, friends, Leroy loved people! And after all, isn't that the important thing? Not whether a person is a member of this or that particular denomination, but that he or she has Christ in their heart."

Ginny squeezed Paul's hand. Apparently she too felt her uncle's heart was full of love. All down the aisle, members of the family were weeping again.

"And then Azalea told me something else that made me very happy. She told me, 'People loved Leroy!' That's right, people loved Leroy. That's the important thing I want you to understand here today. Leroy loved people. People loved Leroy. When we have love in our hearts a place will be made for us in the kingdom of heaven." He bowed his head and began a final prayer.

Knowing that Leroy waited on the far side of those pearly gates made Paul's life here seem all the more precious. And as for love, he thought he loved Ginny and he thought he loved Azalea. Dr. Rupple was an admirable man, and Dan Pauling was probably a good friend if he wanted one. He couldn't think of Bena in terms of love and there was no one else to consider. Maybe that would change. Maybe he didn't understand what was expected of him.

The service was over. Ginny squeezed his hand again. Azalea cried into a sopping hanky. Da Bena was bent. She shook with emotion. Even Dan Pauling, who had known Leroy less than five minutes, was misty-eyed. Down the entire row, tears were being blinked back or shed openly. Only Paul and Camilla remained unmoved.

They returned to the house and gathered in the dining room for a brief and somber meal. Then Dan Pauling, more and more a member of the family, saw to the departure of Mr. Brant and Mrs. Ramona. The rest of them went on with their lives— mourning and, in some cases, packing for the university.

IN THE END

Those papers in the bedroom, I've been looking through them. They're a gold mine, Paul. A gold mine." Dan Pauling was remaining behind. He whispered this as they loaded the bags into the back of the powder blue Plymouth station wagon. "I can't believe you're turning your back on the actual Fennel Family Papers. You know that old woman would let you back in if Azalea and Ginny insisted."

"I've seen enough," Paul said, slamming the door on the baggage.

"I just don't want hard feelings if I come up with something. You know there's never been anything done on the closing of the Caladium Keyhole, and somewhere in all that paper I've got a hunch I'm going to find what it takes. There's an article in this, Paul. I mean a blockbuster."

"Myth," Paul said.

"A mythical body of primary sources. What graduate student hasn't heard of the Fennel papers?"

"Trash," Paul said. "Good luck, though."

The time had come. Everyone had gathered in the dining room to say good-bye. Everyone except Camilla who had retired to her room after the meal.

Azalea hugged Dr. Rupple and he hugged Ginny and shook hands with Paul. Dan hugged Azalea, kissed Ginny on the cheek, and patted Paul on the back—telling him to take care of "our girl." Brown Jack bowed to everyone and melted away. Da Bena hugged Ginny. She hugged Azalea. And then she shook Paul's hand, declaring that she had "raise him up" as best she could in the short time given and that he was "de man of the family now and must do the right thing." Everyone laughed and then Azalea began to cry and she and Ginny had to say their good-byes to Adam all over again. The time had truly come, but now Camilla stood in the doorway.

"Oh, Camilla," Azalea said, smiling through her tears. "I knew you would see us off. No matter what happens, we're still a family." Azalea took a step forward but Da Bena's lanky arm drew her back.

"You were never a Fennel," Camilla snapped. "Marrying this nephew of mine didn't make you a Fennel."

Azalea's face lapsed into the frozen crooked-mouth smile.

"Dere is plenty enough Fennels left in this house." Da Bena spoke with a low menace. "You let these peoples go, Camilla."

"I'm stopping no one who doesn't belong here and as far as I'm concerned that means only Virgina should stay."

Saying this, she pulled an ancient revolver from the folds of her skirt and, holding it with both hands, pointed it straight at Paul. The hammer had already been cocked back. Dan Pauling was at his side and he gave a low whistle of disbelief.

"Camilla, this has gone far enough," Dr. Rupple said and moved forward.

"Stay out of this, Martin. If you approach another step I'll pull the trigger."

"I'll bet that's the same revolver Captain Jack used to murder Virginia's third husband," Paul said.

"Yes sir, Master Paul. That the very same gun," Da Bena declared.

"Shut up!" Camilla cried.

"Dat the same gun. The poor man surrender he fort and that crazy Jack come up behind 'em and blow he head clean off."

Dan Pauling had slipped pad and pen from his breast pocket. But the pen scratched against the paper, leaving only an occasional trace of ink.

"I will not have such sentiment uttered in this house. I am sorry, Bena, but I must ask you and your husband to leave this house as well."

"You know that Brown Jack Simmons ain't my husband. He got him a real wife on the road."

"I know no such thing."

"Jack be my half-brother same as he be your half-brother. Me and him have the same momma just the same as you and him have the same daddy."

"No!" Camilla shrieked. Her hands trembled violently. The gun was still aimed at Paul.

"They're all Fennels," Dan Pauling whispered in awe. He continued to scratch with the dry pen.

"Of course, the young gentlemans is right. Everybody knows we is all the Fennels."

Paul glanced about the room. No sign of surprise on anyone's face.

"But, Da Bena," Dan Pauling asked eagerly, "sharing a mother with Brown Jack wouldn't make you a Fennel . . ."

"Unless," Paul added, "unless her mother was a Fennel to begin with."

"Dat is so," Da Bena declared. "I very proud that my Ginny has found such a smart boyfriend."

"So your mother Bena was also the Captain's daughter," Paul confirmed.

"Shut up!" Camilla screamed once more.

"Captain Jack was Da Bena's grandfather. The Captain fathered Da Bena's mother before he married Gladys and gave her Jack Junior who would sire Adam."

The ink suddenly gushed from Dan Pauling's dry pen and flooded over both pad and hand.

"And then," Paul concluded, "he fathered Brown Jack off his own daughter."

Brown Jack stuck his head through the pantry door.

"Dat is correct," Da Bena said. "And that was my momma and her name be Bena and her momma who that same man catch and bring straight from Africa, she be name Bena. And after she have Brown Jack she come to the mainland and find a good black man and that my pa."

"And," Paul said, pointing his finger straight at Camilla who pointed the gun straight back at him, "after fathering Da Bena's mother, Jack Junior, and Brown Jack, Captain Jack Fennel also went to the mainland and built this house for the little girl who was to be your mother."

"I will not listen to another word," the old woman roared, and Paul saw her finger tighten on the trigger.

"Why is any of this important?" Ginny asked.

The question distracted Camilla. Adam's hand moved, or seemed to. It was impossible to say, things happened so fast. The wheelchair spun forward and crashed into the old woman just as the gun fired.

The noise was tremendous and the room flooded with dense blue smoke. But Paul was still alive and he wondered for a moment if the gun hadn't exploded. No. No, Dr. Rupple had it in his hand.

Disarming, comforting, and congratulating each other, people seemed to be moving everywhere in the room. Only he and Dan Pauling remained transfixed. His office mate was using ink-stained fingers to examine the bullet hole in his coat pocket. His face was drained of color and his mouth hung open in unscholarly amazement.

"Were you hit?" Paul asked.

"No," Dan Pauling said. "Just passed though the cloth and struck the wall." He indicated the shattered plaster behind them. "Got my pipe, though. Look at this." He withdrew the shattered remnants of his briar-wood.

"Be thankful it wasn't in your mouth."

"Oh, I am. I am."

"I'll wait for you to pack, but hurry."

"Pack? I'm not leaving here till I've been through those papers. Didn't you hear what they were saying? This place is a gold mine."

"It's a graveyard."

"Ginny's right. You are paranoid."

Paul laughed and shook his head.

"Don't laugh, buddy. I don't think you realize what you had your hands on here. Don't blame me that you let it slip through your fingers."

Paul could linger no longer. He joined Ginny and Azalea at Adam's side, agreeing that indeed the invalid was the hero of the day. Then it was good-bye again to Dr. Rupple and Brown Jack, and even good-bye to Camilla, who had resumed her place at the head of the table. And finally it was time to say good-bye to Da Bena.

Paul found her alone in the kitchen. She'd gone there to fix Camilla's tea.

"We're going now, Da Bena. I don't want you to worry. I'll take care of everyone." Paul felt awkward. Shy.

"Yes, I knows you do that, and I ain't want you for worry about these here. Me and Jack can tend 'em just fine."

"Go easy on Dr. Pauling. He's really excited about the papers."

"Dem old paper! You best take that young gentlemans with you."

"He won't go."

"Bena just have to do her best then. But this old nigger woman ain't make no promise. No sir."

She smiled broadly and Paul laughed and the steaming cup of tea was ready to be delivered.

"Just admit to me one thing. All this from the very beginning. You arranged it, didn't you?"

"Hush, boy. Ginny warn me about you."

"You wanted to free her from the Fennels, from Virginia, and her father, and Camilla and the rest."

"You talk such trash."

"Bena, it's all you. Fate. Destiny. Everything." Paul circled his good hand at the soot-stained ceiling.

"Everythin'?" She hid the piano-key teeth behind spidery fingers. "Everythin'?" Paul thought she meant to laugh but the next words came low. Almost a whisper. A conspiracy. A confidence. "No. No. You forgets about Adam."

"Adam?"

"Ain't Adam goin' do what he goin' do?"

"Adam?"

"Ain't Paul goin' do what he goin' do? He make up he own mine. Ain't for Bena to know. Ain't for she to say."

Paul heard the melodious chuckle. Self-consciously he wrapped his arms around the skeletal creature. There was little enough body beneath the folds of the gray sacking, but he held on dearly.

"Good-bye, doctor," he said, stepping back at last.

"Now why you call me that? You know Bena ain't no doctor." She cried and laughed at the same time.

"Why, you're a doctor the same as me."

"Dat ain't no kind of doctor at all!"

They delivered the tea to Camilla. It was time to collect Ginny and Azalea and say good-bye all over again.

"Good-bye! Good-bye! Good-bye!" Ginny pulled the Plymouth station wagon out of the drive. Azalea settled in the back seat, removed her cross-stitch from the paper bag, and set to work.

Paul hung his cast-covered arm across the window frame. The Fennel house was already fading into the distance and soon Port Ulacca would be left behind. It was hard to imagine a future with either of these women, but that was what he wanted. It was harder still to imagine himself as a department head, but that was what Bena had foreseen. True, he had killed a man, and not just any man. Paul had killed a man who was loved by an entire community. It was the kind of thing Curly Whitman would have done.

But in truth, Paul had set his sights elsewhere. He had something to tell his students. And he didn't need tenure or an article to do it. He could simply address them in an open and honest manner. He could tell them—he could tell them that despite what they would learn about the world in his class—and despite the armies of despair arranged against them—they must take responsibility for themselves and for the people around them. And above all else they must not be afraid.

Behind him Azalea gave a sniff. She was wiping her eyes on the corner of her cross-stitch.

"Bena could have moved it," Azalea explained. "I'm so proud of Adam. As proud as I can be, but Bena could have moved that wheelchair without touching it."

"I doubt it," Paul said.

"I've seen her move cars in the driveway, and she could change the TV channels from the other room. It wouldn't have been hard for her to roll a wheelchair."

"I saw Adam's hand move," Paul assured her. "It was a very distinct movement."

Satisfied, Azalea resumed her stitching, and Paul turned back to find Ginny smiling at him. Ahead of them lay miles of clean uncluttered highway. Yes, he was beginning to understand. There was plenty to smile about.